THE DOOR TO THE LOST

THE DOOR TO THE LOST

JALEIGH JOHNSON

Delacorte Press

Text copyright © 2018 by Jaleigh Johnson
Jacket art copyright © 2018 by Hannah Christenson
Map illustrations copyright © 2018 by Kayley LeFaiver

Visit us on the Web! rhcbooks.com

Educators and librarians, for a variety of teaching tools, visit us at RHTeachersLibrarians.com

Library of Congress Cataloging-in-Publication Data
Name: Johnson, Jaleigh, author.
Title: The door to the lost / Jaleigh Johnson.
Description: First edition. | New York : Delacorte Press, [2018] | Summary: "After a mysterious accident that closes a portal to another world, magic is banned in Talhaven. But there are those like Rook who are stranded in Talhaven and still have the power to wield magic. Living in exile, a stranger offers Rook and her friend safety, but appearances can be deceiving and the pair soon find themselves in serious danger" —Provided by publisher
Identifiers: LCCN 2017038305 | ISBN 978-1-101-93316-9 (hc) | ISBN 978-1-101-93317-6 (el)
Subjects: | CYAC: Fantasy.
Classification: LCC PZ7.J63214 Doo 2018 | DDC [Fic]—dc23 LC

The text of this book is set in 12-point Goudy Oldstyle Std.
Interior design by Jaclyn Whalen

Printed in the United States of America
10 9 8 7 6 5 4 3 2 1
First Edition

To Tim, for always having my back and for reminding me every day what's most important. Love you so much.

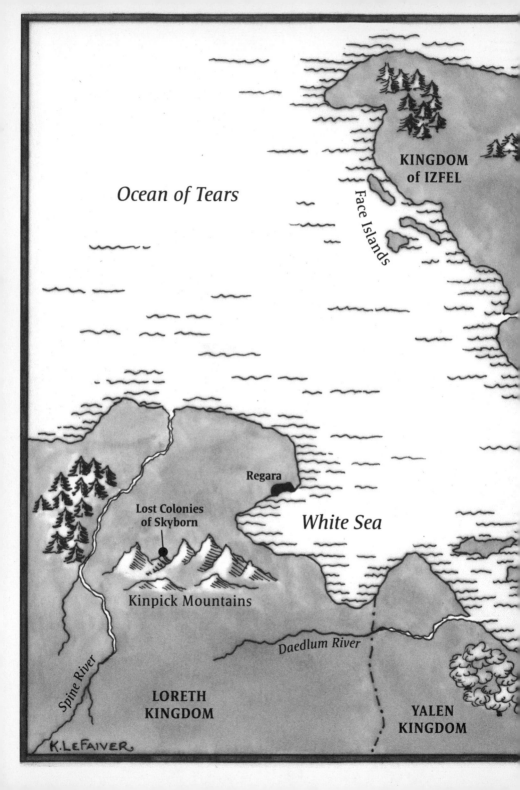

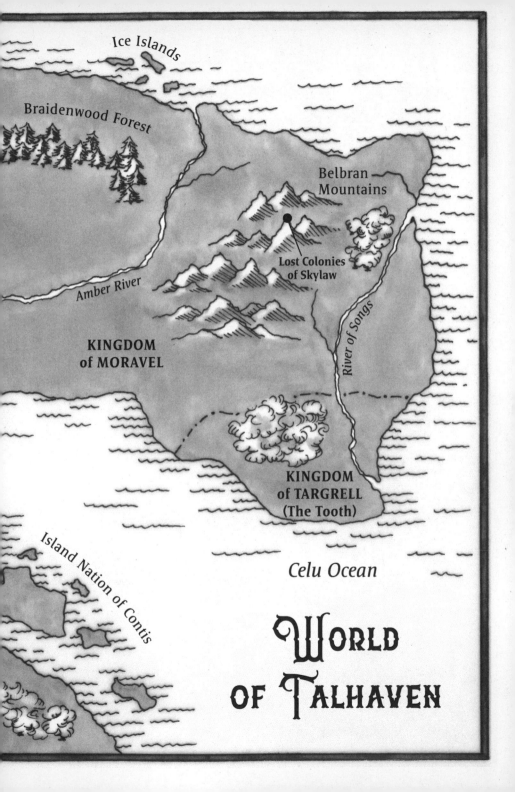

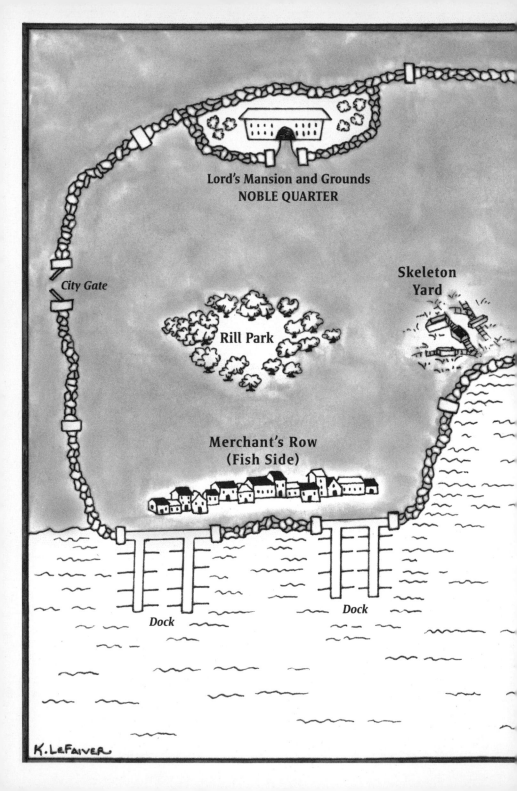

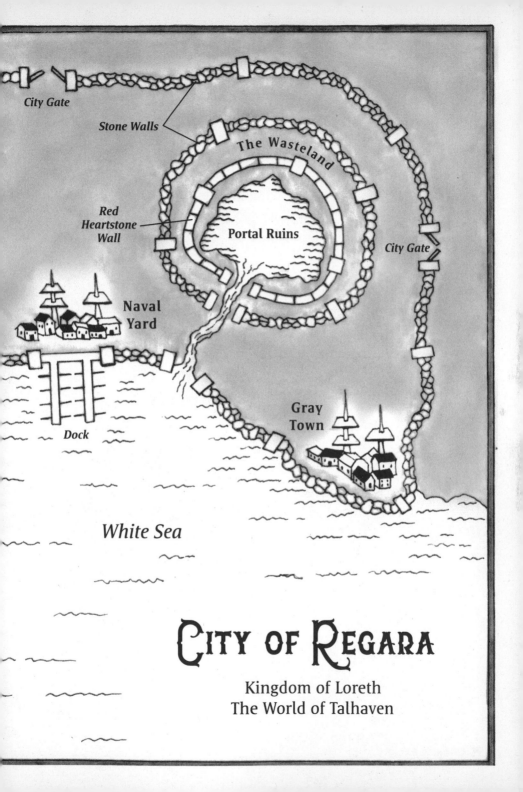

City Gate

Stone Walls

The Wasteland

Red
Heartstone
Wall

Portal Ruins

City Gate

Naval
Yard

Dock

Gray
Town

White Sea

City of Regara

Kingdom of Loreth
The World of Talhaven

PROLOGUE

IN THE WORLD OF TALHAVEN, magic is dying.

The people of Talhaven had no warning this was going to happen, just as they'd had no warning of the Great Catastrophe. They believed magic was a safe, wondrous force that would always be there to light their homes, fly their skyships, and make their lives easier.

They were wrong.

The magic that remains in the world is unstable, dangerous—never more so than in the city of Regara, where the Great Catastrophe struck. Now the people of Talhaven fear magic. They have outlawed its use, and blame those who first brought it into their world for all their misfortune.

The wizards from Vora were responsible. Long ago, they opened a magical doorway between their own world and Talhaven, and brought their magic with them. They called it animus, spirit energy, and traded it in exchange for natural resources Vora lacked. All was well for many years, and the peoples of both worlds thrived.

Until the day of the Great Catastrophe, when the magical doorway connecting the two worlds exploded.

Every building within four miles of the portal was destroyed. Hundreds of people in the city of Regara were killed or injured. In the aftermath of the destruction, the magical door was gone, never to appear again.

No one could explain how the disaster had happened or why the remnants of magic were suddenly unstable. Perhaps the greatest mystery of all, however, was that minutes before the explosion, hundreds of Vorans came through the magical doorway. Three hundred twenty-seven of them, to be exact.

They were all children.

The people of Talhaven didn't know what to do with these strange survivors, for the rest of the Vorans were gone, and the children claimed to have no memory of the world they'd come from. They didn't even know their own names.

And just like everyone else from their world, they all had magic.

The people of Talhaven named them exiles, and some even blamed the children for the disaster that had destroyed the portal between worlds and corrupted the remaining magic. Others wanted to use the children's magic for their own ends. So the exiles did the only thing they could think of to protect themselves: they used their magic to escape and went into hiding.

But no one can hide forever.

1

THE DOOR TO SKELETON YARD

"YOU CAN'T RUN FROM US, EXILE!"

That's what you think. Rook pelted down the backstreets of Regara's merchant district and docks, her lips twisted in a grim smile. For as long as she could remember, Rook had been running, and she was getting very good at it.

She reached out and snatched the rail of the nearest building's fire escape, using her momentum to swing around the corner into a dark alley. Her foot splashed down in a deep, fishy-smelling puddle that had swallowed a portion of the cobblestoned street. Mud and icy water soaked her socks and pant legs. Rook ground her teeth in irritation.

It was time to get out of here. Obviously, the Night Market wasn't taking place in Fish Side tonight, but that hadn't stopped the constables from laying a trap for anyone who came looking for it here.

The problem with holding a secret, movable market once a month was that, well, it had to be secret, and it had to keep moving. It wasn't exactly something you could advertise. Come one! Come all! Get your black-market magic here! We've got the goods that can—*literally*—blow away the competition!

"Cut off the alley! We've got her!"

The voices echoed from two streets behind her, and were closing in fast. Rook barreled toward the brick wall that dead-ended the alley, her piece of yellow chalk already clutched in one sweaty hand. She skidded to a stop and drew a rectangle as tall and wide as her body on the uneven surface of the bricks. Her thoughts centered on her next destination, repeating it in every beat of her pounding heart.

Skeleton Yard.

Skeleton Yard.

Oh please oh please let the market be at Skeleton Yard.

Fear and magic flooded Rook's veins. Both sensations were as familiar as breathing, but still, she faltered. Would her power take her where she asked this time? Lately, it had been failing her more and more often.

The yellow scrawl on the bricks snapped into rigid lines with a *crack,* as if an invisible hand had picked up one end of each and tugged it into place. A puff of chalk dust sparkled in the air, and the lines began to glow. Brightly they shone, until the chalk could no longer contain the light, shooting golden rays out from the wall.

There came the deep rumble of stone scraping stone, and one by one, the bricks in the wall popped free of their mortar and pushed outward with a loud *kachunk kachunk kachunk* sound. Dust choked the air, blurring the scene before Rook's eyes. The stone scraping changed to the cadence of wood creaking and warping, a shrill sound that rang in her ears.

Then, as quickly as the noises began, they stopped. When the mortar dust settled, it revealed a startling sight—a cherry-wood door nested within the surrounding bricks, as naturally as if it had always been part of the builder's plan.

But the transformation didn't end there. Tendrils of gold light sprang from two points along the left side of the door, coiling in the shape of leaves and ropey vines that melted into the wood and solidified into polished brass hinges. Rook shifted her attention to the right side of the door, where a small mushroom of light sprouted into a shiny doorknob. She could just make out her distorted reflection on its surface.

The instant the knob became solid, Rook seized it and yanked the door open. Behind her, uniformed constables poured into the alley, shouting and blowing shrill whistles. Rook ignored them and focused on the open field beyond the door's threshold, lit by silvery moonlight and smelling of wild mint and wet grass.

Anywhere is better than here. Rook dove through, slamming the magical door in the faces of the constables.

2

THE DOOR TO FRENZY

WITH A FLICK OF POWER inside her, Rook severed her connection to the door. The cherrywood blurred and ran like smeared paint before vanishing, leaving behind the scarred white planks of a supply shed.

She was safe.

Rook leaned against the wall to catch her breath and calm her thundering heart. That had been too close. At least her power hadn't failed her. As near as she could tell, it had taken her to the edge of the old railyards, which really was nothing more than a cluster of abandoned flatcars and rusted track bordering an empty, weed-choked field.

Well, not entirely empty.

Mist and moonlight curled around the rusted white skins of four train cars arranged haphazardly in the field, like a bone that had been broken in four pieces. Warm lantern light shone from within the cars, which told Rook she'd chosen the right place this time.

The Night Market was in Skeleton Yard.

Rook pushed off the shed and made her way as quietly and cautiously as possible across the field toward the train cars. She kept an eye out for constables, even though she knew the ones that had been chasing her were halfway across the city, cursing at how they'd lost the exile with the wild black hair yet again.

But that was Rook's gift, to create doors that led anywhere in the world. A talent that had saved her more than once, even if the magic didn't always work the way she wanted it to.

Rook climbed a set of rusted metal steps to the nearest train car. Tethered to a post alongside it were half a dozen horses belonging to patrons of the market. Most of the horses were alive, but a couple of them were still-functioning mechanicals that stomped the ground with metal hooves while clouds of steamy, false breath escaped from their sculpted nostrils. There was just enough animus left inside them to keep them moving, but not for much longer. The blue lights in their eye sockets flickered constantly, a reminder that their magic was failing, no longer reliable.

Rook opened the metal door at the top of the stairs and stepped inside. The market was already in full swing, and there were at least a dozen people browsing. The train's passenger seats had long ago been ripped out, replaced by hastily constructed market stalls or, more often, rugs spread out on the floor and stacked with wares. Most of the merchants were local or came in from the neighboring kingdom of Yalen.

Everything they brought was as colorful and temporary as possible, so the Night Market could come and go quickly if the constables—or worse, the Red Watchers—found them.

But Rook's purpose here wasn't magic. She couldn't have afforded it even if she wanted to buy a trinket. Luckily, the market attracted a wide variety of vendors. The smell of roasted Yalish chickens, hot spices, and cinnamon bread filled the air in the cramped car. Rook's stomach reacted with such raw longing that for a moment she was light-headed.

She made a beeline for the source of the scents—Gert Truevale's stall. She was a middle-aged woman with skin not unlike the consistency of a yeast roll and eyes the color of dried cherries.

Gert looked up from a basket of bread as Rook approached. Her lips pressed tightly together, fashioning an expression that, while not exactly welcoming, respected a paying customer.

"Look at you, out of breath and covered in muck," she said, eyeing Rook's sweaty face and drenched pants. But she stopped what she was doing and began wrapping up three loaves of bread in brown paper. "You want the usual, little mouse?"

Rook nodded. "Yes, please." While she waited, she combed her fingers through her wild hair. It was impossible to tame it, but at least she could make sure none of the natural white strands at the base of her neck were visible beneath the dye that covered the rest.

One of the first things she'd learned upon her arrival in this world was that the children of Talhaven didn't have white hair. If she wanted to blend in, she needed to change hers. The color she'd chosen—black with just that hint of white—reminded her of a rook, a common crow. That was how she'd come up with her name, since she didn't remember her real one.

Rook cast a furtive glance up and down the car to see if she was attracting any other attention. Most of the patrons of the market kept to themselves and didn't ask questions, but you could never be too careful. It didn't take much to make people suspicious of children out alone at night. Gert knew her secret, and for a few extra coins, she kept quiet, but Rook wasn't made of money, and the last thing she wanted was for anyone else to find out she was an exile.

"Don't suppose I can interest you in some baubles?" Gert casually gestured with her free hand to an assortment of random objects arranged in neat rows on a small table. There were Targrell gems, a Contis Island shark tooth charm, and even some forever violets from the kingdom of Izfel. Those were especially hard to come by. They looked odd sitting side by side with the fresh-baked scones, but this was the Night Market, after all, and it seemed every merchant, baker, tailor, and fishmonger dabbled in illegal magic remnants, weak trinkets left over from a time when animus was everywhere and its power wasn't feared.

Her curiosity getting the better of her, Rook picked up a

pair of spectacles with opaque black lenses. "What do these do?" she asked skeptically. As many trinkets turned out to be fakes as not, even in the Night Market, but Gert was usually reliable.

The older woman put the three loaves in a sack and handed it to Rook. "Careful!" she said. "Don't smudge the lenses! Picked those up from a Meddler in Gray Town. Put them on and you can see through other people's eyes. Works up to a mile away, he promised me."

Rook quickly put the glasses back on the table and wiped her hands on her pants as if they'd left a stain. "You shouldn't be dealing in Meddlers' goods," she admonished Gert. "Half of them don't know what they're doing."

And the other half did, which made them even more dangerous, in Rook's mind. Meddlers were people who'd learned through experimentation—and the occasional loss of limb— how to shape the bits of leftover animus, creating their own magical trinkets. Sometimes these trinkets worked, but most often they didn't. Other times they worked—with side effects. Ever since the Great Catastrophe, it was illegal to create or trade in this volatile magic, and that was how the Night Market had been born.

Gert sniffed derisively. "Well, we can't all flick our fingers and make the magic dance for us, can we?" She held out her open palm to Rook. "That'll be ten, little mouse. No more credit. You're already too much in debt to this market."

Rook bit back an angry retort and sighed. She'd meant

to warn Gert, not offend her, but somehow she'd done both. And she couldn't afford to lose the woman's favor. Not when this was the safest place to buy food in the city. So Rook threw in an extra coin when she paid for the bread, though it hurt her gut to do it.

She glanced at a pocket watch on Gert's trinket table to check the time. It was getting late. She needed to leave soon. Drift would be waiting for her at the meeting spot, and she'd worry if Rook was late. She tucked the precious bag of bread under one arm and moved off quickly down the train car. Hands thrust more magical trinkets under her nose as she went.

"Divination rods! Guaranteed full of animus!"

"Try on a vest, girl? A colorful vest with infinite pockets! Hide your valuables! Hide your pets! Hide anything!"

The merchant grinned and flapped the vest like a washerwoman snapping a wet towel. When Rook paused to look, he slipped his large, russet-brown hand into a pocket that couldn't have been more than two inches deep, yet his whole forearm disappeared into the fabric. Dark eyes dancing, he pulled out a handful of butterflies that took flight, iridescent blue and orange specks that zigzagged around Rook's head once before vanishing.

"Pretty," Rook said, smiling politely but shaking her head as the man shooed a butterfly off his nose and tried to get her to put on the vest.

She pushed her way through the crowd and out the

opposite door of the car for a breath of fresh air. Not that the scenery of Skeleton Yard was much to look at. Mostly it was just another reminder of how magic was fading from the world.

The ruined cars had once been part of the Hover Project, a sleek, tubular train that whizzed along on a cushion of air and magic—the first of its kind and a marvel of overland travel. At least, that was the intention. The Great Catastrophe had happened before the train could be completed, so it had been abandoned along with so many other innovations that relied on large amounts of animus.

It had been two years since the disaster, and those two years had taken their toll. The skyships no longer flew, and the moon globes that once lit all the houses in Talhaven had gone dark, replaced by candles and crude gaslights. It was a different world now, but some people still held on to magic and its wonders as hard as they could, while others wanted nothing to do with it.

Or with the children like Rook who wielded it.

Rook huffed out a breath. She shifted the sack of bread and turned to go back inside the car. She still needed to get eggs and a couple of wheels of cheese, if she could make her coin stretch that far, before she went to meet Drift.

A distant shout made her freeze, her hand gripping the door latch. She couldn't make out any words, but it sounded like the shout came from one of the other train cars. The Night Market had its own eyes and ears, watchers who kept a lookout for trouble. Had the constables found them? Rook fished in her pocket for her chalk, just to be safe.

And then a second shout echoed from somewhere off to her left, louder, urgent.

"Frenzy!" the voice screamed.

Rook went cold all over, the skin of her arms erupting in gooseflesh. A Frenzy mob, in Skeleton Yard? It had to be a mistake. The outbreaks almost never happened here, so far from the populated areas of the city. The Night Market chose places like this for that very reason.

Rook bolted back into the train car, shoving past the other patrons and merchants who were crammed at the windows to see what all the commotion was. She ran right up to Gert's stall, dropped her sack of bread, and snatched the black-lensed spectacles. She needed to see what was coming. Swallowing her trepidation, she pushed the spectacles onto her face, wondering whose eyes she'd be seeing through.

"Hey, no free samples!" Gert snapped, tugging on Rook's arm, but Rook just batted her hand away.

"Do these things work?" she demanded. "All I see is black!"

"Course they work," Gert said, sounding annoyed. "Just give them a minute."

Rook was afraid they didn't have that long.

Not if the Frenzy had found them.

3

THE DOOR TO SNOW

Snow-white eyes, pitch-black tongues
Run and hide, the Frenzy will come

It was the warning all children knew, exiles or not: Run
or the Frenzy will tear you apart. As Rook repeated the words
in her head, the black lenses on her face suddenly expanded,
filling even her peripheral vision until she was truly blind. For
a second, Rook's chest heaved with panic. She should have
known better than to take a risk on Meddlers' goods.

Just as she was about to tear the spectacles off her face, a
pinprick of light appeared, slowly widening to reveal a view
of the field outside. In the moonlight, she could just make
out a slice of the harbor on her right. The vision blurred at
the edges, bobbing up and down in a way that made Rook's
temples throb. What was she seeing?

It was through someone else's eyes, Rook realized, just as
Gert said. And that someone was running. Fast. That was

what was causing the motion. But Rook didn't see what they were running *from*.

"How do these work?" Rook groped for Gert's arm. Luckily, the woman was still standing right next to her. "Can I move to someone else?"

"Absolutely." There was a note of pride in Gert's voice. "Fellow I bought them from said to turn in the direction you want to see, tap the lenses twice to jump to another set of eyes. They work up to a mile away," she repeated, ever the saleswoman.

Rook tapped the lenses twice. The vision changed so abruptly she was almost sick. When she recovered, she was facing one of the white train cars at the farthest edge of the yard, bordering the nearby theater district.

And there they were.

Rook squeezed Gert's arm so hard the woman squealed. There were six of them, and judging by their dress—suit jackets and ties for the men, lacy blouses and light coats for the women—they'd just come out of a show. They'd probably taken a wrong turn heading for the cafes and restaurants and accidently strayed too close to the Night Market, to the magic all gathered in one place.

That was when they'd changed.

Now they walked stiffly across the railyard like dolls balancing on wobbly legs, their eyes gone white, black tongues darting between their teeth. The Frenzy illness was yet another scar on the world, a side effect of the Great Catastrophe.

No one knew why some people reacted to magic in this way, becoming mindless monsters when exposed to large quantities of it. But those people were dangerous now, and if they weren't removed from the market and its magic soon, they would tear the place apart and attack anyone who strayed into their path.

"We have to get out of here!" Rook shouted, her eyes still tracking the group shambling across the yard. "Gert, warn the others. Six Frenzy victims headed this way. Tell everyone to pack up and run!"

Rook tore off the spectacles, and her vision went black as the image of the Frenzy mob disappeared. She blinked, waiting for the darkness to clear, while Gert snatched the spectacles from her hands and shouted for the market to pack up. Footsteps pounded toward the exits. Fabric whipped and metal clanged as the merchants yanked their stalls down.

But Rook was still blind.

Panic blossomed inside her. Someone bumped into her from behind, and Rook stumbled, her arms outstretched, but there was nothing to hold on to, nothing but a black abyss. She didn't know which way was out or where to run. She rubbed her eyes until they burned, as if the darkness were something she could wipe away.

"I see them! They're coming!"

Rook recognized the terrified voice. It was the merchant who'd tried to sell her the vest of deep pockets. Still shouting, he ran past her, accidently shoving her into the wall, and there came the clatter of objects falling to the floor.

"Watch where you're going, girl!" shouted another voice. "Get moving!"

"Wait, please!" Rook shouted after the fleeing merchants. "I need help! I can't see!"

Her only answer was the sound of the train car door slamming. Outside, there were the echoes of running footsteps and more shouts, but inside the car, a space of quiet had fallen. Rook was alone.

Well, at least the merchant who'd shoved her had shown her where a wall was. Turning, Rook felt along its smooth surface, trying to see if she had enough space to draw a door. Luckily, she didn't need her sight to do that.

As long as she didn't drop her chalk.

With that ominous thought echoing in her head, Rook clinked chalk against metal and drew a wobbly, probably hideous-looking rectangle on the wall of the train car. She went down on her knees to finish the lines where the wall met the floor. *Take me to safety,* she commanded her magic. *Take me to Drift.*

Heart in her throat, she listened to the screech of metal warping and twisting. When the sounds died away, she stood on her knees and all but lunged for the wall, searching frantically for a knob or latch. The Frenzy must be close. All the magic trinkets were clearing out of the yard, but Rook's own innate power would still affect the victims, keeping them in their monstrous state.

What would they do if they caught her? Rook had never heard of an exile cornered by a Frenzy mob before, and she didn't want to be the first.

In her frantic scrabbling, her hands fell on a square metal latch. With a swell of relief, Rook lifted it and pulled her magical door open. With her other hand, she felt along the ground beyond the threshold to see where her power was taking her.

Her fingers plunged into a pile of cold, wet snow. The scent of pine needles filled her nostrils, a sharp contrast to the stale air of the old train car.

"No!" Rook screamed in frustration and fear.

It was the forest. Again.

Without thinking, Rook slammed the door shut and willed it to vanish. Every time she thought her magic was under control, just when she risked trusting it, it betrayed her. Usually at times like this, when she needed it most. And when it failed, it always seemed to return to that mysterious, snow-covered forest in the middle of nowhere.

Rook had never actually stepped through to that place. Something about it frightened her, as if there was a presence waiting in the trees, eyes watching from just out of sight beyond the threshold.

But this time she should have risked it. Rook berated herself as footsteps rattled on the metal stairs leading up to the train car. She was out of time.

The Frenzy was here.

The door at the far end of the car opened, slamming against the opposite wall, and though Rook couldn't see them, she sensed their weight filling up the room like a nightmare. Teeth clacked together in anticipation, howls and moans growing louder and louder as the Frenzy tore through the train car.

Frantically, Rook drew another door on the wall with one hand. She heard the sounds of a second magical door forming as she searched around the floor, fumbling for a weapon, anything she could use to protect herself or distract the approaching mob.

Her hands fell on a bit of fabric, fingers finding the seams of pockets sewn all over it. It was the vest, Rook realized. A vest to hide valuables.

To hide anything—even magic butterflies.

Rook dug her hand into pocket after pocket, searching for the illusory insects.

The footsteps and wailing were closer.

Louder.

Finally, Rook's hands encountered a soft, fluttering mass inside a pocket as dozens of tiny insect legs latched onto her. Thankfully, they weren't alive, but made entirely of diluted animus. She drew them carefully out of the pocket and threw her hand up in the air in the direction of the approaching mob, hoping the small distraction would buy her enough time to escape.

At first, she heard nothing, but an instant later, there came a confused scuffling, and the moans and howls reached a terrible crescendo as the Frenzy flung themselves after the illusory butterflies. Rook wanted to fold up into a ball and cover her ears, but she forced herself to get to her feet and turn to the door.

Luckily, she found the latch on the first try, yanked open the door, and dashed through, no longer caring where she ended up. Her foot caught on the raised threshold, but Rook managed to pull the door shut behind her before she fell, knees scraping stone as she tumbled to the ground.

"Whoa!" came a surprised voice from somewhere off to her left.

It was the sweetest, most welcome voice Rook had ever heard, because it meant she'd arrived at the right place. She swallowed a relieved sob and banished the door she'd just fallen through. Then she collapsed in a heap, her limbs weak.

She was safe. Safe. No black tongues and colorless eyes waiting in the dark.

"Rook! Rook, are you all right?" Drift's hands came down on her shoulders, coaxing her to sit up. "You're shaking! And filthy! What happened?"

"Trouble at the market," Rook said breathlessly. "I'm blind, but other than that, I think I'm all right."

Drift's hands tightened on her shoulders. *"What?"*

4

THE DOOR TO GRAY TOWN

"STOP RUBBING THEM," DRIFT CHIDED her gently. "Just try to be patient."

For the hundredth time, Rook forced her hand away from her eyes. It felt like someone had poured a bucketful of hot sand into them, but she wasn't about to complain. Apparently, the fierce itching that had started not long after she'd filled Drift in on everything that had happened at Skeleton Yard meant there was some kind of healing going on. Sure enough, over the last few minutes, her vision had slowly been returning. At first, it was just shafts of patchy light piercing the darkness, but gradually she'd begun to make out the blurred shape of Drift's head, then the fine strands of her friend's short, choppy blond hair, and finally her concerned blue eyes.

Once she was certain she wasn't going to spend the rest of her life groping in the dark, Rook breathed a sigh of relief and paused to take stock of everything else. "So, we're in Gray

Town?" she asked, just to be sure, although the answer was obvious once her nose recognized the sulfur fumes in the air.

The smoke-belching factories that dominated this part of Regara had also given the neighborhood its unfortunate nickname. The rest of it was lumber mills and of course the abandoned skyship yards, haunted by the skeletons of half-finished flying vessels that no longer had an animus to power them. It wasn't a pleasant sight, but then again, Gray Town had always been an unpleasant place, even before . . .

Even before the Great Catastrophe.

"We're on Farer's Street in the alley behind the navy warehouse," Drift confirmed. She sat down next to Rook, leaning against the alley wall. "We've been through here before."

Rook froze in the act of reaching up to rub her eyes again. A ripple of fear passed through her. "I remember, but isn't Farer's Street close to—"

"I know," Drift interrupted, and a quick, angry breeze filled the space between them, blowing Rook's hair back. The uncontrolled spate of magic told her better than words that her friend wasn't happy. "It's just a few blocks from the Wasteland, but the clients wouldn't agree to come any farther away. I think they live nearby and wanted to meet somewhere close to their home. Don't worry—Mr. Baroman thinks they can be trusted, and they brought the money, so all we have to do is wait for them to show up and collect."

"Right, simple enough," Rook said, but the fear refused

to go away. With everything that had happened so far that night, she'd almost forgotten they had a job to do.

It turned out exiles weren't the only people who needed to escape or hide. The Frenzy sickness had caused some citizens of Regara to abandon the city entirely for fear that they too might fall victim to the strange, terrifying illness. But while these people tended to leave the city by normal means, there were others in Regara—thieves, people being hunted over a debt, even simply those who couldn't afford to travel—who needed another option. People who were desperate enough to trust an exile like Rook to send them far away in the world for a new start.

For these people, Mr. Baroman, a clockmaker in town, was their first contact. The potential clients came to him with their situation, negotiated a fee and a meeting place, and then Mr. Baroman left messages for Drift in his attic, which she checked every few days. If all parties agreed to the terms, Rook and Drift met with the clients secretly somewhere in the city and Rook opened a door to wherever they wanted to go. The clients went through, and that was the end of it. Deal concluded. Everyone was happy, and Rook and Drift had money to survive on until the next job.

Drift rested a hand on Rook's shoulder. "Tell me what you're thinking," she said. "How many knots in your stomach?"

Rook bit her lip and considered the shape of her worries,

how they coiled inside her like sleeping snakes. "Three," she decided. "One's for the door I have to make." After the way her power had failed earlier, Rook wasn't in a trusting mood where her magic was concerned.

"Not a worry," Drift said, waving a hand. "You've already faced a Frenzy mob tonight. This will be nothing. Clear skies and smooth strides."

"A knot for the Wasteland," Rook said, wishing she shared Drift's confidence. "We're so close to it."

Drift nodded, not even bothering to try to reassure her on that one. Every person in Regara avoided that part of Gray Town when they could help it. Who could blame them?

It was the site of the Great Catastrophe.

"And there's a knot for . . ." Rook swallowed as she tried to dredge up the words. "I lost the bread," she said.

"You what?" Drift's brow furrowed in confusion.

"I bought bread at the market, a whole week's worth, and I lost it when the Frenzy came," Rook said, remembering those fresh-baked loaves with a stab of regret and longing. It was food they couldn't afford to lose. "I'm sorry."

"Hey, it's not your fault a Frenzy mob crashed the market," Drift said. She reached into the pocket of her trousers and pulled out a small cloth bundle. "But that reminds me: Mr. Baroman asked me to give this to you. He got one for each of us."

The object wrapped in the cloth warmed Rook's hands and

filled the dank air of the alley with the tantalizing scent of blueberries. She unwrapped it and pulled out a big fat shroom bun.

Rook's breath caught. "Mr. Baroman got this for *me*? Why?"

Drift counted off on her fingers. "Oh, only because you're amazing, talented, and usually too shy to come with me to his shop, so he's hoping to coax you in more often with a bribe," she said cheerfully.

And what a bribe it was. Shroom bun pastries were little works of art, famous in Regara, but also expensive and time-consuming to make. One half of the pastry was a warm roll with fruit baked into its narrow stem, while the top was a fluffy disc fashioned in the shape of a mushroom cap and dusted all over with powdered sugar.

Rook's mouth watered uncontrollably, but she resisted the urge to wolf down the gift. Food like this was precious. It would have been a crime to devour it—it needed to be *saved*, carefully wrapped, and measured out later to last for as many days as possible.

But it smelled so good and so fresh that it almost made Rook cry.

Drift smiled encouragement. "It's okay," she said. "Take a big bite now, while it's still warm, and we'll wrap up the rest for later. Maybe it'll even give you some courage."

"Courage?" Rook said skeptically.

"Blueberry-flavored courage—the strongest kind," Drift

assured her with a grin. "I had a bite of mine, and let me tell you, it's an explosion of happiness. Just . . . *boom*." She threw up her hands for emphasis.

Rook chuckled, and a tiny sliver of her worry faded away. She bit into the pastry and closed her eyes while she savored the sweet tang of blueberries filling her mouth. Warm, sugar-dusted, delicious.

When she opened her eyes, Drift was still grinning at her. "Boom," she whispered.

"Boom," Rook agreed.

With a wistful sigh, she rewrapped the pastry and tucked it carefully into her pocket. Another bite for later, she promised herself; a reward after this long night was all over.

A hush fell over the alley. The only sound came from an old Regaran sky fleet poster flapping in the breeze above her head, alongside a Wanted sign for world-famous sky pirates. Faded sketches of Red Danna, Merry Teagan, and Gerheart Blake stared defiantly across the alley. As far as Rook knew, none of the outlaws had been seen in over two years, not since the Great Catastrophe.

Drift, never one to stay still for long, stood up and began to pace, keeping watch all the while. A handful of people walked by the mouth of the alley, but Rook wasn't particularly worried about being seen. She and Drift were well hidden in the darkness behind a stack of old crates and trash barrels, and besides, no one lingered on the backstreets of Gray Town at night.

But Drift wasn't just watching for the clients, Rook knew. She marked each passerby to make sure they weren't wearing the gold-and-black uniforms of the Regaran constables— or the armbands of the Red Watchers. Technically, the Watchers were a citizens' group, formed in the wake of the Great Catastrophe, so they had no official authority. But they were notoriously good at hunting down exiles and turning them in to the constables, so no one complained. Once captured, the exiles disappeared, their fates unknown. The Watchers also had a reputation for being not so gentle with the exiles they caught. Point was, you didn't want to meet them in a back alley like this. You just didn't.

Minutes passed, and Rook began to fidget. Patience was not one of her strongest traits. "They should have come by now," she muttered.

Drift heard her but waved her off with a smile. "They're probably just taking their time, being extra cautious," she said. "That's a good thing for all of us."

Unless they'd been caught by the constables and were now leading them straight to this alley, Rook thought. By reflex, she tensed, ready to run if necessary.

Just then, movement at the mouth of the alley caught Rook's eye. Three figures were coming toward them, pressing close to the wall so they were hidden in shadow, just as Rook and Drift were.

A fourth knot, larger and heavier than the others, snapped tight in Rook's stomach. "There are three of them," she whispered to Drift, who'd come to stand beside her. "There were only supposed to be two."

This had never happened before. Mr. Baroman always gave them detailed descriptions of who they'd be meeting and how many people would be present so there were no surprises.

Rook plunged a hand into her pocket for her chalk, her mind fixed on the need to escape. One of the figures approaching might easily be a constable or a Red Watcher. She and Drift might have walked right into a trap.

5

THE UNPLANNED DOOR

"GET READY," DRIFT WHISPERED TO Rook. Wind swirled through the alley, stirring bits of trash into mini cyclones at her feet. "Stand near the wall so you can draw a quick escape door if there's trouble. Whatever happens, get back to the roost."

"Not without you," Rook said.

For the first time that night, a scowl found its way onto Drift's serene face. "We don't have time to argue, Rook. We may have to split up."

Rook never bothered replying to nonsense. She just raised an eyebrow at her friend. Drift must have gotten the message, because she said, "Have it your way. Now stop looking at me like you bit into a lemon."

The strangers arrived.

In front was an old man with patched trousers who walked with a noticeable limp, his left foot turned inward. A teenage boy kept pace beside him with one arm held out, not quite supporting the man, but keeping close by in case he stumbled. Behind him came a middle-aged woman with a worn-out look in her eyes and a faint scar down the center of her left cheek.

Rook watched the scarred woman nervously. She was the one who wasn't supposed to be here. The old man and the boy at least matched the descriptions Mr. Baroman had given Drift. He'd said they were a small family, a grandfather and grandson—the Kelmins. They'd lived in Gray Town all their lives, but after the Great Catastrophe, both the Kelmins had lost their jobs at the skyship factory.

The grandfather had decided to retire while the boy looked for work elsewhere, but one day a group of men came to their house, offering their services as "protection" from burglars. When the Kelmins refused to pay the men, they threatened to burn down their house and promised to come after them if they told the constables or tried to leave the city. They needed to escape Regara in secret, and Rook's magic was their best option.

Drift put on a bright smile as the trio approached. "Hello," she said, keeping her voice low but friendly. "We're so glad you made it here safely. And it looks like we've picked up an extra guest." She said it politely, but she glanced pointedly at the woman, silently waiting for her to explain her presence.

Before the woman could reply, the grandson spoke. "She's with us," he said shortly. "It's fine."

They waited, but no further explanation seemed to be

coming, so Drift stuck out her hand. "Well then, let's introduce ourselves," she said, a bit reluctantly. "I'm Drift, and this is my friend Rook."

There was an awkward pause as Mr. Kelmin and his grandson looked down at Drift's outstretched hand. By the expression on their faces, she might as well have been holding out a poisonous snake and encouraging them to pat its head. The woman said nothing, but the grandson shifted so that he stood slightly in front of the old man.

Drift's friendly smile never wavered. She lowered her hand and took a step back to give them all some space.

Finally, Mr. Kelmin seized his courage. "It's a pleasure to meet you both," he said, his voice quiet and scratchy, as if he were getting over a cough. "My grandson and I are thankful for your assistance."

Thankful but still afraid of dealing with exiles. Rook felt a rush of anger, though she knew she shouldn't be surprised by the Kelmins' attitude. Some of their other clients had reacted the same way, especially in neighborhoods like Gray Town that were next to the Wasteland. The people of Regara had taken magic for granted for so long they never expected it to turn on them. When it did, they needed somebody to blame.

Taking a deep breath, Rook tried not to scowl at Mr. Kelmin. He was at least making an effort to be polite. "Mr. Baroman told you how my . . . how this works, right?" she asked.

Her gaze darted suspiciously to the woman. She hated doing this when they still didn't know if the woman was a threat, a Red Watcher or a constable waiting to ambush them.

"The clockmaker said you . . . well, that you could *transport*"—Mr. Kelmin's voice quavered on the last word— "us to safety. I have a cousin in Siranta, a village on the Island Nation of Contis. We'd thought to try to book passage there across the White Sea, but we couldn't raise the money to get that far, not in time anyway." He stared down at Rook, a doubtful expression in his eyes. "Can you really help us get there?"

Rook nodded. "I can send you anywhere in this world you want to go." She glanced at Drift. This next part was going to be tricky. It always was.

Drift cleared her throat and smiled her most easygoing smile. "We're glad to help. All we need is for one of you— probably Mr. Kelmin, since it's his cousin—to take Rook's hand so that her magic can get an impression of that village from your thoughts. Kind of like molding a piece of clay," she explained. "It won't take a minute, and then we'll be ready to go."

She made it sound as simple as a walk in the sunshine, but it wasn't. Really wasn't. Rook's power—when she used it to create a door for someone else—involved touching a person's mind and getting a glimpse of the feelings nearest their heart. Nobody, no matter how open-minded about magic, wanted an exile that close.

Sure enough, a look of horror twisted the grandson's face. "Wait a minute, y-you mean she's going to read his mind? No one said anything about that! Grandfather, it's a trick! You can't let them do that to you!"

His words made Rook lose her grip on her temper. She squeezed the piece of chalk in her hand, snapping it in half. "Fine with me," she said, and turned to Drift. "We can leave now. They don't want our help."

"Rook, now, let's not be rude," Drift said, at the same time Mr. Kelmin was trying to quiet his grandson. The conversation was deteriorating fast.

And then the scarred woman, who'd been standing silent as a ghost behind the Kelmins, spoke for the first time.

"Everyone, please lower your voices," she said. Her tone was soothing, yet it carried an unmistakable ring of authority that cut through the chaos of the moment. "Let's all calm ourselves and think clearly."

Rook glanced at the woman, her suspicions still aroused even though the woman spoke reasonably. "Who are you?" Rook asked, tired of being polite. "Mr. Baroman didn't say anything about you being here. I don't see a red band on your arm, but that doesn't mean you aren't a Red Watcher in disguise."

"My name is Lily," the woman said, fixing Rook with such a clear, penetrating gaze that Rook lost some of her bravado. "I'm not with the Red Watchers. The Kelmins are my friends."

"It's true," Mr. Kelmin said, giving Lily a grateful smile. "She offered to help us when no one else would."

Lily took the old man's hand and squeezed it affectionately. When she turned back to Rook and Drift, her eyes were sharp. "I came to make certain they escaped the city and that they weren't being taken in by charlatans who *claim* to have magic but might just be trying to wring as much money from them as possible."

"That's not what we do," Drift said quickly. "You can trust us. We're the real thing."

"Oh?" The woman raised an eyebrow. "Perhaps you'd care to give us a demonstration?"

Drift bit her lip, considering. "Fair enough," she said, "but I'll need some room."

The Kelmins and Lily obligingly backed up several feet. Rook stayed where she was, but for the moment, everyone had lost interest in her. They had fixed their attention on Drift, waiting to see what trick or talent her friend might display. They were probably expecting something horrifying. Was the boyish little blond girl about to turn into a hideous monster with fangs and boils before their very eyes? Rook gritted her teeth. They had no idea the beautiful things Drift was capable of.

Although they were about to find out how she'd gotten her name.

With all eyes on her, Drift held her arms out from her sides and conjured a light wind that whistled through the alley and fluttered her bangs. The breeze was fine and cool against

Rook's cheeks. Just knowing it came from her friend eased some of the turmoil inside her.

But Drift was just getting started. She flicked her slender fingers and brought forth a heavier, more focused wind. It came from beneath her, blowing her hair straight up and effortlessly lifting her six inches off the ground.

Mr. Kelmin gasped. The boy grabbed his grandfather's arm, digging his fingers in. They stared at the hovering girl, and even Lily looked impressed.

Drift turned to Rook and extended her hand. Clearly, she had one more demonstration in mind. Rook reached up and took Drift's hand and immediately felt a sharp updraft beneath her feet. She relaxed into the wind and let it lift her up to hover beside Drift. Hand in hand, they stood before the Kelmins and Lily, smiling, as if floating in midair were the most natural thing in the world.

"Is that proof enough for you?" Drift asked. The whole time she was addressing the group, she watched the alley entrance to make certain no one else was witnessing the display. "Will you trust us?"

The Kelmins and Lily exchanged a look. "I—we believe you," Mr. Kelmin said hesitantly. He stared as Drift guided herself and Rook back to the ground, then he reached into his pocket and pulled out a small pouch that jingled with coins. He gave it to Drift. "Here's the payment we agreed on—it's not much, but it's all the money we can spare."

And with that, he held out a trembling hand to Rook.

Rook didn't wait for him to change his mind. She took Mr. Kelmin's hand in a firm grip and closed her eyes. "Think of the place you want to go—no, the place you *need* to go, more than anywhere else in the world," she instructed. "The magic reacts to feeling, and the place you feel the strongest about at this moment is the place it will take you."

She had no idea if Mr. Kelmin was listening to her, but the older man's grip tightened. Rook felt an answering jolt of power inside her, and a sweet, flowery scent filled her nostrils.

With the magic in place, Rook released the old man's hand and opened her eyes. Mr. Kelmin looked a bit dazed. He held his hand extended for a second longer before dropping it. He gazed at Rook in wonder.

"That was . . . so strange," he whispered. "I was thinking of my cousin's house. It's a very old place. We played there as children. There were wild orchids growing in the field behind the house, and every summer we'd pick some for our mothers. For a moment, just now, I thought . . . well, I thought I smelled the orchids. Isn't that the oddest thing?"

Rook didn't answer, didn't tell him that she smelled the orchids too. Full of the power of Mr. Kelmin's happy memory, she turned to the alley wall and began to draw.

Nerves fluttered inside her. She was never comfortable with so many people watching. Still, her magic did its work. When she'd finished joining her lines, golden light poured from the chalk drawing, snapping into place to create a plain wooden door with a worn brass knob, something you'd probably see in any common household in Regara.

Everything was going to be all right, Rook told herself. She just needed to send the Kelmins through the door, and then she and Drift were free to go home and eat the rest of their shroom buns.

She reached for the knob and eased the door open. There was a soft hiss of air, and a cold wind danced over Rook's skin. Too cold for the Island Nation of Contis. Snowflakes swirled at her feet, and the familiar scent of pine needles filled the air even as a rush of foreboding swallowed her heart.

It was back. The strange, dark forest that haunted her, twisting her magic to return her doors to this same spot. Rook stared into the blackness as that sense of eyes watching fixed on her and intensified. She tried to pull back, but somehow she couldn't make herself close the door.

Behind her, Drift spoke up. "We're off the mark a little bit, but not to worry," she said, and put her hand on Rook's shoulder, giving it a reassuring squeeze. "We'll just let Rook rest for a few minutes before she tries again. Right, Rook?"

Rook forced herself to turn and look at Drift. Concern filled her friend's eyes. Rook knew it wasn't because she'd made a mistake. Never that. It was because Drift saw that Rook was afraid.

"Y-yes, we'll try again in just a minute," Rook said. She started to close the door and banish the forest, but to her surprise, Lily stepped up and stood in her way.

"Where does it lead?" she asked curiously, peering among the dark, snow-laden trees. "Do you know?"

"I don't want to know," Rook said, and again tried to shut the door, but Lily stood calmly in its path.

"It could be Braidenwood Forest," Mr. Kelmin said, a note of awe in his voice. He pointed to the ridges of bark on the closest tree, interwoven like strands of hair. Rook stared at him blankly. "That's in the northern part of the kingdom of Izfel," he explained. "Braidenwood trees only grow up there, and it's very cold, so there aren't many people. In fact, some stories say the forest is haunted, covered in strange mists that make it impossible to see."

Rook clenched her jaw and took a step back. Just her luck to repeatedly open a door to a haunted forest. "If that's true, then what are we still staring at it for?" she asked, irritated that Lily refused to get out of the way.

"Wait," Lily said, cocking her head as if listening to something. "Do you hear that?"

Rook started to say no, when she realized she did hear something. It was a soft, rapid sound, like raindrops pattering on a rooftop.

Or feet crunching snow.

Then, in the distance, Rook caught movement, a large, shadowy form bounding through the dark forest, shaking snow and icicles from the trees as it arrowed straight toward them.

"Get back!" Rook cried, shooing Lily and the Kelmins

away. She pushed Drift aside with her other hand, forgetting to be quiet, not caring who saw them in the alley. Something was coming. She heard its harsh breath as it neared the door, so fast, a blur of claws and fur.

Lily and the Kelmins scrambled out of the way, pressing themselves against the far wall of the alley. "Shut the door!" Lily shouted.

Rook grabbed the knob and flung the door closed, but instead of clicking into place, the wood slammed into something solid. There came a muffled thump, followed by a high-pitched squeal, like an animal in pain.

Then the door burst open, and a huge shadow landed in the alley right in front of Rook.

6

THE DOOR TO SHADOWS

FEAR FROZE ROOK'S BOOTS TO the cobblestones as she stared at the creature occupying a large portion of the alley. It stood on four legs and was covered in a generous coat of red, white, and black fur. If Rook didn't know better, she would have sworn the creature was a fox. She'd seen them sometimes running wild in Gray Town, sniffing at trash cans or making dens in the ditches behind the factories.

But never this big. The creature was larger than a wolf, lips curled back to reveal rows of long, thin white teeth. It shook itself, spraying wet snow across the front of Rook's shirt. Even with the freezing droplets hitting her skin, she still couldn't find the strength to run. The creature threw its head back and let out a deep-throated howl.

A scurrying movement came from behind her, and then Drift was there, seizing Rook around the waist. She felt herself lifted into the air, out of reach of the fox. On the ground,

Lily had grabbed Mr. Kelmin and his grandson and was backing them slowly toward the alley mouth.

Suddenly, there came another commotion to their right. Footsteps and voices filled the air. Rook twisted in Drift's grasp just in time to see three constables step into the alley.

"That's where the shouts were coming from, and then I heard— Look!" one of the constables cried, pointing. "Exiles! And a Wasteland monster! Block the alley!"

"Oh no," Drift whispered. She carried them higher, aiming for the nearest rooftop. "We have to get out of here."

Below them, Lily and the Kelmins were running toward the constables, their hands in the air. "Help!" Mr. Kelmin cried. "Shoot the beast! Shoot it!"

The fox, as if sensing the danger, flattened its ears and pressed its big body into a crouch. A snarl escaped its throat, and the patches of red and white fur on its body darkened, turning all to black.

And growing.

Rook's mouth fell open. Inky black shadows poured from the fox's body, wreathing it like smoke. The shadows broke apart and drifted in pieces to fill the alley. Slowly, they reshaped themselves, lengthening and sharpening into dark replicas of the fox, complete with pointed ears and bushy black tails. They had no eyes, but the shadow creatures' mouths were unnaturally wide, opening in unison to let out a chorus of howls.

By that point, Lily and the Kelmins had reached the constables, who ushered them quickly out of the alley and then formed a line to block the entrance, trapping the shadow foxes.

"Shoot it!" one of the constables shouted, just as the foxes burst into motion, passing beneath Rook and Drift and sprinting to the mouth of the alley.

Cracks of pistol shot filled the air, ricocheting off the alley wall. Drift surged upward, lifting Rook over the edge of the nearest roof and dropping her on the slanted tiles. Rook fell to her knees, scraping her skin on the rough surface. More shots rang out from below.

Rook pushed herself up and began a half run, half climb to the top of the roof, throwing one leg over the peak, then the other, and sliding down the tiles on the opposite side. She didn't have to look back to know Drift was behind her. She felt the rush of wind and heard her friend's labored breathing as she flew through the air.

When she reached the edge of the roof, Rook shouted, "Have you got me?"

"Always," Drift called back.

That was all Rook needed to hear. She leaped from the rooftop, legs and arms pumping, soaring over another empty alley. But she wasn't going to make it to the next rooftop, not by a long shot.

Just as she was starting to fall, Drift snatched her out of the air. A quick surge of wind bore them aloft again, boosting

Rook the rest of the way to the next rooftop. Behind them, the frightful howling continued.

"They can't kill it," Rook said as Drift flew over her shoulder and landed on the roof tiles just a few feet above her. "They're shooting at shadows."

"Well, one of them isn't a shadow," Drift said. She craned her neck to try to see behind them down to street level. "I'll be right back—I need to get a better view."

She leaped off the roof, the wind carrying her to the top of a nearby metal tower rising up between the warehouses. It was an old skyship docking station, abandoned and rusting, with an empty animus crystal still fastened to its peak. The crystal was useless now, of course, its magic entirely spent. But from the platform at the top of the tower, Drift had a clear overhead view of the surrounding streets.

Rook didn't want to look. More screams shattered the air, and then came the sound of running feet from several directions at once. Drift jumped off the tower and zoomed back to the roof where Rook was crouched.

"The townspeople have seen it," Drift reported, her face grim. "They're running."

Rook's heart sank. If the constables didn't stop them, the fox creatures would be free to terrorize everyone in Gray Town.

"This is my fault," Rook moaned. Her magic had betrayed her in the worst possible way this time.

"Hey, now." Drift slid down the roof tiles until she was near enough to put her arm around Rook. "If anyone's to blame, it's me. I should have gotten that woman out of the way and slammed the door as soon as we saw that it wasn't the right place. The constables will take care of the monster, but then they'll be looking for *us*. We need to get out of here."

Drift was right—beating themselves up about it wasn't going to help. They had to get to safety. Rook stood, and the two of them scrambled to the peak of the roof and down the other side. Drift wrapped her arms around Rook and a fresh wind launched them into the air. They flew to the next rooftop, and the next, until an imposing wall of gray stone loomed before them, the barrier that encircled the Wasteland and guarded the citizens of Regara from what lay within.

Dread stirred inside Rook, a fear unlike anything she'd ever felt before. She wanted to tell Drift to hurry, to get them as far away from that wall as possible, but she could feel Drift's magic weakening. The wind that boosted them had gone from a gale to a feeble puff. Drift had used too much of her power all at once during their escape.

"Are you all right?" Rook asked over her shoulder.

"Think so . . . Just need . . . quick rest," Drift said, breathless. She landed them on the peak of the nearest roof and sagged against Rook's shoulder.

Rook steadied her, but her attention was still on that massive wall. Sailors claimed it was the first thing they saw when approaching the Regaran port, miles before the rest of the city came into view.

And the sky above the wall was always a different color than the sky over the rest of the city.

Today it was blister red, clouds swirling in a towering vortex, almost as if the wind was blowing in different directions on the other side of the wall. It probably was. The Wasteland obeyed no laws of nature.

Two years ago, the area had simply been Lake Caralan, the site where the Voran wizards had constructed a permanent magical portal between the world of Talhaven and the wizards' world of Vora. For years, ships from Vora had sailed out of the great stone archway housing the portal and on to every trading port in Talhaven, carrying animus crystals filled with magic that would change people's lives. It was, or so the stories went, a time of cooperation and prosperity for both worlds.

After the Great Catastrophe, the area around Lake Caralan was forever changed. The portal explosion had released a huge amount of magic into Regara, but it had somehow become corrupted. Overnight, strange plants grew on the wreckage of buildings, creating a wilderness in the ruins. Terrible sounds came from within, the shrieks of animals exposed to the soured magic. It transformed them. Made monsters of them. Soon after, the first cases of Frenzy started showing up among the Regarans.

No one knew how to get rid of the dangerous magic, so to save the city and protect the people from this new disaster, the mayor of Regara ordered that the lake and surrounding area be walled off completely from the rest of the city.

In the two years since, the rest of Regara had managed to recover, but after all that had happened, could anyone blame people for being afraid of magic and the exiles? With a wince, Rook remembered the looks on the Kelmins' faces. Many Regarans had lost loved ones in the portal explosion, and others were now threatened by a strange, violent magical illness. The exiles and their power would always be a reminder of these tragedies.

"Sorry," Drift said, breaking into Rook's dark thoughts. "I'm better now, and I think we're far enough away from the constables that we can fly down here." She nodded to the trash-strewn alley below them. "Get ready to draw the door to the roost."

They stepped off the roof, letting Drift's wind cradle them until their boots landed on the cobblestones. Rook looked around. Behind them was a dead end, and the mouth of the alley was almost completely blocked by a dozen overflowing trash cans. The shouts from the constables were barely audible in the distance. Now was the time to escape.

Taking out her chalk, Rook sketched the hasty outline of a door, not even bothering to make it a normal-sized entry. She and Drift would have to duck going through it.

She was finishing the last line when Drift screamed.

7

THE DOOR OUT

ROOK WHIRLED JUST IN TIME to see the giant fox rise from where it had been hiding among the trash cans. None of its shadows was anywhere to be seen, and the fox's fur had returned to its original red, black, and white color, but the sheer size of the creature made Rook tense with fright.

She grabbed Drift's arm and instinctively pulled the other girl behind her. Not that it would do much good. The thing was big enough to rip through them both like paper. But if Drift managed to get in the air fast enough—

As if it had heard the thought, the creature leaped, closing the distance between them in an instant. Its bulk filled the narrow alley even without its shadow doubles.

They were trapped. The beast was too close—if they tried to fly away, it would tear them out of the air before they got more than a foot off the ground. And there was nothing but a bare alley wall behind them.

"Go," Rook hissed at Drift. "I'll distract it while you fly away."

"Save your breath," Drift said, clamping her hand on Rook's wrist. "I'm not going anywhere."

Rook dared to take her eyes off the creature, glaring at Drift over her shoulder. "Don't be stubborn," she said. "This is *my* fault. I don't want you dying because I was stupid and—"

"Wait," Drift interrupted, tightening her grip on Rook's wrist. *"Look."*

Rook turned, half expecting to see the creature's open mouth waiting to take a bite out of her. Instead, the giant fox was lying on the ground, resting its head on its paws. Its eyes were half closed, and the beast's tongue lolled out the side of its mouth like a puppy's.

"What's it doing?" Rook whispered as she slid back a step to put some distance between themselves and the creature.

"I don't know," Drift said, backing up with her, "but once we get far enough away, you need to brace yourself, because I'm going to take off *fast*. Like hair-standing-straight-up-on-your-head fast."

"But the door's finished," Rook said, nodding to the alley wall. It was a plain white rectangle with hinges in the shape of silver half-moons. "If we can just get through it, we'll be safe."

"Leave it for now," Drift said. "We'll lead this thing away and then circle back and use the door to get home."

Good enough, Rook thought, and braced herself for a wind gust to end all wind gusts.

Just then, the fox raised its head and *whimpered* at them.

Rook stared at the creature, her curiosity temporarily overcoming her fear. If she didn't know better, she would have sworn the fox was *begging*—but for food, attention, or something else?

Drift tugged Rook's waist, preparing to fly, but some strange compulsion made Rook hesitate. "Wait," she said, putting her hands over Drift's to stop her taking off. "I think it's . . . I don't think it wants to hurt us."

Drift let out a squeak of disbelief. "Are you serious? That thing's dangerous! Didn't you see the way it *pulled darkness out of its body?*"

"Yes, but it was surrounded by strangers with pistols," Rook pointed out, "and it didn't know where it was. Maybe it was just scared."

Drift was silent, as if she was thinking that over. "I suppose it's possible," she said after a moment. "But how do we know it won't go from scared to angry? Or hungry? We should go."

"But we can't just leave it here," Rook said. "If the constables find it, they'll kill it."

And that, too, would be her fault.

"Then what do you suggest?" Drift asked. "We can't stay here all day. The constables will track us all down eventually."

"I have to try to send him back where he belongs," Rook said. "Back to that forest."

"But you've already made a door to the roost," Drift said. "What are you going to do with that one?"

"I'll change it," Rook said. She gently disengaged herself from Drift's grasp and sidled up to the door, keeping one eye on the huge fox. He watched her just as keenly, his bushy tail swishing back and forth like a broom.

Rook reached out and laid her hand on the silver doorknob. She closed her eyes and let the magic flow out of her and back into the door. It was a trick she'd learned not long after she'd arrived in this world.

The constables had taken all the exiles and housed them in temporary dormitories where sailors usually stayed when they were in port. It was a cramped space, and it smelled like dirty laundry. Rook secretly got up in the middle of the night, sat on the floor beside her bed, and practiced making doors. She tried not to draw the attention of the other children, but most of them were too busy conducting small, hesitant tests of their own powers to notice her. They were all hoping the same thing—to use their magic to escape.

With each door Rook created, she had only one destination in mind.

Take us back to Vora, she'd silently beg before opening the doors. She had no memory of what that world looked like, but she'd heard one important detail from the few Regarans who'd been allowed on the other side of the portal.

In Vora, the sky was red, as red as it ever was over the Wasteland.

So Rook practiced her magic in the dead of night, searching desperately for that blazing sky. Each time, her doors opened to a different place, but it was always in the world of Talhaven. Never home, a family waiting for her with open arms.

Undeterred, Rook kept going, testing her powers. One of those tests was to see how many times she could change the destination of a door once she'd created it. She'd discovered that three was her limit. Any more attempts and she ended up bent over a bucket throwing up.

That was how Drift found her one night: head in a bucket, white hair flopping all over, next to a tiny green door the size of a shoebox. Drift had gotten her a glass of water and a damp rag to clean herself up, and then the two of them had sat on the floor, talking for hours. They whispered about how they felt so lonely, though neither of them could remember what or who they should be lonely for. Rook had made over a dozen doors that night, but she'd had no idea she would also make a friend.

The doorknob warmed under her fingertips. Rook opened her eyes and turned the knob. She was more cautious this time, opening the door a crack, just wide enough to let in a rush of snowy wind. Beyond the door loomed the dark forest and the pine trees with their icy skins. For once, Rook was relieved that her magic had returned to the haunted forest.

The destination a success, Rook turned to face the giant fox. She wasn't quite sure how to coax it through the door. Maybe if it smelled the forest, it'd be drawn back to where it belonged. She opened the door a little wider.

"Do you smell that . . . er . . . Mr. Fox?" she asked, opening and shutting the door to fan the wind into the alley. "It's your home. It's okay now. You can go back to the forest." The fox swung its head toward her, and Rook pulled the door wide, stepping to one side of it. "Go home! You're free!" she announced.

And she waited.

And Drift waited.

But the fox just sat in the middle of the alley with its tongue lolling out the side of its mouth.

Rook shifted her weight from one foot to another, kicking at the cobblestones. Maybe it was better if she approached the creature more like a dog.

"Come on, boy!" she called, slapping her thigh. When that got no reaction, she put her fingers in her mouth and whistled. "Over here! Be a good boy!"

The fox's ears twitched, and slowly it pushed itself up to its full, impressive height. Drift let out a gasp. "Be careful, Rook," she said.

"It's all right," Rook assured her, though she really had no way of knowing that. She just had a feeling. Staring into the fox's warm, intelligent eyes, she was sure the beast wasn't going to hurt her.

Rook gestured to the open door again. The creature ambled over and stood in front of her, its head almost at eye level, its tail thumping the ground.

Now Rook was getting impatient. The constables were

coming, their distant shouts getting louder as they tracked the fox. They had to get this done. She made a shooing motion in the fox's direction—not enough to startle it, she hoped, but just enough to get it moving through the door. It wasn't as if she could push it through.

"Go on, boy," Drift chimed in, clapping her hands gently and pointing to the door. "Don't you recognize your home? Your family must be missing you."

Rook gulped, trying to imagine an even larger mama and papa fox running around the dark forest. Why couldn't the beast just *move* so she could shut the door and close off the haunted place?

Then, before Rook could react, the fox stretched out his head to sniff at Rook's pocket, the one that held the shroom bun. Rook went absolutely still. She had to fight the urge to scramble backward and put space between herself and the creature. The fox inched closer, snuffling around her, nudging his head against her flank. His nose left a wet mark on her pants leg.

As she stood there, a familiar burning sensation spread through Rook's chest. She was exhausted from running and jumping off rooftops, but that wasn't what caused the feeling. It happened when she left a magical door open too long. She was getting weak, just as Drift had earlier when she'd used too much magic flying them from rooftop to rooftop.

Rook's legs wobbled and she gripped the door handle for support. "Please," she said, involuntarily reaching out toward the fox. Her hand froze in midair. What was she doing? This wasn't a dog to be petted! "You have to go now. I can't keep the door open. Don't you see—if we leave, you'll be stranded here, with no family and no way to get home!"

Desperate, Rook reached into her pocket and took out the shroom bun. Without even looking at it, she hurled it through the doorway into the dark forest, where it landed with a soft thump in the snow. The fox's head snapped around to follow the movement, but it stayed where it was.

"There!" Rook shouted. So much for blueberry-flavored courage. "Go get it. Eat up!"

But the fox didn't budge. Rook stared helplessly into the creature's eyes. They were amber colored, with little flecks of black at the center. White whiskers twitched along its snout as it stared back at her steadily.

Rook's vision swam, and the world tilted. Her hand slid off the doorknob and her legs gave out. The door swung shut with a sharp click, but Rook didn't see it. She caught a streak of red in front of her eyes, and then she was falling. Somewhere far away, she heard Drift cry out her name.

8

THE DOOR TO ROOK'S ROOST

As Rook swam slowly back to consciousness, she felt her cheek resting on a strange bed of something soft and prickly. She took a deep breath, inhaling the scent of damp fur and wildness. Her eyes flew open.

The fox, she discovered, was stretched out on the ground beneath her. It must have caught her when she fainted. Drift was kneeling beside them, feeling Rook's forehead with the back of her hand. "Are you all right?" she asked.

Carefully, Rook pushed herself up off the fox's back and into a sitting position. "I think so," she said. She thought she'd only been out for a few seconds, but the burning sensation in her chest from having kept the door open too long had disappeared. She glanced over at the door and saw that it had vanished.

Frustrated, Rook clenched her hands into fists. The constables' shouts still echoed in the distance as they hunted for the fox. It sounded like there were even more of them now.

"I'll rest a minute and then open the door again," she said. She'd push aside her fear and drag the fox through the door herself if she had to, but she was getting the beast home.

Drift's mouth pressed into a line, while another line formed between her brows. "No you don't," she said. "You've already worn yourself out, and we've stayed here too long." As if to emphasize this, footsteps sounded from the next street over. Too close. The constables were searching for them street by street. At this rate, they'd find them in minutes.

Rook wobbled to her feet and grabbed Drift's arm. "Then let's take it with us," she said, nodding at the fox.

Drift blinked. "Back to the roost? You can't be serious!"

Rook swayed on her feet. The fox sprang up and pressed its big body against her to steady her. A sane person probably would have jumped back, screamed, or tried to run away, but Rook was discovering she was too exhausted to be afraid. She abandoned all sense and flung an arm over the fox's back, leaning against it for support.

"I don't think it's dangerous," Rook said. Quite the opposite, the creature seemed perfectly content to serve as Rook's crutch. Its lips pulled back from its teeth, not in a threatening way, more like a goofy, foxy grin.

"Maaaaybe," Drift said reluctantly. "But will it fit in the roost?"

Rook shrugged. "Only one way to find out," she said. With the fox walking beside her, she stumbled over to the wall and raised a hand to sketch yet another door. "It's only temporary,

Drift, I promise. As soon as I get my strength back, we'll send it home."

Assuming they could even get back to their hideout. This time, when she drew the door, Rook's lines were so haphazard that when they snapped into place, they formed a circle instead of a rectangle, and a black doorknob appeared in the center, surrounded by bright orange wood. A pumpkin door, Rook thought, but she didn't have time to be critical. The footsteps and voices were almost on top of them.

"Let's go," she said, pulling open the door. She didn't hesitate. She dove through with Drift at her heels, and the fox followed close behind.

As the door swung shut, Rook found herself in a familiar underground tunnel. After the humid, smoke-ridden air of Gray Town, the cool draft blowing through the passage dried the sweat at Rook's neck and went a long way toward clearing her head.

The door vanished, and for a moment it was pitch black. Still, Rook wasn't afraid. In fact, she was so relieved she almost felt like fainting again. Her magic hadn't failed her this time. This was the path to the roost, the way home.

They waited in the dark, and as their eyes adjusted, Rook could make out soft light shining down on them. Starlight. Strewn along the tunnel ceiling was a glittering field, a perfect replica of the night sky.

As it always did when she gazed up at the strange ceiling, the magic inside Rook stirred. She started down the tunnel,

Drift and the fox beside her. It ended in a blank wall, unremarkable but for a light coating of yellow chalk dust—the faded remnants of many, many other doors.

Rook stepped up to the wall and added yet another. Her magic doors took many different forms, but the way to the roost was always the same: a small yellow door with a black latch and matching hinges in the shape of stars.

She undid the latch, pushed the door open, and was greeted by the welcoming scent of woodsmoke filling a warm living room. A gray stone fireplace dominated the opposite wall, and a fire burned behind the iron grate. Neither Rook nor Drift had lit one before they left, yet a fire was always waiting for them when they came home, just as the house was always the perfect temperature, no matter the season. It was all part of the magic of the place, an unexplainable wonder they had gradually grown accustomed to over the past two years.

There were two beds, one on either side of the fireplace. A blue patchwork quilt was crumpled up in the center of Rook's bed, its surface peppered with stars done in bright yellow cloth. Drift's quilt was red and lay neatly folded at the end of her bed. A large orange sun was sewn on the front and a blue moon on the back. They'd found them inside a pair of wooden trunks that sat at the foot of each of the beds when they'd discovered the roost. The only other rooms were the kitchen and a small washroom at the back of the house.

Once everyone had filed in, Rook closed the door and banished it. Slowly, all the tension and fear of the past few hours fell away. This was the one place where she and Drift could relax.

Drift wandered across the room and plopped down on her bed. On the wall behind her, she'd hung drawings from her sketchbook, the only luxury she owned. Most of them were of birds, dogs, or dolphins she'd seen swimming in the harbor, but some of them were sketches of Rook's doors.

Rook had hung nothing on the wall above her own bed, but there was a single small window, in itself a mystery. The window didn't open, and its glass panes refused to break, no matter what you tried to smash them with.

It was dark now, but outside the window, Rook knew, there was an open field, with nothing but tall, wavy grasses in shades of green and yellow as far as the horizon. Rook spent many nights staring out the window at the millions of stars overhead. Her favorite was one bright red star visible only on certain nights. She'd only ever seen it out this window.

They had stumbled on the mysterious house by accident while running from the Red Watchers, not long after Rook and Drift first met and escaped their captivity together. Drift had been terrified at the time that they were going to be caught. With the angry, red-banded citizens closing in, Rook had taken Drift's hand and asked her to think of the place she most wanted to go. Wide-eyed, Drift had shouted, "I don't care! Far away from here."

Good enough.

Rook drew the door and found the star tunnel to the blank

stone wall. When Rook drew a second door, it led them to the magical house. There were no entrances to Rook's Roost— that was what Drift had named the place—except through the doors Rook created. So neither of them knew exactly where in Talhaven the house was located.

Rook asked Drift later what she had been thinking when she'd imagined where she wanted to escape. Drift replied that her mind had gone blank, and all she could think was that she wanted to go someplace that was completely safe, someplace no one would ever find them if they didn't want to be found.

The roost had fulfilled the wish of her heart.

Now there was a fox the size of a giant wolf bounding around in the middle of it.

It skidded to a stop next to the fireplace, stuck its paws out, and performed an impressive full-body stretch. Then it shook from head to tail before collapsing on the braided rug with a contented sigh.

"Hey, don't get too comfortable," Rook warned. "Remember, you're going home as soon as I've rested."

The fox rolled over onto its back, four paws sticking up in the air, and closed its eyes.

Rook shook her head in exasperation and sat down on the edge of her bed. She no longer felt any fear of the beast. The only problem was, the fox took up all the space in front of the fire and then some, making the house feel even smaller than it usually did.

Drift stood and headed to the kitchen, emerging a few minutes later with two glasses of water, one of which she handed to Rook. She glanced down at the fox, raised an eyebrow, and then went back to the kitchen, returning with a bowl of milk, which she carefully placed on the floor in front of the fireplace.

"Do foxes drink milk?" she asked Rook.

Rook shrugged.

They got their answer when the fox rolled to its feet, sniffed the bowl curiously, then lapped at it with a long pink tongue. After a few seconds, the lapping became gulping, and suddenly the milk was gone and the fox was licking the bowl so hard it looked like it might scrape the paint off.

"Hungry beast," Rook remarked.

Drift laughed. "I'll see what else I can find."

She returned to the kitchen and this time came back with a wedge of slightly stale cheese Rook had bought on a previous visit to the Night Market. Drift broke it up into bite-sized chunks and knelt by the fire, intending to drop them into the empty bowl, but the fox darted forward and snatched a piece from her hand so fast that Drift barely had time to yelp. The fox parked itself in front of her and whimpered, waiting for more.

Rook giggled at the expression on Drift's face—a look somewhere between shock and laughter. "Well, you really are tame, aren't you?" Drift said. Hesitantly, she held out her hand, palm up, offering the rest of the cheese. The fox wolfed the chunks down in one great bite, then ran its enormous tongue over Drift's empty palm, checking for crumbs.

"Eew," Drift said, yanking her hand back and wiping it on her pants. "We're going to have to teach you some manners."

"Yeah," Rook laughed. "Don't you know it's not polite to drool all over the hand that's feeding you?"

The fox sat back on its hindquarters and stared dolefully at both of them.

"No," Drift said, holding up a finger. "One meal at a time."

"Besides," Rook said, standing and stretching. "I've rested enough. It's time for me to send you home."

In response, the fox collapsed on the rug and turned its head away from her.

"That's not going to work," Rook said, hands on her hips. "You can't stay here, no matter how nice the fire feels. You're too big for this house. You belong in the open forest where you can run and hunt and play with the other giant foxes."

She reached into her pocket and fished out her chalk. When she approached the wall opposite the fireplace, the fox let out a high-pitched, mournful whine that filled the whole house. Rook whirled to find the creature staring intently at her.

Drift's brow furrowed as she glanced between Rook and the fox. "It really doesn't want to go," she said. "Maybe we let it sleep here, just for—"

But Drift didn't finish the sentence. Her face had gone very still. She had reached into her pocket, and there was the sound of dozens of coins jingling. Rook's stomach turned over as Drift pulled out the money pouch Mr. Kelmin had given them in the alley. It held the coins they'd been paid for a job they'd failed to do.

A job *Rook* had failed to do.

It was a long moment before either of them said anything. In the end, Drift was the one who broke the silence. "I . . . In all the confusion, the running, I forgot I had these," she stammered. "I guess we should go to Mr. Baroman, see if he can help us find the Kelmins so we can try again to get them out of the city." Her eyes were downcast as she spoke.

Rook knew what she was thinking. After witnessing a giant beast jump through one of Rook's doors and create menacing shadow doubles of itself, the Kelmins, already skittish of magic, might not want to have anything to do with her or Drift ever again. And if that was the case, they obviously couldn't keep the Kelmins' money, not without having completed the job.

But when Rook met Drift's eyes, she saw the pain there, the conflict. It mirrored her own feelings.

They *needed* that money. In the early days, after their escape but before they started working with Mr. Baroman, they'd come close to starvation more than once. Sometimes, Rook had to open doors to people's pantries to pilfer food, but they'd almost been caught more than once, and they'd both hated resorting to stealing. It wasn't a state Rook ever wanted to be in again.

And it would be so easy to keep the money, Rook thought, tell Mr. Baroman they'd lost it in the chaos after the fox's appearance. Or they could never go back to the clockmaker's shop at all, just take the coins and stay away.

No. Rook considered herself many things, but she wasn't a thief. Not anymore, and not from someone like Mr. Kelmin, who needed the money as much as they did.

"We'll take care of that tomorrow," Rook said to Drift, "but we need to send the fox home tonight. It doesn't belong here, and it doesn't need to get tangled up in our problems."

Yet, when she stared across the room, she couldn't help but think that the fox looked at home sitting there by the fire. It sprawled on the rug as if it were *his* spot, and he was just coming back to it after a long time away. He'd already shed a generous amount of red and white fur on the rug too, and it didn't seem to matter. It felt *right,* but it couldn't feel right, and that was why Rook had to get him out of there, before she or Drift accidentally got attached to him.

The floorboards creaked as Drift rose to her feet and came over to where Rook stood. "You're right, of course," she said, putting on a smile the way she always did to make Rook feel better. "But you have to admit, he'd have made an *incredible* guard dog."

Rook glanced over at the fox, who was once again sitting

up and watching them intently. "No argument there," she said, relieved that Drift wasn't angry with her over this mess. She turned back to the wall to finish her other lines.

A loud yip startled her into juggling her chalk, but somehow Rook managed to keep from dropping it. She spun to glare at the fox.

"Stop that," she scolded. "You're going home, and that's the end of it."

The fox lifted his head and yipped again.

And suddenly . . .

He changed. Rook didn't know how to describe it. For a split second, the fox's body shimmered. Rook thought he was about to throw out the shadow forms she'd seen in the alley, but this time there was a flash of light, bright enough to make Rook shield her eyes.

When she dropped her hand, the fox had vanished. In his place, a boy sat on the braided rug, his bright red hair sticking up all over his head, a profusion of freckles scattered across his cheeks. He grinned, and there was a small gap between his crooked front teeth.

Rook stared. Drift stared.

The boy held out his hand. "Cheese?" he asked.

9

THE DOOR TO A LULLABY

ROOK GASPED, THE PIECE OF chalk sliding from her fingers. It clattered and rolled across the sloping wood floor, lost in the dark space beneath her bed, but neither she nor Drift paid any attention.

They were too busy staring at the fox who'd suddenly become a boy.

Rook guessed he was younger than they were, maybe nine or ten years old. He was skinny, fragile as a baby bird, barefoot and dressed in faded trousers and a baggy green shirt. Loops of string wound around his elbows to contain the loose sleeves.

"Wh-what just happened?" Drift demanded. "Somebody didn't pull a weird switch on us, did they? I mean, he *transformed*, right?"

"He did," Rook said, finding that though her voice still worked, her mouth had gone cottony. The boy had transformed, and that meant . . . She hesitated, but once the word popped into her head, it all made sense. Why hadn't she guessed it before? The fox's size and intelligence, the magic he'd displayed in the alley, all of it pointed to one thing.

"He's an exile," she said, "a shapeshifter."

Drift huffed and threw up her hands. "Well," she said to the boy, "you might have warned us! Or changed back to a human as soon as we were inside the house! I mean, you take up half the room!" Her eyes widened. "I . . . *I fed you cheese from my hand!* And then you . . . you . . . Eew!" She wiped her hand on her pants again, obviously remembering the fox slobber.

But Rook's thoughts were going back further than that, to the alley in Gray Town, when the fox and his shadow doubles had faced down the constables, pistol shots ringing in the air. Rook flinched in horror at the memory of what had almost happened. She stumbled over to her bed and sank down on the mattress. Why hadn't the boy transformed back then? The constables almost shot him in his animal form, but they never would have drawn their weapons if they'd seen a little boy in the alley.

Or would they? a tiny, mistrustful voice whispered in Rook's head. Would the boy really have been safer if he'd changed right in front of the constables? Would that have stopped them firing? Or would their fear and mistrust of the exiles have overridden everything? Rook shivered and ran her hands up and down her arms.

Across the room, Drift was still ranting and didn't seem to notice Rook's distress. "What were you doing in that forest?" she asked. "It's all the way across the ocean!"

That was an excellent question. Rook and Drift hadn't encountered any exiles in Regara since their mass escape, but Rook hadn't expected them to end up so far away.

When Rook glanced at the boy, she noticed that he had ducked his head and was plucking at the loose threads of the rug. He didn't answer Drift's question. Actually, he hadn't spoken at all since he'd transformed, except to ask for cheese.

Rook slid off the bed and sat cross-legged on the floor next to the boy. She moved slowly, not wanting to frighten him. The boy looked up at her from under a tangle of red bangs.

"Hey there," she said, "what Drift's trying to say is that was an impressive transformation. Top-notch. It just shook us up, that's all. Do you have a name?"

The boy blinked. Like the fox's, his eyes were a vivid shade of amber, and there was still a hint of wildness in them, as if he was only gradually adjusting to being human again.

"Fox," he murmured.

Rook bit her lip. Not quite what she was looking for, but she nodded encouragingly. "Definitely got that part, but what do you call yourself as a human?" She assumed that he, like all the other exiles, had no memory of his real name and so had chosen one for himself.

The boy pressed his lips together in concentration and

rolled his eyes toward the ceiling. His fingers never stopped toying with the rug. Rook waited, leaning forward as if she was about to hear an important secret.

"*Fox*," the boy said at last, in a tone that implied there was no need for further discussion on that topic.

Rook glanced over at Drift. "Fox," she repeated.

Drift shrugged. "Fine by me," she said. "My name's Drift and that's Rook. Do you want some more to eat?"

The boy's head whipped around. He fixed Drift with a look that was exactly like an animal begging. "Cheeeeese," he said, putting as much longing as possible into the word. "Please," he added.

Drift's lips twitched. She was fighting a smile, and Rook recognized the sparkle in her eyes. Despite her shock—and the fox drool—Drift already liked this boy.

Rook did too.

So much for not getting attached.

"Cheese for Fox, half a shroom bun for Rook and me," Drift said. She held up a hand to stop Rook's protest. "We've got mine left, we're sharing it, and that's all there is to say. I'll be right back."

While Drift went to the kitchen, Rook scooted closer to Fox. It was hard to get a decent look at him under all those baggy clothes, but he didn't seem to be hurt or starving. His clothing was clean, and it looked like it had only been a day or two since he'd last had a bath.

He's been living somewhere safe, Rook thought, or had someone taking care of him. But how had he ended up so deep in that haunted forest?

"Fox," she said, "can you tell me where you come from? Have you been living with anyone? A family, maybe?"

The boy stopped playing with the rug and stared off into space. Rook couldn't tell if he was going to answer her or not, but she waited patiently while he sorted through his thoughts.

He looked up at her. "Sank," he said.

"Sank?" Rook repeated, raising an eyebrow. "What is that? A family name? A city?" She wished, not for the first time, that she had a map of this world. She'd opened doors all over Talhaven, but there was still so much she didn't know about its geography.

The boy shook his head. "Sank," he repeated. He shifted to face the fire, stretching his hands out to warm them.

Drift came back into the room carrying two plates. She must have heard the word "Sank," because she looked as confused as Rook felt. "I don't recognize the name," she said. "I could ask Mr. Baroman about it, but . . ." She glanced at Fox, then turned to the boy. "Are you sure you didn't make that up?"

He seemed mesmerized by the pile of cheese and bread on one of the plates. "Chewy," he murmured.

"Yes, the cheese is chewy," Rook said, getting the littlest bit impatient. "Although not really, because it's going stale, but that's not important right—"

"No," Fox interrupted, wrinkling his freckled nose in annoyance. "Sank chewy. That's where . . . that's where I was. Sank chewy."

Rook and Drift exchanged a quick glance. "Are you trying to say 'sanc-tu-ary'?" Drift asked, pronouncing the word clearly.

Fox stood up, snatched the plate out of Drift's hands, and plopped back down on the rug, arranging the cheese feast in his lap. "Sank chewy," he repeated, and began to eat, wolfing down the food with just as much enthusiasm as he had when he was in fox form, though with a bit less slobber.

"I guess he's been living at some kind of sanctuary," Drift said. She'd cut the shroom bun in half, with equal portions of blueberry filling on either side, and put it on the other plate. She offered one piece to Rook.

"But what does that mean?" Rook asked, accepting the gift with a grateful nod.

Drift shook her head. "I don't know." She took a bite of her bun. "We can't be sure where most of the exiles ended up. They might have found families or safe places to stay, just like we did."

They heard stories floating around Regara sometimes, of exiles popping up here and there throughout the six kingdoms. Stories like the time a bridge collapsed in the city of Terren's Bluff after an exile child had supposedly driven over it in a carriage. Or the time a servant boy had jumped from the roof of a noble's three-story mansion, but instead of falling to his death, his arms had transformed into hawk's wings, and he flew away.

Of course, some of the exiles had been recaptured by the authorities and brought before the ruler of whichever of the six kingdoms they'd been caught in. Rook knew even less about the fate of these children, but she suspected some of them might have been held in secret, forced to use their magic as a tool for the kingdom . . . or maybe a weapon.

Best not to dwell on that too much, Rook thought with a shudder. She had enough worries of her own. But she couldn't shake the feeling there was more to the boy's story than he was telling.

"So, Fox," Drift said when the boy was nearly finished eating, "do you think the people at this sanctuary will be missing you? Earlier, Rook was trying to send you home through the door she made. She can make another one for you now if you like."

The boy glanced up from his meal. A look of confusion and irritation passed over his face. "Why?" he asked.

Rook offered Drift a raised eyebrow. It translated roughly to: *Is it just me, or is this kid acting like he's moved in?*

Drift shrugged. She tried again. "Weren't you happy living at this sanctuary?"

"Or did people mistreat you?" Rook asked, digging her nails into her palms as she braced for the answer.

Fox looked at both of them, absorbing their questions and

seeming to rattle them around in his mind like a pair of dice. "No," he said, after some consideration.

"To which question?" Drift pressed.

Fox gave a gusty sigh, as if this was all getting very tiring and silly. "Both," he said.

Rook shot Drift another raised eyebrow, higher this time, that said: *Okay, well, now what?*

"Rook, can you help me take the dishes to the kitchen?" Drift asked politely. She stood and reached down for Fox's plate. He was staring at it with an expression that clearly said he was wishing for more cheese to appear. "We'll only be a minute."

Rook followed Drift and pulled out one of the chairs arranged around their small, circular kitchen table. She straddled it, draping her elbows over the back as Drift took their plates to the sink.

"What are we going to do with him?" Drift asked, leaning against the counter.

"Send him back?" Rook offered, but she heard the uncertainty in her own voice.

"I don't think he'll go," Drift said, shaking her head. "What if this sanctuary wasn't a good place?"

"What if it was, and people are out looking for him right now, worrying to death?" Rook countered. "He said he wasn't mistreated there." She tilted her chair forward on two legs, tracing circles with her finger on the kitchen table.

"Do you really think so?" Drift asked. "That he found someone from this world to take care of him?"

"I don't know," Rook said. "All I know for sure is I like him. But you saw how much he ate."

Drift winced. "Enough for three foxes."

Their food shortage was a real, ongoing problem. The clients who paid them to escape the city could never afford much, and almost all of the money went for food, fuel for the stove, and any other survival necessities. Now they were facing the possibility of having to return the coins the Kelmins had given them. In the midst of all that, taking on another mouth to feed and clothe was unthinkable.

And yet . . .

"I think if he doesn't want to go back to the forest, we should let him stay here," Rook said. "He's an exile. We have to look out for each other."

"I agree," Drift said. "I'll just have to come up with a brilliant money-making scheme, that's all."

She was smiling, but her eyes were shadowed. Rook didn't need to guess why. In the time she'd been with Drift, her friend had considered herself the leader in their partnership. Rook was the girl who made doors. Drift was the girl who made plans. Now she felt it was her responsibility to take care of them all.

Rook rocked back in her chair, putting all four of its legs on the floor. She stood up and went to the sink to help Drift wash the dishes.

When they came back into the living room, Fox was curled up on the rug in front of the fire, back in his fox form, sound asleep.

Drift made a noise of surprise. "Well, that's no good. He can't sleep like that. He needs to be in a bed."

Rook shrugged. "He looks pretty comfortable to me."

"He takes up half the floor!" Drift lowered her voice as Fox snuffled in his sleep. "And he sheds."

Rook couldn't argue with either of those facts, but she had to admit the sound of a fox snoring was kind of adorable. "We don't have any extra beds, so unless he's going to share one of ours—"

"Not as a fox!" Drift interjected in a fierce whisper.

"Then I say we leave him where he is," Rook said, with an exasperated smile, "and let him be what he is."

Drift gave up and sighed. "You're right," she said. "We need to get some sleep too."

They took a few minutes to change into nightclothes before crawling into bed. Rook pulled the quilt of stars up to her chin, and though she thought she'd be asleep as soon as her head hit the pillow, she found that her mind was awake, replaying the events of the day.

It happened again, Rook's hands curled into fists that crumpled the cloth stars. When she needed it most, her magic failed her, opening a door to a place she didn't want to go. Today that failure had brought disaster down on all of them. Luckily, Fox hadn't been hurt, and as far as Rook knew, he hadn't caused any real harm other than scaring people, but it could have been so much worse.

"Can't you sleep?" Drift whispered from the other side of the room.

Rook rolled onto her side and looked over at her friend. The glowing orange coals of the dying fire illuminated Drift's concerned face. Between them on the floor, Fox slept the deep sleep of a content, exhausted animal.

"No," Rook said, pushing her tangled hair out of her eyes. "You?"

"Wide awake," Drift said. She shifted, tucking the edge of her blanket beneath her chin. "What happened today wasn't your fault, you know."

Rook resisted the urge to hide beneath her blankets. How did Drift always know what she was feeling? She must have a special type of magic, something that only worked on Rook. But that was silly, she told herself. How was it possible for someone to have magic meant for only one other person in the world?

"Rook," Drift prodded.

"It *was* my fault," Rook said. "My power failed. You could have been hurt. Fox could have been hurt."

"But we weren't," Drift said, pushing herself up on one elbow. She jerked her chin in Fox's direction. "He's fine, and what if . . ." She hesitated, lips pursed. "I think it's a *good* thing Fox ended up here. Don't you? I mean, what if he was meant to be with us?"

She had a point. Despite their worries about having enough food, Rook *was* glad Fox was with them. But she was still uncertain. "If that's true, why can't you sleep?" she asked quietly.

"Easy—Fox's snoring," Drift said, flopping back onto the bed and fluffing her pillow. "He's facing toward me, so it's much louder over here."

That coaxed a giggle out of Rook. "You poor thing," she said.

"Hey, Rook, do you think . . ." But Drift didn't finish, which made Rook raise her head to look closer at her friend.

"What is it?" she asked.

Drift looked uncomfortable. "I know I shouldn't ask, not when you're feeling this way, but do you think we could see if there's any music out there? It might help both of us sleep."

Rook smiled in relief. "Sure," she said. What Drift asked for was easy enough, and this small use of her power wouldn't hurt.

She slipped out of bed, crouching on the floor to retrieve the piece of chalk she'd dropped earlier. Wiping the dust bunnies off it, she crawled back into bed and sketched four quick lines on the wall beside her.

A concert hall or a theater—that was what they needed. I want to hear music, Rook thought, imploring her magic to listen. Music to fall asleep to. It wasn't so much to ask.

With a small creak and a series of pops like popping corn, a plain metal door barely bigger than her hand appeared in the wall. In its center, there was just enough room for a gold knob the size of her thumbnail.

Using her finger, Rook pried the miniature door open. Its hinges squeaked as it swung toward her. Beyond the door, there was little to see except a dusty wood floor lit by wavering candlelight, and the shadow of a small, polished object. Rook reached through the door and felt along the floor until her fingers found the mystery. She drew it back through the door and into the light. It was a slender violin bow, dropped by its owner.

"I think you found the right place," Drift said. Rook heard the smile in her friend's voice.

Carefully, Rook slid the bow back through the opening before someone missed it. Then she pushed the door almost shut, leaving only a thin crack separating the house and the concert hall, a small, in-between place to fill with music.

As Rook lay back on the bed, a soft melody began to play somewhere beyond the door. It was a single flute at first, unaccompanied by other instruments. The high, pure notes drifted into the room like a welcome guest. A moment later, the violin joined in, and the two musicians played the song together as if they had done so since birth. A lullaby, just as Rook had asked.

"Thank you," Drift murmured, and Rook could tell the music was already working, making her friend drowsy. Soon she'd be adding her own soft snores to Fox's rumblings on the floor.

Rook pressed her cheek into her pillow and let the slow, whistling notes of the flute wash over her. Because the door was so small, she could keep it open for almost an hour without feeling weak, and she never had to worry about anything larger than a mouse coming through.

That she could handle.

But she still couldn't sleep, even after the music ended and she'd pushed the little door shut. The rest of the house was quiet and still. Fox slept on his back with his legs kicking air as if he were running in his sleep. Drift flopped on her stomach with one arm dangling off the bed.

Rook stared up at the ceiling. Drift was right. She was glad Fox was here . . . except it wasn't enough. The real problem was her magic. If she were able to use it the way she needed to, to cross over to another *world* instead of just other cities and kingdoms in Talhaven, none of them would have to stay here and be in danger.

They'd be back in Vora. Back home.

10

THE DOOR IN THE DARK

GIVING UP ON SLEEP, ROOK tossed back her blankets and got out of bed, tiptoeing around Fox to get to the kitchen. She ran a glass of water from the tap and drank it down in large gulps. It soothed her a little, but she still felt restless, tapping her bare foot against the cold stone floor.

If she was going to be awake all night, she might as well put the time to good use.

Rook crept into the living room and found her chalk on the bedside table along with her journal. She collected both and went back through the kitchen, stopping to light a candle and slip it into a brass holder. When she had everything she needed, she made her way down a short hallway to a tiny closet at the very back of the house. In a normal home, this was the area where there would have been a back door.

Rook stepped inside and shut the closet door behind her. Turning to the back wall, she put the candle and the journal on the floor and knelt beside them. The flickering flame cast her shadow in a large, gloomy swipe across the wall.

She held the chalk in her hands and considered how big to make the door. She was *not* letting anything dangerous into this house. She would rather die than put their only sanctuary in jeopardy. But today had been a harsh reminder that she had to keep practicing her magic, no matter what. She, Drift, Fox, and the other exiles didn't belong in this world. Magic was dangerous now, a poison to Talhaven. It had created the Frenzy sickness, the Wasteland, and who knew what else. They needed a door home to Vora.

And Rook was determined to make it.

Rook had never told Drift about these late-night practice sessions. She wouldn't have understood. Drift was happy enough in Talhaven, ever since they'd found this house. She said the place felt familiar, like coming home, so she wasn't longing for a way back to Vora. And she trusted Rook's power, never accepting what dangerous, uncertain things her doors could be.

Rook had tried to explain it to her, that a door meant *risk*—abandoning safe, familiar places for something new. Piling your hopes at the threshold and waiting to see if the world beyond would stomp all over them.

It very often did.

"But a door is also the place where you welcome people to your home," Drift was always saying. *"Throw it open wide, say 'Come in!' and maybe you make a new friend."*

Drift was right, of course. All of those things were true.

But this was also true: open doors can let precious things slip out.

Or terrifying things come *in*.

Rook cracked open her journal and flipped to an empty page. Practicing like this made her feel more in control, and it had also given her brief glimpses of every corner of the world of Talhaven. She made notes on the things she found and collected samples. She had a tiger stone snatched from the banks of the Amber River in the kingdom of Moravel. She'd touched the warm golden sand on the Island Nation of Contis and brought a handful of it back with her. She'd even caught a glimpse of the lost colonies of Skyborn, situated high in the Kinpick Mountains. The settlements, once vibrant trade centers built thousands of feet above sea level, were now ghost towns wrapped in mountain mists, abandoned when the skyships could no longer reach them.

And, of course, she'd opened more than one door to that dark, snow-covered forest where Fox came from. She still couldn't understand why her magic kept returning to that spot.

In the end, it didn't matter. She'd seen beautiful places and mysterious places, but none of them had the telltale red sky of the world of Vora. None of them was home.

And so, by the light of her small candle, Rook drew yet another rectangle on the back wall of the closet, determined to try again, to ask her magic to grant the wish of her heart.

It was a larger rectangle than the one she'd drawn to hear

the lullaby, but much smaller than the one that had lured
Fox. The lines snapped into place and formed an unstained
wooden door like the ones in the treehouses built for the children in Rill Park. A gold latch the size of a hoop earring appeared opposite intricate hinges worked in the shape of roses.
The whole thing was small, delicate, and lovely.

Yet Rook froze up when she put her finger on the latch.
Her stomach was tied in knots again, one for every door she'd
ever made and every risk she'd ever taken.

The consequence of opening a door is that you have to
deal with what's on the other side, she reminded herself.

She was just about to tug on the latch when she heard a
sound. A soft, gentle tapping coming from somewhere in the
closet. At first, Rook thought it might be a mouse scurrying
along the baseboards outside the circle of candlelight. Just
a harmless creature searching for food. But then the sound
came again.

And that's when Rook realized it wasn't a tap.

It was a *knock*.

Knock. Knock. Knock.

Coming from the other side of the door.

Rook dropped the latch, but the sound persisted, getting
louder.

Knock. Knock. KNOCK.

No one had ever knocked on one of her doors before.
Rook's heartbeat sped up. No one had ever been *waiting* on
the other side.

KNOCK. KNOCK. KNOCK.

Now the sound was urgent, angry.

Let me in, the knock demanded.

LET. ME. IN.

Rook slapped her open palm against the door, calling up her magic in a rush. *Go away! Go away!* she commanded, and her magic responded. The door vanished, leaving behind only the ghost of itself in faded chalk lines.

Snatching her candle and journal, Rook backed out of the closet and hurried down the hall through the kitchen. The flame guttered and died as she ran, and she tossed the candle-holder into the sink, wincing at the clatter.

When she got back into the living room, Drift and Fox were both still asleep in the same positions Rook had left them in. Relief flooded her that she hadn't woken them. She moved quietly to her bed and dove under the covers, yanking them up over her head. She crammed her fingers in her ears to block out every sound and curled into a tight ball.

Just let me sleep, she begged. Sleep and pretend this whole night never happened.

As she lay there, her heartbeat slowly returned to normal, her breathing steadied, and eventually, far into the night, Rook slept.

When she woke again, she was still buried in her nest of blankets. She was also covered in sweat, her hair plastered to her cheeks and neck. She had no idea how long she'd been asleep. It might have been a minute or an hour. Cautiously, she peeled back the covers and peeked out.

Watery sunlight filtered through the window above her bed. It painted the far wall in strokes of gold and illuminated one of Drift's drawings, a sketch of navy ships lined up in Regara's harbor. Rook rolled onto her side toward the fireplace, hoping to catch another hour of sleep before the rest of the house woke up.

A hint of red and white fur just below the level of her bed caught Rook's eye. She leaned over and discovered Fox curled up on the floor, his bushy red tail tucked around his body like a blanket. On either side of him was a shadow arranged in the same shape, so that together they formed a ring of sleeping foxes around her bed.

Protecting her.

Somehow, Fox had known she was scared and appointed himself and his shadows to be her guards all through the night.

Rook stared down at the strange scene until tears blurred her vision. She reached up, dabbing them away with a corner of her blanket, and then she lay back down and closed her eyes.

11

THE DOOR TO FISH SIDE

ROOK AWOKE NEXT A FEW hours later, this time to an empty living room and the sounds of breakfast being prepared. Her stomach immediately started growling at the thought of scrambled eggs. She climbed out of bed and made her way to the kitchen to see Drift already at the stove, cracking eggs on the side of a cast-iron skillet. Fox sat right next to her in his animal form, watching every move she made with rapt attention.

"Good morning, Rook," Drift said brightly. "Did you sleep well?"

"Mmm," Rook said, still only half awake. She stumbled into a chair at the kitchen table, leaning forward with her chin on the tabletop, her eyelids drooping.

"What's wrong?" Drift asked, taking half a step toward her. "You look like you haven't slept at all. Did you have a nightmare?"

Rook shook her head. "No, no, I'm fine," she said. "Just a headache, that's all."

It was a lie, and not a very good one, but the last thing Rook wanted to do was talk about her strange door and the person knocking on it in the middle of the night.

Drift frowned, as if she saw right through Rook, but she was distracted when Fox pressed his wet nose against her hip, staring at the cooking eggs. She elbowed him aside and added three strips of bacon to the pan. Grease sizzled and popped, and Fox's body went rigid as a hunting dog. His tail thumped the ground.

"If you want breakfast, sit with Rook at the table," Drift said breezily, flipping the eggs with her spatula. She gave Fox the side-eye. "As a boy. Not a fox."

In response, Fox tilted his head and whined.

Watching the two of them, Rook put her hands over her mouth to smother a giggle. But Drift heard it. She glanced over her shoulder at Rook, eyebrow raised, but Rook just stared innocently at the table, as if she found the patterns in the wood fascinating.

When Drift turned back to the stove, she gave a yelp of surprise. Rook glanced over and saw the source of her distress.

There was no longer any bacon in the skillet.

"*You!* How did you—" Drift waved her spatula like a sword, driving Fox back from the stove. "It wasn't even cooked yet!"

Fox just stared at her grease-spattered spatula and panted.

This time Rook couldn't contain her laughter.

Using a hot pad, Drift pulled the skillet off the stove and brought the eggs to the table. "*Rook!*" she bellowed. "Stop enjoying yourself, go change out of your pajamas, and then set the table." She tried to sound strict, but her lips twitched the whole time, as if she was fighting a smile.

After breakfast—Fox had eaten in his animal form, despite Drift's best efforts—Rook settled on the rug in front of the living room fire, and the others joined her.

"All right," Drift said. "Fox, last night you said you didn't want to go back to your sanctuary. Is that still how you feel?"

Rook watched Fox's expression, searching for some clue as to what he might be thinking, but his furry face and amber eyes gave nothing away. Then, quick as a blink, he transformed, and there was the red-haired, gap-toothed boy sitting between them on the rug.

"I want to stay here," Fox said as soon as he was able to speak.

"Are you sure?" Rook asked. "You'd be leaving your home and—"

"Not home," Fox interrupted her, sounding annoyed. "Sank chewy."

Rook held up her hands. "All right," she said. "You're welcome to stay, but if you ever change your mind and want to go back, just tell me."

"Everything will be fine," Drift said. "We just need to make a quick trip to see Mr. Baroman and make some arrangements." She sounded confident, as if they didn't have a worry in the world.

Rook knew better. Their food supplies were dwindling,

and the way he ate, taking on Fox was like adding two people. The money the Kelmins paid them would help so much, but they might not be able to keep it. They had to go see Mr. Baroman, who would know whether the Kelmins still wanted their help.

She went over to her bed and started putting her boots on. Drift moved to do the same, and Fox performed another blindingly fast shift back to his animal form. He sat up straight on the rug, ears flat, a soft whine lodged in his throat.

"It's okay," Drift said. She walked over to Fox and scratched him behind the ears. "Rook and I will be back soon."

"Before you can finish a nap," Rook said, nodding toward the fireplace and the soft braided rug.

Fox swung around to look at the inviting nook, but then he pushed himself up and moved to sit in front of Rook, blocking her path to the wall. He obviously didn't want to be left behind.

Rook put her hands on her hips. "All right, the truth is we need to see this friend of ours *quietly*, and if we take you with us, there's a bigger chance we'll attract attention."

She watched Fox mull this over. Finally, he let out a sharp yip that made Rook jump. Then, tail dragging, he ambled over to the rug and flopped down dramatically, laying his head on his paws. Rook bit her lip to keep from grinning. She was sure they had just witnessed the fox version of a tantrum.

"Good then," she said, turning to the wall. For just a second, as she pressed the tip of her chalk against the wood, she remembered the door she'd made last night, and the ominous, insistent knocking.

Her hand wavered.

"Rook?" Drift asked, concern in her voice. "Are you sure you're all right?"

Rook swallowed her fear and nodded, not turning from the wall. "Fine," she said. "Everything's fine." Quickly, she sketched a door to the star tunnel. She didn't want to risk any more questions from Drift or give Fox the chance to change his mind and try to follow them.

When she and Drift passed through the plain wooden circle she'd conjured, she turned and waved to him, but he was still sulking by the fire. Sighing, she closed the door and banished it.

At the end of the star tunnel, Rook sketched a second door, and this time she and Drift emerged in the dim attic of Baroman's Lively Clocks and Cherished Curiosities. The only light in the room came from a small round window off to their right. A thick film of dust caked the glass, partially obscuring the view of the waterfront, the docks, and the foamy mouth of the White Sea. Wind hissed through cracks in the old wood-beamed ceiling, carrying the reek of silver trout and salt water. They were in the merchant district now, but everyone who lived anywhere else called it Fish Side because of the smell.

Mr. Baroman had a reputation as the best pendulum clockmaker in the city. Rook didn't know exactly how they worked, but she knew that hidden somewhere among the cogs and gears, the ceramic figures and wooden box frames, was a tiny crystal of animus to make the scenes depicted in each clock feel real. They didn't require much, so the animus might last for another few years.

Rook went over to the attic door and pressed her ear against the wood. Voices drifted up from the shop, but that wasn't unusual for this time of day.

"Are you coming downstairs with me?" Drift asked, sounding surprised. "You usually don't."

"I need to explain to Mr. Baroman what happened," Rook said. It had been her magic that failed. She couldn't hide up here in the dark while Drift spoke for her.

They made their way quietly down a narrow, creaky staircase overrun by cobwebs. At the bottom, an old wooden door with a loose knob led into the main store. Drift put her hand out but stopped short of opening the door. Rook bumped against her back, and the two of them spent a minute jostling in the tight space.

"Sorry! I didn't expect you to stop," Rook whispered when she'd regained her balance. "What's wrong?"

"Nothing, it's just I can't remember if Mr. Baroman ever shuts this door," Drift said. "Usually when I come down, it's cracked. That way I can peek into the shop and make sure no one's around before I go in. Maybe it's because he's not expecting us but . . . I don't know."

"Uh-oh." Suddenly, Rook wasn't feeling so good about this

visit. She squeezed past Drift and pressed her ear against the door to listen.

There were several voices in the shop, though Rook couldn't make out what they were saying. "Open the door an inch," she whispered to Drift. "Do it *very* slowly."

Drift nodded and eased the door open so Rook could get a look into the shop.

What she saw made her stomach plummet to her boots.

Mr. Baroman stood near the front door, his back to Rook. He was making large swinging gestures with his hands, as if he were demonstrating how to cast a fishing line. His audience was a group of three: two men and one woman. All of them had a blue, shield-shaped patch over their left breast pockets, indicating that they were members of the city merchants' guild.

But they also wore thick red armbands above their right elbows.

Mr. Baroman was talking to the Red Watchers.

Panic seized Rook. What were they doing here? Had Mr. Baroman told them about her and Drift? But that didn't make sense. It was foolish to betray them when he had just as much to lose if people found out he was working with exiles.

Or were the three Watchers searching for the girls after what had happened yesterday in Gray Town?

"Red Watchers," Rook hissed. She pulled the door shut, trying to be quiet, but it still closed with a *click*. Rook froze.

Even standing across the room, there was a good chance the Watchers had heard the sound.

Sure enough, the voices paused, then grew louder. They were approaching the door.

"We have to get out of here," Drift said. "Up the stairs, quiet as you can!"

Rook didn't need to be told twice. She backed up, willing her body to be light as a feather so her weight wouldn't make the stairs creak. Drift was right behind her.

They came through the attic door and closed it behind them just as the downstairs door was opening. Now they heard Mr. Baroman's voice clearly.

"This drafty old attic isn't fit for company," he was saying. "Mice nests everywhere. You really shouldn't bother with it."

It didn't sound like he was trying to turn them in, Rook realized. From his words and his tone, it seemed like Mr. Baroman wanted the Watchers to leave. She didn't have time to be relieved. She yanked out her chalk, but her hands were shaking so much she dropped it as soon as it was out of her pocket. It rolled across the floor and disappeared between boxes of spare clock parts. Frantically, Rook dove for it, but Drift grabbed her shoulder.

"There's no time anyway," she said. She wrapped an arm around Rook's waist, and a quick gust of air lifted them from the floor and blew through the attic, demolishing cobwebs and knocking over some figurines on a table by the window.

As the dust settled, Drift guided them to the rafters near the dark peak of the attic roof. There, in the shadows, a wide shelf jutted from the wall. It looked like it had been built to take advantage of the empty space at the top of the attic and could only be reached with a ladder. There were a couple of boxes stacked on the shelf, and beside them, just enough space for two desperate exiles.

Drift quickly deposited Rook on the shelf and, with a last gust of wind, settled in beside her. Rook crammed her body as far back against the wall as possible to hide herself from view. Though she was scared, she had the presence of mind to reach for Drift's hand. Fingers clasped, Drift put her other hand over her nose to hold back any sneezes that might come from kicking up all the dust.

They sat side by side, suspended above disaster, as the attic door swung open and the Red Watchers came into the room.

12

THE DOOR TO RED WATCHERS

"I HOPE YOU'LL EXCUSE THE mess," Mr. Baroman said as he entered the attic behind the Watchers. His voice sounded strained to Rook, though she couldn't see his face from her position up on the shelf.

"Do you mind if we look in some of these bigger boxes?" one of the men asked, though his companions were less polite. Rook heard them already moving things around, sliding boxes across the floor and sifting through their contents.

Looking for hidden exiles.

Rook squeezed her eyes shut and begged them to be quick, to not look up. She begged the wood shelf not to creak, and for Mr. Baroman not to break down and decide to confess that he'd been helping exiles.

Minutes crawled by, until Rook's fingers ached from clutching Drift's so tightly, and her legs were cramped from keeping them tucked up against her chest. But she didn't dare move a muscle. If they were seen, it was all over.

"Nothing here," the woman said at last, sounding disappointed. "I'm sorry we've wasted your time, Mr. Baroman, but you understand we had to check. We're searching all the parts of town where the girls have been spotted before. We thought we'd sweep the area again, just to be sure."

"Don't worry, we're going to find them," one of the men added, and there was no need to see his face to tell he was furious. "We'll double our patrols and pull in more volunteers from the citizenry. We have to catch them before they let loose another creature from the Wasteland."

"Disgusting, ungrateful little monsters," said the other man, and Rook had the distinct feeling that if he'd been on the street he would have spat after uttering the words. "They come to this world, wreck our city, and then run amok with their freakish magic, ripping creatures from the Wasteland to terrorize poor folk who can't defend themselves. You can bet they're having a great laugh at us all right now, wherever they are, seeing the damage their 'pranks' caused."

Rook wanted to cover her ears, but she couldn't risk moving, so there was no way to block out the words.

The Red Watchers and the city constables—and who knew how many others?—thought Fox was a creature from the Wasteland she'd let in on purpose to torment the people of Regara. Search parties were sweeping the streets and shops looking for them. The situation was so much worse than they had known.

"Rubbing it in our faces is what they're doing," the woman

said bitterly. "This city used to be a wonder with all its magic. You know I loved the way those skyship docks were lit up at night, tall towers sparkling like they were covered in stars. I'd take my children outside to watch the ships fly in from all over the world. Now the magic's nearly gone, except what these exiles have. Something so precious, and look how they use it! Why can't they put their magic to work for us and restore some of what we lost?"

"Ah, but it's been proven the children don't have the strength to refill the animus crystals with magic," Mr. Baroman offered hesitantly. "Only the adult wizards from Vora had that power."

"Maybe they'll learn it someday," one of the men said ominously. "Maybe we'll *make* them. In the meantime, we're going to catch these exiles instead of just talking about it. We've taken up enough of Mr. Baroman's time—we need to be going."

"Oh, not at all, not at all," Mr. Baroman said, his wheezy voice drifting in with the sound of more boxes being shifted. "I understand you must be thorough in your search. Why don't I show you that pine-forest clock we were talking about earlier before you leave? Ma'am, didn't you mention that your aunt likes squirrels? I think she'd really enjoy what this clock has to offer."

There were murmurs of agreement and the sound of footsteps headed toward the attic door. Mr. Baroman kept up the friendly chatter with the Watchers all the way down the stairs, until Rook heard the sound of a door closing, and the voices cut off. For a moment, she couldn't make her body uncurl from the shelf, until she felt Drift's hand at the small of her back.

"I think it's safe now," she said, and before Rook could answer, a breath of air lifted her from the shelf. Rook forced her stiff limbs to straighten as Drift guided them down. When her feet touched the ground, Rook's legs gave out, and she sank to her knees on the dusty attic floor.

Drift knelt beside her and, without saying a word, pulled her into a tight hug. Rook buried her face in Drift's shoulder. For the next few minutes, the only sound in the attic was their unsteady breathing.

Eventually, the downstairs door opened again, and there came the sound of a single pair of quiet footsteps. Rook tensed, but it was only Mr. Baroman this time. He peeked into the attic and saw the two of them on the floor. His aged, wrinkled face softened with relief.

"When I heard the attic door, I thought you two might have been up here hiding," Mr. Baroman said, shuffling over to them. He had thin, gnarled brown fingers, and his white beard was clipped close to his chin in the style of his homeland, the kingdom of Targrell across the sea. "But I wasn't sure your magic would keep you safe."

"We have the worst luck in the world, showing up just when the Red Watchers come for a visit," Drift said. Her voice quavered, but she smiled at Mr. Baroman. "Good thing for us you got rid of them as quick as you did."

Rook nodded in agreement. She was so grateful Mr. Baroman hadn't betrayed them. All he would have had to do was say that exiles were hiding in his shop, and she and Drift would have been taken away. Instead, he had gone out of his way to protect them. She never would have expected someone from Regara to do so much for an exile, especially after hearing the hateful words of the Red Watchers.

"Are the two of you all right?" Mr. Baroman asked. "The news came in from Gray Town early this morning that a monster had gotten loose from the Wasteland, but when the constables started passing out sketches of your faces, I feared the worst. What happened out there?"

"It wasn't a monster, and it wasn't from the Wasteland," Drift said. "We found another exile, a boy who can transform into a giant fox."

Mr. Baroman's eyes widened in surprise, and he made a little tutting noise. "I can see why that gave the constables a fright," he said.

Afraid? The constables? *They* were the ones with pistols pointed at a ten-year-old boy, Rook wanted to shout, but she kept her mouth shut. This wasn't Mr. Baroman's fault.

"There's no need to worry," Drift assured him. "The boy was never going to hurt anyone, and he's staying with us now, so he'll be safe. We came to see you because of this." She pulled out the pouch containing Mr. Kelmin's money and reluctantly handed it to Mr. Baroman. "Can you tell Mr. Kelmin and his grandson that we're very sorry we couldn't complete the job, and we'd be more than happy to try again if they give us another chance?"

Mr. Baroman took the pouch. "Thank you for returning the money," he said gravely, "but I'm afraid Mr. Kelmin and his grandson have already found another means of leaving the city in secret—a sympathetic merchant who's going to give them free passage on her ship. I will have just enough time to send the coins to them before they depart."

So that was it, Rook thought, her hopes slipping away. They wouldn't be able to help the Kelmins or keep the money. The whole job had been a disaster from start to finish.

Seeing her face, Mr. Baroman's expression softened. "You did what was right," he said. "I'm sure it wasn't easy to give this back, but the important thing right now is that the two of you remain safe. You should return to your home and stay there for the time being."

Rook would have loved nothing better, but she shook her head. "We can't," she said. "We have three of us to feed now, and we're out of money."

"Is there any chance you have another job for us?" Drift asked. "We need clients now more than ever."

Mr. Baroman's face creased in a look of distress. "My dear, I don't think you understand," he said. "The constables and the Red Watchers—they know your faces. They know your powers. Word of this incident is spreading through Regara as we speak. Any clients I might have been able to contact for you . . . well, there's a good chance that . . . once they hear that you're being hunted . . ." His words trailed off into uncomfortable silence, but Rook understood all too well.

"No one will hire us after this," she said quietly. "They'll be too afraid."

Drift reached for Rook's hand, but Rook pulled away. "This uproar will all die down after a few days," Drift insisted, trying to be reassuring.

Mr. Baroman shook his head. "I wish I could agree with you, but the authorities seem very determined to track you down. I'm afraid they see your magic as a threat."

"Then maybe it's time we leave," Rook said quietly. They could start over in another city where no one knew their faces or their magic.

"Rook, are you sure?" Drift asked, though she didn't sound opposed to the idea.

Rook shrugged. "It won't be easy," she admitted. If they tried to get jobs, any employer they approached was bound to ask questions. Questions about their parents, about where they lived and why they needed work. No matter where they went in the world, people would be on the lookout for escaped exiles. Up until now, their situation with Mr. Baroman had been the safest, best opportunity to make money.

"It may not be so terrible to start over," Mr. Baroman said, giving Rook a sympathetic pat on the shoulder. "Not everyone in the world is out to hunt and hate exiles."

"Don't be so sure," Rook muttered.

Mr. Baroman pursed his lips, looking unhappy. "Well, if

you need money immediately . . . I wasn't sure if I should tell you this, but I did receive a message just before the Red Watchers arrived, from a client who expressed interest in your services. I'm not sure how she'll feel after this upheaval, but if you want, I could reach out and see if she still wishes to hire you."

Drift's face brightened. "That might be just what we need," she said. "One last job, and then we can start over in a new city. Sure, it's a risk, but it's also a chance for a new beginning."

Rook nodded slowly. "No matter what, we need the money," she said. "Where does the woman want to go?"

"She didn't say where, and she didn't mention what she was running from," Mr. Baroman replied. "She just said it was urgent that she leave the city and offered to pay double your normal asking price if you could meet her immediately."

"Double?" Drift said breathlessly. "Did you hear that, Rook?"

Rook heard. It was exactly what they needed, enough money to keep the three of them comfortably fed until they could make a new life for themselves.

Which also made it seem too good to be true.

"I don't know," Rook said. "The Red Watchers are combing the city for us, and suddenly a client shows up who wants to pay a lot of money to meet with us. What if it's a trap?"

Drift fell quiet, thinking it over. "Where does the woman want to meet?" she asked after a moment.

"In Rill Park, at midday tomorrow," Mr. Baroman said. "Apparently, she lives nearby."

Rill Park wasn't a place they used very often. It was the largest public park in the city and drew big crowds in the spring and summer. There were only a few places that were quiet and secluded. One of them was a small grove at the center of the park that was restricted because there were fire hornet nests and thick beds of poison ivy around the trees. They'd used the place as a meeting spot only a handful of times, and Rook had drawn the clients' door on the trunk of a wide old harringwood tree.

"I don't like it," Rook said. "I have a bad feeling."

"The park *is* awfully exposed." Drift nervously ran a hand through her hair. "But do we really have a choice, Rook? We have Fox to think about now. We have to get money somehow."

Mr. Baroman cleared his throat. "If you need money to last until you can leave the city, I have a bit set aside that I—"

"No," Rook interrupted. "Thank you. Thank you for everything you've done, but we can't take your money."

The very last thing she wanted was for anyone to offer her charity, even kind old Mr. Baroman. The only reason they let him help them as much as he did was that he had agreed to take a share of the money from each job they did. In Rook's and Drift's minds, that was fair. He shared in the risk; he took part of the reward. Rook didn't want to be more of a burden to this world than she already was.

"You're very kind to offer," Drift said, smiling. "If you can get us this last job, it will be more than enough help."

"If you say so," Mr. Baroman said reluctantly. He shifted, his back slightly hunched from years of bending over work-tables to construct his clocks. "Though are you sure you want to do this?"

"No," Rook said, "but Drift's right. We don't have a choice. We have to take care of ourselves and we have to take care of Fox. He's one of us."

Mr. Baroman nodded. "I understand. Do you have enough food to last until I contact the client and get everything set up?"

"Yes," Rook and Drift said at once, although truthfully, since they'd left Fox home alone, Rook wondered if there would be any food at all when they got back. But that was their problem, not Mr. Baroman's.

With the plan decided, Rook forced herself to get up off the attic floor. Her legs were cramped from kneeling so long and being curled up on the shelf before that. She limped to the boxes in the corner to find her lost chalk. Outside the attic window, the voices of children laughing and playing in the streets drifted up to her.

What was it like to be a child of this world and not an exile with a magical gift you couldn't control? What were the normal children of Regara doing right now, at this time of day? Playing kickball or hide-and-seek? What must it be like not to have to worry about where your next dinner was coming from, let alone the next insult?

Disgusting, ungrateful monsters.

The words burned in Rook's ears. She knew she would re-member them for a long time. Yet another reminder that they didn't belong in this world. They had to find a way to escape it. *That* was the new life the three of them needed most.

She found her chalk wedged between the boxes—luckily, it hadn't shattered into a dozen pieces. Drift was saying good-bye to Mr. Baroman and thanking him again for all his help.

"It's the least I can do," Mr. Baroman said solemnly. He hesitated, his gaze falling on Rook. "Please let me say again, not everyone in Regara feels the way the Red Watchers do. I'm afraid it will never be easy for the exiles to live in this world, but that's our fault, not yours. We let ourselves rely too heav-ily on magic—a power we didn't earn or fully understand—and now that it's gone, we need someone to blame, so we look everywhere but at ourselves. But there *are* people in this world you can trust. If you give us a chance, we will help you in any way we can."

For a moment, Rook was speechless. She'd never heard such words from anyone in Regara. Even Drift, who always knew exactly what to say in these situations, could only whis-per, "Thank you."

At least there was one person in the city who was on their side.

THE DOOR TO BIRDS

WHEN THEY ARRIVED BACK AT the roost, Rook and Drift stepped from the star tunnel into the living room, and Rook's jaw dropped.

"Oh" was all she managed to say as she tried to figure out what exactly was covering the living room floor. At first glance, she thought it was snow.

She blinked and realized it was actually paper.

Fox was sprawled on his stomach on the rug with Drift's sketchbook lying open beside him. He had a piece of paper in his hands, and he was folding it with quick, expert twists, fingers moving fast and sure. He'd already removed dozens of the sketchbook's pages, folding each of them into the same shape.

Birds.

Coming up beside Rook, Drift opened her mouth to speak, but the only sound that emerged was a surprised squeak. Rook crouched at the edge of the rug and picked up a handful of the birds. There were paper cranes, hawks, doves, owls, and other birds she didn't recognize. Each one was a tiny work of art, as if they were done by someone who'd been practicing paper folding for years.

"This is—" Rook began.

"My paper," Drift interrupted, sounding as if she was in a daze. "*All* my paper."

"Fox," Rook said, balancing a dove in the palm of her hand, "what is this?"

Fox looked up from his paper folding in surprise, as if he hadn't been aware that either Rook or Drift was in the room. "Birds," he said.

In the short time she'd known him, Rook had discovered that when asked a question, Fox always told the truth. He just left out all other vital bits of information.

Rook cringed at the amount of paper the boy had gone through. She picked up the sketchbook—thankfully, it still had a few pages left—and tucked it under her arm, out of Fox's reach. The boy was too busy adjusting a crane's wing to notice.

"Did you have to make so many of them?" Drift asked faintly.

"Yes," Fox said. He chewed his lip as he examined the bird's beak, which was just a bit crooked. He refolded it.

"Fox, pay attention," Rook scolded him. "This paper belongs to Drift. It wasn't yours to take." She scooped up the birds nearest the fireplace and moved them onto her bed so they wouldn't catch any errant sparks.

Fox froze and dropped the crane he'd been working on. He looked up at Drift, his eyes wide. "This was wrong?" he asked.

"Well, it would have been nice if you'd asked first," Drift said, looking pained. "I would have given you some paper—not all of it, but some."

Fox's freckled cheeks reddened. He picked up the crane he'd been working on and began unfolding it, careful not to tear the delicate edges of its wings. But when he'd flattened it out, there were creases all over the paper that wouldn't go away, no matter how much he smoothed it with his hands. His face scrunched up in misery.

"Ruined it," he whispered. "I'm sorry."

"I know—it's all right," Drift said. In the face of Fox's misery, she seemed quick to forgive. "Here, let's just make it into a bird again." She tried to refold the paper, but her hands didn't have nearly the same skill as Fox's. "Where did you learn how to do this?" she asked.

"Messages," Fox said. He took the bird from her and absently refolded it back into a crane.

"Messages," Rook echoed, confused. "You mean instructions? Did you read a book on how to make them? Or look at pictures?"

Fox paused in the act of pinching a corner of paper between his thumb and forefinger. He looked up at Rook and shook his head. "It was a message," he said.

A strange, unsettling feeling crawled up Rook's spine. She reached out and put a hand on Fox's arm, forcing him to look up at her. "What does that mean?" she asked. "Someone taught you how to do this? Who was the *message* from?"

A line formed between Fox's brows, and he shrugged. "Don't know *who*," he said. He held up his hands. "They just know."

Rook sat back, releasing Fox's arm so he could fold his paper. She and Drift exchanged a glance. He had to mean someone from his past, Rook realized. Like the rest of the exiles, Fox had lost his memory when he passed through the magical portal to Talhaven. He remembered that someone had taught him how to fold paper into birds, but he didn't know who it was.

Still, there was something about the way he'd said "message" that made Rook's scalp tingle. She felt like she was missing something important, but she didn't know what it was, and she didn't think Fox knew either.

"Hey," Drift said, breaking the silence that had fallen in the room. "I think we have some string in the closet. Why don't I go get it and we'll hang these birds up to make them fly!"

Fox looked up. A hopeful smile broke through the misery on his face. "They'll fly?" he asked.

"They will when I'm done with them," Drift assured him.

They found some string on a shelf in the closet alongside some tacks that neither Rook nor Drift remembered buying. They used it to attach strings to the cranes, hawks, and other avian species, and one by one attached them to the ceiling.

Soon there was a flock of paper birds soaring over the living room, a separate group nesting in a circle on the mantel, and a pair on the nightstands next to Rook's and Drift's beds.

"Can I have some of the leftover birds?" Drift asked, cradling an owl in her hand. "I'd love to do some sketching on them, maybe define their plumage and faces. What do you think?"

Fox sprang up from where he'd been sitting on the floor and quickly scooped up a whole handful of birds, depositing them in Drift's lap. He ducked his head, a shy smile spreading over his face.

"I think that's a yes," Rook said, grinning.

This was one of the times she was reminded how much she loved Drift. Rather than being angry at seeing so much of her sketching paper folded into animals, Drift used it as an opportunity for a new art project and a way to show Fox that his talents were appreciated. She always saw the best in every situation. And in every person.

"Can we have some music, Rook?" Drift asked as she stood on her bed to hang the last of the birds from the ceiling.

Rook got her chalk and went to the wall above her bed. With a few tiny flourishes, she sketched a fist-sized circle, and it changed before her eyes into a little round door, the kind that might fit on a birdhouse. There was a yellow flower painted on it, no bigger than a coin. Rook pulled the door open and left it while she went to gather up the string and tacks.

A few minutes later, the sound of a piping flute drifted

through the door, a march that made you want to tap your foot in time with the music. Hearing it, Rook felt some of the pain of their earlier encounter with the Red Watchers fade away.

"Perfect!" Drift said, and with a wave of her hand, she conjured a gentle breeze. She used the song's rhythm to swing the birds back and forth as if they were dancing in flight. Fox jumped off the bed and landed on the floor in fox form, bounding around the room in playful circles.

And then, without even meaning to, they all started dancing, driven along by the happy music. Rook twirled in a circle while Fox yipped and wiggled, trying not to knock her over in the small space. Laughing, Drift swept her hands out, and her wind lifted Rook six inches from the floor so that she was dancing on air. Fox jumped up and barked, his tail swishing back and forth in wild joy.

Soon Rook was sweating and giggling, her feet tapping the air to kept time with the flute player. She and Drift clasped hands and spun until they were both dizzy. Rook let herself fall to the ground and sprawled on her back, watching the birds spin above her head. Fox dove after her and they wrestled until Rook was laughing so hard she thought she'd never be able to stop. She threw her arms around Fox's neck and hugged him, her cheek buried in his thick red coat.

As she held him, she looked up and noticed Drift still hovering in midair, gazing down at the two of them. She was smiling, but there was a strange look in her friend's eyes, one Rook had never seen before. Drift caught her staring, and she spun in a playful circle, breaking eye contact. When she turned back around, she was grinning, and the expression in her eyes had vanished, leading Rook to think she'd imagined it.

But she could have sworn that just for an instant, in the middle of all that joy and laughter, her friend had looked . . . lonely.

THE DOOR IN THE TREE

THEIR JOURNEY TO RILL PARK began with an argument, Rook and Fox against Drift.

"Fox absolutely *cannot* come with us!" Drift said, for maybe the tenth time. "Rook, you of all people should know how dangerous it is if he's seen in his fox form!"

Rook did know how dangerous it was. People would immediately assume that Fox was a monster escaped from the Wasteland, the constables would be summoned, the Red Watchers would give chase, and they would all probably be captured.

But she also knew that she couldn't leave Fox trapped in the house. If something happened to her or Drift, he would be stuck without a door, and she couldn't rely on the house's unpredictable magic to set him free.

Besides, Fox knew they were going on an important mission. He obviously wanted to help and was determined not to be left behind this time. Rook knew this because Fox's contribution to the argument was to sit in his giant fox form in front of the wall where Rook created her doors to the outside world. He was alert and tense, ready to dart through as soon as a way out appeared. Even if she agreed with Drift, there was no way he'd let them leave the house without him.

"We're going to be in the woods at Rill Park," Rook pointed out. "The place we'll come out has trees and big boulders everywhere to hide us. No one will be able to see Fox."

While she spoke, Fox remained sitting by the door. The only thing that moved was his ear, twitching in response to the cracks and pops from the fire. He stared at Drift, full of fox resolve.

Drift sighed and relented, but she didn't look happy.

Their decision made, Rook went to the wall and sketched a quick door out into the star tunnel. When they were all through, she closed the house safely away. Now, even if there was a trap waiting in Rill Park, no one would be able to force their way back through the door to find the roost. All they'd see was a strange, dead-end tunnel.

At the end of the passage, she drew a different door, tall and narrow, one more suited in shape to a tree. As she drew, Rook imagined the space in Rill Park—the deep shade of the harringwood grove, with large, smooth boulders rising up to form a wall off to one side. If she concentrated, she swore she could smell the fresh-cut grass and hear the sparrows chattering in the trees.

When she'd connected the lines, the door that appeared

was slender and white, a candle without a wick. Its hinges were black and shaped like arrowheads. The door handle had a button at the top to release the latch.

"Is everybody ready?" Rook asked.

"Ready," Drift said, recovering her usual confidence.

Fox yipped excitedly, and Rook took it as agreement.

Swallowing her nerves, she opened the door.

Dappled sunlight fell on Rook's face, brightening the end of the star tunnel. She stepped out into a grove of harringwoods, their red trunks and thick, tulip-shaped leaves hanging over her head like a protective umbrella. Insects buzzed all around, and the air smelled of lilac bushes and the sweet rill flowers that gave the park its name.

Turning, Rook looked up. The door she'd just passed through opened out of one of the largest harringwoods in the grove. Its trunk was so thick it would take all three of them joining hands to wrap their arms around it. A crow cawed loudly somewhere close by, startled into flight by the sight of something that should not be: three figures emerging like spirits from the trunk of the great old tree.

Rook held the door open while Drift stepped out, and Fox came bounding behind her. He skidded to a stop, kicking up small clumps of dirt and grass, ears twitching every time a bird chirruped.

"Do you hear anything, Fox?" Rook asked. They appeared to be alone in the grove, but she didn't have Fox's keen senses to tell her for sure.

Fox cocked his head and listened. The wind ruffled his red and white fur. Then his ears flattened to his head, and he uttered a low growl.

"I don't like the sound of that," Drift said. "I think someone's coming." She took up a position at the front of the group, with Fox crouched next to her. Rook stayed in the rear, keeping the door that led to the star tunnel open in case they needed to dive back through it. They had rehearsed the escape plan before they left the house, but her hand still trembled on the door handle as she waited for whoever was coming to show themselves.

A woman stepped into the shade of one of the harringwood trees. Rook recognized her immediately, but it was Drift who spoke first.

"It's you," she said in surprise. "Lily."

Rook relaxed and let the door in the harringwood tree swing closed and disappear before it could start to drain her magic.

"Hello, girls." The woman smiled, deepening the crease her scar made on her cheek. She crossed the grove toward them, but when her gaze rested on Fox, she stopped in her tracks.

"It's all right," Drift said, putting her hand on Fox's head. "He's not from the Wasteland. He's an exile, like Rook and me. A shapeshifter. Show her, Fox."

Fox eyed Lily, and Rook wondered if he recognized her from their last encounter in the alley. If so, he might not look kindly on the woman who'd run screaming to the constables to get away from him.

But Fox seemed more curious than anything, and after a moment of mutual appraisal, he shifted to his human form, red hair aflame in the sunlight. Rook blinked, and he shifted again, back into a fox. Lily's eyes widened during the transformations. Rook waited for signs of fear or disgust to cross her face, but to her relief, Lily didn't look the least bit repulsed.

"Extraordinary," she said, venturing a few steps closer. Now that she knew Fox wasn't a threat, she appeared just as curious about him as he was about her. She held out a hand but seemed unsure what to do with it. Fox helped her out by scooting forward and bumping her fingers with his nose. Lily chuckled and scratched his ears. "I see you enjoy being a fox more than a human," she said.

Rook had been thinking the same thing, but she was surprised Lily had seen into Fox's heart so quickly. The woman was perceptive.

Now that she'd gotten over her surprise at seeing Lily again, Rook was confused. "What are you doing here?" she asked. "Why do you need to escape the city? Is it because you helped the Kelmins?"

Lily turned her attention from Fox and regarded her steadily. "Not exactly," she said, and though her voice was calm, Rook felt a shadow of tension fall over the grove. "I'm sorry, but I haven't been entirely honest with you girls."

Rook's uneasiness grew, threatening to become panic. She

took a step back. "I was right—you're a Red Watcher," she said. Her gaze swung to Drift. "It's a trap!"

A gust of wind shook the grove as Drift's own fear surged. Their group closed ranks, clustering together for protection, but Lily held up her hands in a calming gesture. "Wait, please," she said, soothingly. "I *swear* to you, I'm not a Red Watcher. I'm only here to ask for your help. But you see, I don't need a door."

"What do you need, then?" Drift asked suspiciously.

Lily lowered her hands. "Regara is in great danger," she said. "I need your help to save the city."

It was the last thing Rook had expected her to say. Before she or Drift could think of a response, Fox tensed and growled another warning.

"What is it?" Drift asked, laying a hand on Fox's back. "Did you hear something?"

A second later, Rook heard it too. More footsteps approached the grove, and multiple figures stepped out from behind the trees.

Rook's blood froze in her veins. There were four of them, and they were all wearing the uniforms of Regaran constables.

It had been a trap after all, and they'd let Lily lead them right into it.

15

THE LOCKED DOOR

THE CONSTABLES SURROUNDED THEM. Rook, Drift, and Fox instinctively tensed, ready to fight or run, but Lily held up her hands again, turning a pleading look on the constables.

"Captain Hardwick, I asked you and your men to wait until I'd had a chance to explain the situation," she said tersely. "You're frightening the children for no reason!"

"I thought you'd learned by now that you're not the one giving orders," replied the captain, a heavyset man with a dark beard and thick mustache whose eyes tracked every movement the three exiles made. There was a badge pinned to his chest, a stylized *R* on a silver-wave background, the city crest of Regara.

Rook cursed herself. How could she have been so stupid? She'd trusted Lily and banished the door back to the star tunnel, cutting off their escape route. Beside her, Fox's lips pulled back in a snarl. His fur darkened, and his shadow lengthened, flowing like spilled ink across the ground. Lily and the captain were too busy arguing to notice, but the other constables shifted uncomfortably, their hands dropping to their pistol hilts.

Rook realized if she didn't stop Fox, one of the constables was liable to shoot him out of fear.

Dropping to her knees beside Fox, she threw her arms around his neck and whispered in his ear. "It's all right," she said. "We're caught, but just wait. Wait for a chance to escape. Please, Fox. Don't do anything right now."

She didn't know if she was getting through. She tightened her grip on his muscled shoulders. No wonder he preferred being a fox. In this form, he was strong and powerful, and right now, every instinct was telling him to use that power to protect himself and his friends.

But that didn't make him invincible.

"Please," she repeated in a choked voice. "I don't want to lose you."

Her soft plea was like its own magic. It drained the fight out of Fox, and his growl tapered off to a soft whine.

"Good boy," she murmured, relief making her weak in the knees. She stayed on the ground beside Fox to keep him calm, while Drift stepped forward to address Lily and the captain.

"What do you want with us?" she demanded. "If this is about what happened with Fox, I'm telling you, he didn't come from the Wasteland. We weren't trying to hurt anyone."

"That's not why we're here," the captain said. His eyes

narrowed. "Although your antics in the city *are* what first brought you to our attention."

"We'd heard rumors of two powerful exiles," Lily cut in, "one of whom could fly, while the other had the power to open doors to anywhere in the world." She gave Rook a small smile. "I thought I'd heard of every type of magic still out there, but yours is an ability I've never encountered before. I had to see for myself if you were real."

"That's why you helped the Kelmins," Drift said, her cheeks flushing in anger. "You were just trying to get close to us."

"Yes," Lily said, looking guilty. "I didn't want to lie to you then, and I'm truly sorry for the ruse that brought you here now. You've both impressed us with the extent of your powers, but they've also made you nearly impossible to track down. We needed a way to find you, because I knew you were the ones to help me. I told Captain Hardwick as much."

"You'd better be right," the captain said. "Your continued freedom depends on it."

Rook's ears perked up at that statement. Her freedom? What did that mean? Was it possible that Lily was as much a prisoner as Rook and her friends?

The captain nodded to the other constables. "We need to get going. We'll explain the situation once we get to the wall."

"The wall?" Rook said, thinking she must have misheard. "You can't mean we're going to the Wasteland?"

No one answered her. The nearest constable stepped forward and seized her by the upper arms, dragging her to her feet. Rook struggled, kicking and jerking to try to break his hold, but his grip was too strong. Another constable grabbed Drift and got a blast of wind in his face that left him cursing and stumbling. Fox snarled and snapped at the man holding Rook, tearing the hem of his uniform as he started pulling her toward the edge of the grove.

Lily stepped forward, raising her voice above the chaos. "Stop," she said, appealing to Captain Hardwick. "Please, there's no need to treat them this way. You'll hurt them!"

"Then you'd better do something," Hardwick told Lily. "Or I'll have my men subdue them." His voice was calm, though his eyes were hard as stone.

Rook saw anger flash in Lily's eyes. "As you wish," the woman said. Reluctantly, she stretched out a hand in Rook's direction.

Before Rook knew what was happening, a wave of dizziness crashed over her. Her legs went wobbly, and she sagged in the constable's grip. If he hadn't been holding on to her so tightly, she would have fallen to her knees. It felt like all the energy was being pulled out of her at once.

Drift yanked away from the other constable and was beside her in an instant. "Rook, what's wrong?" she demanded. "Are you all right?"

"I—I don't know," Rook said. She shook her head, willing the dizziness to go away. She was suddenly so tired she wanted to lie down in the grove and sleep for days. Fox pressed against her other side, his fur warm but his body trembling in fear. Rook was afraid too. What was happening to her?

As if she'd spoken the question aloud, Lily's voice cut through Fox's whimpering and Drift's soothing whispers. "Don't fight it, Rook," she pleaded. "If you fight it, it will only take more of your energy."

"Stop!" Drift whirled to confront Lily. "What's happening?" she cried. "What did you do?"

Lily clasped her hands in front of her. "It's all right, Drift," she soothed. "I just temporarily drained Rook's magic. That's my power."

Rook opened her mouth to speak, to say that that was impossible. There were no more adult wizards in Talhaven. But she felt herself slipping, her mind sliding into a cool, dark pit. She knew she should have been afraid, but a voice at the bottom of the pit promised safety and sleep, and she was so very, very tired.

"Rook! Rook!" Panic filled Drift's voice. Fox's frantic yips echoed in Rook's ears, his head nudging her arm, but all those sensations seemed so far away and unimportant.

And then Fox's human voice rang out, surprising Rook enough to keep her conscious. "Who are you?" he asked, directing the question at Lily.

When Lily answered, her voice was formal and proud. "My real name is Dozana Atrathk, of the world of Vora." She glanced at Drift, her face softening. "And I am your mother, child."

Shocked silence fell. Drift's face drained of all color. Rook wanted to say something, desperately wanted to reach out to her friend, but before she could react, the constable who'd first grabbed her picked Rook up and slung her over his shoulder. Rook kicked feebly, but her strength was gone.

Sunlight blinded her as the man carried her out of the grove. She lifted her head and caught a glimpse of a carriage parked on the road leading out of the park. A team of four black metal horses was tied to it, and another constable sat in the driver's seat. There was no one else in the park. They must have cleared the area before springing their trap.

The constable opened the carriage door and laid Rook on the bench inside. Rook tried to pull herself up to a sitting position, but only managed to lean her cheek against the wall. She tried to fight it, but her eyes slid closed. A moment later, she felt other people climb into the carriage, heard Fox's and Drift's voices. They were still together. That was something to be grateful for.

She managed to open her eyes long enough to see Lily—Dozana—and Captain Hardwick settling themselves on the bench opposite her. The captain reached over and pulled the carriage door shut, locking it. Then he pounded the roof with his fist, three sharp raps, and the carriage started to move.

The last thought in Rook's head before she succumbed to sleep was that they were on their way to the Wasteland.

16

THE WRONG DOOR

THE BOUNCING OF THE CARRIAGE woke Rook. She wasn't sure how long she'd been out, but it couldn't have been more than a few minutes. Heavy curtains covered the carriage windows, letting in only thin beams of light and giving away nothing of their location.

Carefully, Rook sat up. Fox was beside her in his human form, propped sleepily against her shoulder, and Drift sat on his other side on the bench. She was wide awake, but staring straight ahead with a dazed look on her face. Dozana and the captain were deep in agitated conversation across from them.

"What's going on?" Rook asked quietly, reaching over Fox to tug on Drift's sleeve.

Drift turned to her, and her eyes lit with relief when she saw Rook was awake. She scooted closer on the bench. "Are you all right?" she asked.

"I think so," Rook lied. The truth was her head felt like a swarm of bees had taken up residence, and were rearranging the furniture, but she didn't want to upset Drift any more than she already had. While she talked, Fox stirred and sat up, rubbing his eyes.

"You both got hit pretty hard with that magic," Drift said. "It drained Fox so much it transformed him back into a human."

"What about you?" Rook asked. "Did you try flying?"

Drift shook her head, looking ashamed. Her gaze kept returning to Dozana's face. "I . . . I was distracted," she said. "I'm sorry."

Rook understood. Finding out that your mother was alive and in Talhaven was enough to knock the wind out of any of them. Speaking of which, she couldn't help remembering how Dozana's magic had affected her, the dizziness and exhaustion coming on all at once. Rook hadn't been able to do anything about it. She'd never felt magic that strong.

Then again, she'd never watched an adult Voran perform magic. Not that she remembered, anyway.

Dozana Atrathk. A wizard of Vora. How? How was it possible?

From all that Rook had heard, the only Vorans who'd originally come through the magical portal were the ones in charge of negotiating trade and sailing ships full of animus crystals from Lake Caralan down the channel to the White Sea. At the request of the Vorans themselves, traffic through the magical portal was strictly regulated. Only the rulers of the six kingdoms of Talhaven, their guards, and a few merchants were ever allowed on the Voran side of the portal, and as few wizards as possible entered Talhaven in return, just enough to distribute animus and collect their own goods in return.

But by accident or design, those wizards had all been on the Voran side of the portal when the Great Catastrophe happened. Rook and everyone else had thought there were only children left in Talhaven after the explosion destroyed the magical portal.

Obviously, they'd been wrong.

"I want to go home," Fox said, interrupting her thoughts.

Rook's stomach tightened. "I know, Fox. We all do."

Captain Hardwick drew a corner of the curtain back to look outside. "We're nearly there," he said. "I sent men ahead to clear and secure the area. There won't be any civilians nearby."

Dozana leaned forward in her seat to address Rook, Drift, and Fox. "I know you have questions and that you're afraid," she said. "I'm so sorry for all this." She looked at Drift, her expression pained. "You don't know how much I wish we could have found each other under different circumstances, my daughter. I wanted to seek you out long before now, but I . . . I wasn't allowed." She swallowed. "I promise you, from now on, I'll do everything in my power to protect you."

Rook glanced over at Drift, who looked stunned. Tears welled up in her friend's eyes, but she blinked them back. "I— I'm sorry," she said, her voice thick. "I still don't . . . I don't remember you."

Dozana nodded, and there was no masking the sadness in her eyes. She reached out hesitantly and put her hand over Drift's. "All that matters is we're together now," she said. "We'll get through this. I swear it."

"You said Regara is in danger." Drift met Dozana's eyes, her gaze intent, as if searching for something familiar in the woman's face. "From what?"

"The Wasteland," Dozana explained. "After the city completed construction of the walls around the area of the portal explosion, the guards patrolling the top of the gray wall started to notice something strange."

"In the Wasteland?" Rook scoffed. "That whole place is one big nightmare. You can take your pick of strange."

"Not like this," Hardwick spoke up. "Lake Caralan has become a giant whirlpool, and the area around the remains of the portal's stone archway is thick with magical energy, animus running wild. And it's growing stronger by the day."

"My best guess," Dozana said, "is that the walls surrounding the Wasteland—particularly the inner, red heartstone wall, because it naturally binds magic—have trapped the power that was released by the portal explosion. Instead of being allowed to dissipate naturally over the past two years, it's been slowly building up. That's why you see the sky change colors over the Wasteland."

"If the magic has nowhere to go," Drift said, "eventually, won't it . . ." Her voice trailed off and she gasped.

"It will explode again," Dozana confirmed. "But this time, I'm afraid the effects will be ten times as devastating."

"If that's true, the whole city will be wiped out," Rook said, gripping the edge of the bench for support.

"No, it won't," Captain Hardwick said, in a voice so intense it startled Rook. "The mayor of Regara has been taking steps to prevent another catastrophe. That's why we've risked gathering you three together and working with Dozana. You're going to use your magic to save the city, no matter what."

"I won't have the children put in danger, Captain," Dozana interjected.

"You don't get a say in the matter," the captain shot back, his tone sharp. "You follow my orders or you'll be dealt with."

Dozana fell silent, her face pinched with anger. Rook glanced between them in alarm. She realized her earlier guess had been right. Although she was helping the constables, Dozana seemed to be as much a prisoner here as Rook, Drift, and Fox.

The carriage rolled to a halt. Captain Hardwick glanced behind the curtain again, then leaned over to unlock the door. He jumped out and motioned for Dozana and the others to follow.

Climbing out of the carriage, Rook blinked in the sunlight and craned her neck to look up at the massive gray wall towering over her. She'd never stood at the base like this before. The sheer height of it made the guards walking on top look like toy soldiers.

A shout drew Rook's attention to a small crowd forming in the yard of one of the houses closest to the wall. That was strange, Rook thought, since Hardwick had said they were clearing the area of people.

Seeing the commotion, the carriage driver and three of the five constables who'd been waiting for them near the wall broke away and moved off to intercept the people. Rook turned to see what was going on, but the captain towed her in the opposite direction with a firm grip on her arm.

"Keep moving," he said. "Don't look."

The tightness in his voice sent a chill through Rook. Ignoring his warning, she glanced over her shoulder, straining to see what was happening.

The constables had formed a semicircle in front of the crowd. Through a gap, Rook caught a glimpse of a woman in stained work clothes shoving one of them, trying to push past. Even from this distance, Rook could see that her eyes had gone completely white.

She had succumbed to the Frenzy sickness. The constables were holding the woman back, pinning her flailing arms against her sides. She shrieked like a wild animal and spat on them. Rook shuddered. The Frenzied were sometimes drawn to the gray wall, where they would run their hands over the stones as if they could sense the magic churning within like soup bubbling in a pot. They would pace the wall all day and night until they collapsed if the constables didn't pull them far enough away to bring them back to their senses.

If Dozana was right and the magic in the Wasteland continued to build, more and more people could be claimed by the Frenzy.

"Rook," Drift said, her voice hushed.

"I see her," Rook answered. Nearby, Fox whimpered.

"Don't look," Dozana said from behind them, echoing the captain's advice. "There's nothing we can do for her." Gently, she urged them forward with a hand at each girl's back.

The remaining two constables met them at the wall. Rook watched as they saluted the captain, who acknowledged them with a curt nod.

Dozana leaned in and said something to Hardwick that Rook didn't hear; then she came over and held out a new piece of chalk to Rook. "The effects of my power have probably worn off by now, so you can use this," she said. "The constables have cleared a section of the wall of moss and dirt for you to draw the door on a smooth surface. You'll need to create a passage that comes out in the Wasteland near the inner, red heartstone wall. *Near* it, not over it," she added firmly. "About a mile away should be far enough."

"Why not go all the way past the inner wall to the lake?" one of the constables asked. He was a skinny young man with two small crescent scars marring the tawny skin beneath his left eye, which he rubbed nervously when he spoke to Dozana. "The less of the Wasteland we have to travel on foot, the safer we'll be."

Dozana shot the man an irritated glance. "Because red heartstone has been proven to trap magic," she explained, as if speaking to a child. "That's why the city used it to build the inner wall. *Only* the inner wall, because red heartstone is very rare and they didn't have enough to surround the entire Wasteland. But it's strong, so strong that Rook's powers will be disrupted if she tries to create a door through it or anywhere near it. It's wiser if we appear some distance into the outer ring of the Wasteland, at least a mile from the red heartstone wall. We'll travel the rest of the way on foot and climb over. It's not a fraction as tall as the gray wall, so we'll be fine."

There was nothing but confidence in her voice. Still, the two constables exchanged wary glances. Rook wondered if they realized what they had gotten themselves into. If they understood the danger of poisoned magic at all.

"Whenever you're ready, Rook," Dozana said, pointing to the cleared spot on the wall.

"Wait," Rook said, swallowing the ball of fear rising in her chest. "What is it you think we can do to stop the magic from exploding? You've seen what our powers are. They won't help you."

"It's not so much how your powers manifest," Dozana said, "as the amount of raw magical talent you possess. You see, every Voran is a wizard. Every Voran has a certain amount of animus inside of him or her, which can be harnessed, drained, and replenished. That raw power is what I will need in order to cleanse the magic from the area. When the time comes, I'll show you what must be done." She turned to Captain Hardwick, her jaw tightening. "Are your men prepared to follow my directions once we're inside the walls? Because the Wasteland is no place for people who lack a working knowledge of magic. If you insist on bringing them along, they'll need to do as I say."

The captain's eyes narrowed. "We will protect you and the children while you guide us to the portal site, where you will work your magic," he said. "We need no more direction than that. Once we've accomplished our mission, the children will be cared for, and you'll go back to a prison cell while the mayor of Regara decides your fate."

"I don't understand," Drift said, her voice shrill as she turned to Dozana. "Why send you to prison? I thought you were helping them?"

Dozana's lips thinned. "I am," she said. "I simply wasn't given a choice in the matter. Do I have your permission to tell my daughter the situation, Captain?"

Rook noticed that Drift sucked in a sharp breath when Dozana said the word "daughter."

"Your story is your own," the captain said dismissively. "You can tell it once we're inside."

And with that, all eyes turned to Rook and the piece of chalk Dozana had given her.

Rook stepped up to the wall. Was she really going to do this—open a door into the Wasteland on purpose? Her fingers trembled so badly she could barely hold the chalk, let alone draw a straight line with it.

If only they had taken Mr. Baroman's advice and stayed at the roost. Or left Regara at once to start over someplace else. None of this would have happened.

There was the sound of claws clicking on the cobblestones, then Fox, back in his animal form, bumped against her hip. The familiar scent of gamey fur and wildness washed over her.

Rook glanced over at Drift, looking for more comfort, but Drift was staring at Dozana, her eyes shining with unshed tears.

Of course she's worried about her mother, Rook thought, but there was a small pang in her chest. She couldn't help feeling that her friend was miles away from her at that moment.

Pushing her fears aside and drawing strength from Fox's presence, Rook put her chalk to the wall to draw. She managed a passable rectangle, which took the form of a heavy-planked wood door with black bar hinges and an iron knob. It might have been the most unremarkable door she'd ever created.

Until she reached for the knob.

There was an ear-splitting crack, and the door's wood planks buckled and warped before Rook's eyes. Nails popped, raining down on the cobblestones. The ones that stayed in place strained to hold the door together. Luckily, the magic was stubborn, and Rook's will was strong.

When the sounds died away, the door before them was still a door, but only just. It had twisted into a crude S shape, some of the planks wrenching free of their nails and jutting out in all directions. The hinges were bent beyond recognition. Rook didn't think she or anyone else would ever be able to open the mangled door.

"We can't do this," Rook whispered. "I mean, *look* at it." It wasn't a door anyone should ever have to walk through. It was just . . . wrong.

"Don't let it frighten you," Dozana said kindly. "What you're seeing are traces of animus on the other side pushing back against the door, cracking and twisting it. All the more reason we need to get the magic out of there."

With shaking hands, Rook took hold of the knob—it was hot to the touch, almost too hot to hold—and wrenched the door open.

The first thing she noticed on the other side was the color of the sky. It was red, but not the warm, golden glow of a sunset over the harbor. This was a dull, heavy red, like blood dripping from raw meat. The color made it impossible to tell whether it was day or night inside the Wasteland. It was more like a perpetual ugly twilight.

The second thing Rook noticed was that it was raining beyond the door. Everywhere else in Regara the sky was calm, the air warm and humid, but not over the Wasteland. Large, dark drops splashed and ran in oily puddles. It didn't smell like a normal rain either, the kind that washed the world and glistened on the grass and leaves. This rain carried the distinct smell of decay.

Wrong. Wrong. Wrong.

"Let's go," Captain Hardwick said grimly, pushing past Rook to take the lead. "Wizard, stay close to the children. My men, bring up the rear. Everyone, be alert."

Forcing her feet to move, Rook crossed the door's threshold as lightning split the sky overhead, throwing distorted shadows across the gray wall. Thunder followed in a rumble that she felt all the way to the soles of her feet.

When they were all on the other side of the door, Dozana pushed it closed, and Rook reluctantly let the magic slip away. She wanted to feel the safety of the city one last time, but it was too late. The door wedged into place with a groan and then faded, protruding nails and all.

17

THE DOOR TO THE SKY

ROOK SENSED THE MAGIC IN the air as they traversed the Wasteland. The pure, uncontrolled animus was all around them, invisible, but she was as sure of its existence as she was of the wind lashing them. It blew her hair back, chilled her skin, and rattled the leafless, gnarled trees that grew from the shells of buildings and cracked city streets.

"Look at that!" Drift pointed to a wrought-iron fence a few feet off to their left. The house behind it had been reduced to nothing more than a pile of stones, but sections of the fence remained intact. Coiling around its black bars was a green vine as thick as Rook's thigh. It had grown so tall that the tip of the vine was suspended twenty feet in the air, where it had wrapped itself around the wheels of a full-size wagon. The wagon now hung upside down from the vine like an oversized grape. It swayed back and forth in the wind, creaking and groaning as if it might snap off at any moment.

Fox growled and sniffed along the base of the vine. He

sneezed, rubbed his nose with a paw, and backed up, obviously not liking whatever it was he smelled. A shadow jumped from his body, and they stood back to back, their mirrored selves sniffing the air, ears twitching as if they expected something to leap out from behind the piles of stone.

"Good idea," Rook told him. "Doesn't hurt to have eyes in the back of your head."

"Keep moving," Hardwick said.

They cut a wide path around the suspended wagon, but Rook couldn't help staring up at it as they moved past. She wondered who the vehicle had belonged to and where they were now, if they had survived the explosion.

She was just about to turn away when suddenly the end of the vine stiffened and curled in on itself, snapping the spokes of the wagon wheels one by one.

"Look out!" Dozana shouted from behind them.

With the spokes gone, the vine uncurled, and with nothing to hold it, the wagon fell, smashing to the ground in a ruined heap. Rook and the others scrambled out of the way of the flying debris. When she looked back at the vine, Rook saw that its tip was now straight and sharp like a spear. Before she could call out a warning, it shot straight toward the group.

Rook dove aside as the vine stabbed the broken street next to her, sending stones flying. Drift launched herself into the air, while Fox howled and shed two more shadows to bark and bite at the length of vine coiled around the wrought-iron fence. Hardwick and his men charged forward, drawing their knives and putting themselves between Rook and the stabbing spear.

"Keep the children safe!" Hardwick ordered. He slashed at the vine with his knife, severing its tip. The vine recoiled and shot into the air as if it had actually *felt* the wound. The other two men went for the base, hacking and stabbing at the plant.

Rook scrambled to her feet to find Dozana next to her. "Are you all right?" the woman asked, concern darkening her eyes.

"I'm fine," Rook said. "I just—"

But she never got to finish. A tickling sensation brushed her ankle, and Rook looked down in horror to see a thinner vine coiling around her leg. It stretched and cracked like a whip, yanking her into the air upside down.

"Rook!" Dozana screamed. She grabbed Rook's hand, trying to pull her from the vine's grip. Rook strained to hold on, but the oily rain made it impossible. Her fingers slipped from Dozana's grasp, and suddenly she was weightless, flung into the sky like a rag doll on a string.

"Help me!" Rook shouted. The ground and the sky blurred as the vine swung her back and forth. She flailed her arms, reaching for something, anything that would make the sickening motion stop and release her from the pressure of the vine squeezing her leg.

"Cut it at the base!" Hardwick and his men were shouting. All the blood had rushed to Rook's face, and she was so dizzy she was afraid she might pass out. She tried to reach up and untangle the vine wrapped around her leg, but it had her in a death grip. Below her, Fox and his shadows howled in a frightened chorus.

"Rook, hold on!" shouted a voice close by.

Rook turned her head and caught a streak of motion as Drift flew past her. Her friend twisted in midair, reaching for Rook's hand. Rook met her halfway, but just as quickly, the vine ripped her out of reach. Rain dripped down Rook's face. She scrubbed it away and looked down to see Hardwick and the others clustered around the base of the vine, hacking and chopping furiously.

"We've almost got it!" Dozana cried.

They were right. A tremor rippled through the plant, and the vine holding Rook's leg loosened. Rook gasped, dropping several feet before the plant caught her again. She was at least thirty feet in the air now, and the ground looked so very far away.

"Um, maybe we should wait until it decides to lower me a few feet!" Rook shouted at the group below, but none of them could hear her over the rain and howling wind.

"Got it!" Hardwick shouted, seconds before the vine stiffened and whipped violently from side to side, knocking Rook back and forth like a pendulum.

And then it let go.

18

THE DOOR TO THE PAST

THE FORCE OF THE VINE'S swing launched Rook into the air. There was a terrifying instant of out-of-control spinning, her stomach heaving . . . and then a weight slammed into her. Hands locked around her waist and buoyed her on a sudden, fierce wind that blew the rain sideways into her eyes.

"Drift!" Rook cried, for even blinded, she knew her friend had caught her. Drift was always there to catch her.

"I've got you!" She was out of breath, soaked to the skin just like Rook. The wind steadied, and Drift angled them toward the ground. As soon as Rook's feet touched the broken pavement, Fox bounded up and pressed his wet muzzle into her shoulder. She wrapped her arms around him and held on.

"Are you all right?" Dozana asked, coming over to them. Hardwick and his men were busy slicing the monstrous vine up into pieces too small to attack.

"I think so," Rook said. She released Fox and reached down to pull up her pant leg. There was a long red mark where the vine had squeezed her, but the pain and dizziness of being swung around like a toy were slowly fading. She looked up at Drift, who was wringing rainwater out of her clothes. "Thank you," she said.

Drift nodded, but her mouth was pressed into a line and she was so pale Rook thought she might faint. "I can't believe this," she said, raising her voice so Hardwick and his men could hear her. "We're in the Wasteland five minutes and the *weeds* are trying to kill us! What's going to happen when we get inside the red heartstone wall? That's where the magic is going to be strongest, right? Around the ruins of the portal site?"

"It doesn't matter," Hardwick said, sheathing his knife and kicking aside a clump of vine. "Get yourself together," he told Rook. "It's time to move."

Now Drift's face was turning red, her hands shaking as she stalked over to the captain. "In case you weren't paying attention, my friend was almost killed just now! The least you can do is let us rest for a minute!"

The captain's stony expression didn't change. "The longer we stay here, the more chance there is we'll be attacked by something even more dangerous."

"Much as I hate to admit it, the captain's right," Dozana said. She put a hand on Drift's shoulder, which seemed to calm her a bit. "You did very well, Daughter, but we need to be even more careful from now on. I'm afraid it was no accident the vine went after Rook and not the rest of us."

"Why's that?" The man with the crescent scars glared at

Dozana, his dark eyes suspicious. "You holding something back, Voran?"

Dozana flashed him a smile of narrowed eyes and many teeth. "I wasn't sure until just now, but I believe Rook may have greater stores of animus inside her than any of the rest of us," she said. "That's what the vine was drawn to—the strength of her magic."

"You mean the same way magic sucks people in and turns them into Frenzied?" asked the other constable. He had hazel eyes and a nose that had been broken so many times it had given up trying.

"The result is the same," Dozana said, "in that the subject's behavior turns violent, but we don't know what makes people fall to the Frenzy or why only a small number are affected. The animus is an easier force to understand. It feeds on itself and grows stronger."

Wonderful, Rook thought as the weight of that knowledge settled on her shoulders. Now she was a magnet for dangerous magic, and it was only going to get worse the longer they remained in the Wasteland.

Hardwick didn't look happy to hear Dozana's theory either. "Jace," he said, pointing to the scarred man, "stay close to Rook. Garrett, you keep an eye on the other two. The wizard can use her defenses to guard us all. Let's move out."

It was only when Hardwick mentioned it that Rook remembered Dozana's power. Why hadn't she brought it to bear on the vine to weaken it? Did it only work on humans? Or was she saving her power for when they were inside the red heartstone wall?

Rook let her questions go for the moment to concentrate on the walk ahead of them. Hardwick kept them on as straight a path as possible going east, but their pace was slowed by the overgrown plants and debris piled in their path. Thankfully, the rain eventually slowed to a light drizzle, and in the distance, they could just make out their destination: a ten-foot wall of copper-colored stones, illuminated by periodic lightning flashes. They were too far away to see many details, but even so, Rook thought there was something strange about the barrier, though she couldn't say exactly what it was.

Ahead of her, Drift quickened her pace until she fell into step beside Dozana. Her expression was a mix of longing and determination. Rook crept forward to get within earshot.

"M-Mother," Drift was saying, her voice tentative, apologetic, "there's still so much I don't remember. I mean . . . I don't remember *anything*."

Dozana smiled sadly and stroked Drift's wet hair. "It's all right," she said. "For now, it's enough that I have you with me again. I've missed you so much, my dear."

Drift leaned into the affectionate touch. Watching them, Rook felt that same pang in her chest, but sharper this time, lingering like a wound.

"But how are you here?" Drift pressed, still as full of questions as Rook. "I thought all the wizards went back through the portal before the explosion."

"Not all of them," Dozana replied. "Some even came here in secret and stayed."

"Why?" Rook spoke up before she could stop herself.

Dozana didn't seem surprised that Rook had been eavesdropping. "To escape the wars," she said soberly.

"Wars?" Drift echoed. "When were the Vorans at war?"

"When *weren't* we?" Dozana countered. She laughed without humor. "I'm happy you don't remember, child. Our people fought over so many things—who should own the land, who should be a king, but mostly who should control all the magic in the world—including the magical portal to Talhaven. It's possible to heal from wars fought over the first two. But wars fought over magic, *using* magic . . ." There was a haunted expression in her eyes. "They cause nothing but devastation. Destruction you can't ever recover from. You just have to run."

A prickle of understanding touched Rook's mind. "Is that what caused the portal explosion?" she asked. "Fighting over it with magic? Is that why our people sent the children through first? Because they wanted us to run away?"

The group halted briefly while Hardwick and Jace kicked aside the skeleton of a dead horse that lay in their path. Rook tried not to look at its bleached white skull as she passed.

She held her breath as she waited to hear Dozana's answer to her question. It was so strange. She should have been angry at being kidnapped, at seeing her dearest friends put in danger. She should have been terrified of the Wasteland they walked through. She was soaked and miserable, her teeth chattering from the chill in the air and the fear churning inside her.

But at that moment, none of it mattered. Dozana could answer the questions that had been piling up in the hearts of every exile in Talhaven. Questions weighing on them so heavily that some nights they could barely breathe.

Who am I?

Where do I come from?

Why was I abandoned here?

"That's exactly what happened," Dozana said, bringing Rook back to herself. The woman's eyes continuously scanned the ground while she spoke, as if she was on the lookout for more plants that might attack them. "Our leaders had gotten wind that a large revolt was brewing, so all the Vorans were recalled from Talhaven to help defend Cherith, the city on the Voran side of the portal. It hardly made a difference. Rival wizards launched a surprise attack on the city, and the results were devastating. We had only minutes to gather as many of our children as we could and put them on a ship. There were *so many* left behind." Dozana's voice cracked, and she quickly cleared her throat. "The children were sent through the portal to safety, while their parents stayed behind and used their collective magic to shield the ship and cover its escape before the city was destroyed. But no one predicted that the magical chaos would travel *through* the portal, destroying it and a portion of Regara. That's what caused the Great Catastrophe."

"But how can you know for sure that's what happened, if you were living here in secret?" Drift asked.

Dozana raised an eyebrow at her. "I never said *I* was living here. I said other wizards were—and might still be, although if they're smart, they'll be deep in hiding. I know what I know because I was on the ship with the children when they came through the portal. I was tasked with being their protector."

Rook felt like her world had been turned upside down. Their families had sent the exiles away to save them from a catastrophe that had destroyed a city, then reached *between worlds* and wrecked part of another. And Dozana had been with them the whole time. Her existence must have been wiped away with all Rook's other memories.

The thought tied another knot in her stomach, but a sudden change in the landscape distracted her. After having trudged down one broken street after another, they were now hiking through a wild clover patch, but it was unlike any clover Rook had ever seen. It was purple and grew as tall as her waist in places. It sprang from the base of what had once been one of the city wells but was now little more than a stone ring in the ground.

And then there were the floating stones.

Dozens of them, some small as her fist, others as big as her head, all of them frozen in the air above the clover patch. Rook might have been more shocked at the strange sight if she hadn't just been used as a juggling toy by a monstrous vine.

Hardwick raised his hand for the group to stop. "What is this, wizard?" he demanded. Rook didn't think she'd ever heard him call Dozana by her name.

Dozana waded into the clover patch but stopped short of walking among the hovering stones. She reached out and tapped one of the smaller ones lightly with her finger, but it didn't move. It was stuck, hovering in midair. She nodded, muttering something to herself.

"What did you say?" Hardwick asked.

"I believe it's a time distortion," Dozana said, pitching her voice so the whole group could hear.

"Time . . . *what?*" Jace rubbed his scars again. He seemed to do it whenever he was nervous. "What does that mean?"

"I told you it was important to have someone with a working knowledge of magic as your guide, Captain," Dozana said. She grabbed the small rock in her fist and pulled. The stone didn't move. Dozana's face reddened with strain. Her arm trembled, but finally she managed to yank the rock out of its position and tossed it to Hardwick.

"Wait, you're saying that time works differently here?" Rook asked, staring at the stone in Hardwick's hand.

"Everything works differently here," Dozana said. "Never forget that. The weather is abnormal, the plants and animals are out of control, and yes, even time is distorted in places, slowed down so much that a shower of stones from an explosion that happened two years ago can still hang in the air, taking years to fall."

"Is it dangerous?" Garrett asked, stepping back from the cloud of stones.

Dozana didn't even look at him. "No more or less so than the rest of the Wasteland," she said. "It's very possible that this whole area is experiencing time distortion of varying degrees. That would explain why it looks like a different time of day beyond the Wasteland walls. But this particular distortion is old and weakening. That's probably why I was able to remove the stone from it. Nevertheless, we should give this area a wide berth, just to be safe."

"But if time is passing more quickly outside the Wasteland, aren't the rest of our people going to wonder what's happened to us?" Jace asked. "Won't they send out a search party?"

"We can't know how fast time is passing outside," the captain said, "and it doesn't change our mission. We press ahead, no matter what."

No matter what? Rook shuddered. They'd just keep going, even if time continued to slip away faster outside the Wasteland? She stared at the stones as they set off again, careful to stay clear of the area. What if they stepped into another distortion without realizing it and ended up frozen forever like the rocks?

The captain obviously understood the risk, Rook thought, but he wasn't turning back, which gave them no choice but to follow.

Their new path led them onto a side street that they'd avoided earlier because it was choked with debris. Their pace slowed even more as they climbed over piles of broken stones, squeezing past trees and bushes that had overgrown the street.

Dozana dropped back to walk on Rook's right side. Drift followed her mother. Jace kept to Rook's left side. The adults were obviously staying close in case some other strange magic popped up to menace them, providing Rook with another opportunity to talk to the wizard.

"You said you'd tell us your story." Rook pitched her voice low and glanced sidelong at the older woman. "About why you're a prisoner."

Dozana's gaze flicked to Captain Hardwick and then back to Rook. "So I did, though there's not much to tell. You already know I was sent here with the Voran children to protect them. I was tasked with the job because of my power. I used it to drain the magic around the ship as we came through the portal, effectively creating a bubble that no harmful magical energy could penetrate. This allowed me to shield the ship from the explosion, and somehow protected me from the memory loss that afflicted the children, but the shock wave threw me into the lake." Her lips twisted. "That was . . . unpleasant. The constables found me during the rescue efforts. They saw me using my power to try to calm the wild magic, and they captured me. Officially, I am a 'guest' of the mayor of Regara, an 'advisor' to help her and the captain here deal with the magical turmoil that plagues the city."

"And once that's done, they'll just lock you up?" Drift

asked, pressing forward to tug at her mother's arm. "But why? You haven't done anything wrong."

"Oh, no?" Dozana gestured to herself. "Am I not a wizard of Vora? I'm the only adult at hand to pay for what my people did."

Jace snorted. "Don't let her play innocent with you." He pointed to the crescent scars under his eye. "She gave me these beauties trying to escape. Almost took my eye out. She's dangerous, just like . . ."

He trailed off, cleared his throat, and looked away.

Anger boiled inside Rook. "Like *us*," she finished, nodding to Fox and Drift.

"Can you blame him?" Garrett said, ripping aside a tree branch covered in rotting yellow leaves. A cloud of biting flies swirled around his face. He slapped them away. "Didn't the exiles bring the Frenzy sickness to Regara? And weren't you two girls the ones who let that fox monster out of the Wasteland?"

Before Rook could reply, Drift chimed in. "We told you Fox didn't come from here," she snapped. "We weren't trying to hurt anyone. And we didn't bring the Frenzy sickness either. We're just as scared of it as you are!"

"It's not their fault," Jace agreed, surprising Rook. She hadn't expected the man to speak up on their behalf. "The Red Watchers can yell and spit all they want, but we're talking about kids here. I don't believe they're making people sick, but they'll grow up with no one to teach them about magic. They're going to make mistakes."

"*I* could teach them," Dozana said. "But I'm too *dangerous* for that, aren't I, Constable?"

Jace rubbed his scars and didn't reply.

Captain Hardwick, silent up to this point, spoke. "It's *what* you'll teach them that concerns me," he said, his voice a low, ominous rumble.

They were climbing over a shifting pile of broken tables and chairs in the ruins of what might once have been a restaurant. Hardwick slid down the debris, and when he'd reached the bottom, he stood up and held out a hand to help Rook. Reluctantly, she took it. His palm had a raised line running across it that felt like a scar.

When she was back on solid ground, he released her but didn't immediately turn away. "The wizard told us that you've been using your power to open doors for people in the city," Hardwick said. "She told us about the Kelmins, that you were helping them escape from some men who were threatening them. Is that true?"

Tried and failed, Rook thought. She looked up, but the captain's face was impossible to read. "It's true," she said.

He nodded. "Your power *is* remarkable," he said. "And that you use it to help people speaks well of your character." Rook was surprised to hear the approval in his voice.

Following the captain's example, Garrett had turned back

to help Drift down the debris pile, but he scowled when she simply flew over his outstretched hand and touched down near Rook. "Doesn't change the fact that the three of them are runaways," he said. "Exiles can't be allowed to run wild. Accident or no, your powers can hurt people. They need to be kept under control."

"Maybe we wouldn't have run if we hadn't felt threatened," Drift said, matching his scowl.

"Have to admit, I wouldn't mind being able to fly like you can," Jace said, and he actually smiled at Drift. It was the first time Rook had seen anything like friendliness in the face of a constable, and she didn't know how to feel about it, or the compliment the captain had paid her.

Drift didn't seem to know either, because she blushed, and an agitated breeze blew across the back of Rook's neck.

"I believe the exiles' magic needs to be monitored so that no one gets hurt," Hardwick agreed as the group moved down a street that was thankfully mostly clear of debris. "But I also think if we trusted each other a bit more, it would make things easier. We've let the Red Watchers have too much sway among the people of Regara. The Frenzy sickness hasn't helped matters either. Instead of letting old wounds heal, people have become even more afraid of magic and the exiles."

Again, Rook found herself surprised at the captain's words. But did he mean them? Did he realize that the words *he* chose to use—calling Dozana "wizard" and referring to Rook, Drift, and Fox as exiles instead of using their names—weren't help-ing Rook to trust him?

"As touching as this conversation is," Dozana said, sar-casm thick in her voice, "we're almost to the red heartstone wall. Everyone stay close."

"Rain's picking up again," Jace said. "Be wise to find shel-ter until it passes."

"Not until we're on the other side of the wall," Hardwick said. "Keep moving."

Dozana was correct. Ahead of them, about fifty yards away, the red heartstone wall stood, blocking their path. As they drew closer, Rook finally realized what had seemed strange about the wall from a distance.

The rain had been falling everywhere, covering the Waste-land in a wet, oily skin.

Except on the wall.

It was as if the stones were waterproof, protected by an invisible barrier that the raindrops couldn't touch.

A shiver that had nothing to do with the chilly rain passed through Rook's body. She didn't realize she'd stopped moving until Dozana rested a hand on her shoulder.

"I promise, nothing will happen to you or the others while I'm here," she said. "I'll protect you all with my life. It's the very least I can do for my child and the children of my home world."

"Keep up, you two," Hardwick called back to them, and Rook reluctantly started walking again.

Bolstered by Dozana's words, Rook hoped that the woman's power would be enough.

Because she had a terrible feeling that whatever lay beyond the red heartstone wall would be far worse than any of them were prepared for.

19

THE DOOR TO POWER

AS THEY APPROACHED THE RED wall, Rook was surprised at how much shorter it was than the gray wall. It ended just a few feet above Dozana's head and would be easy enough to climb. There were no guards watching the area. No one in the city—not even the constables—had ventured this deep into the Wasteland since the explosion that tore apart the portal.

"How is a wall that short supposed to protect the city?" Rook asked.

"Don't underestimate its power," Dozana cautioned. She stepped up to the wall and laid her hand gently against the copper stone. "For two years, it's managed to cage uncontrollable magic. Come here and feel for yourself."

Reluctantly, Rook stepped forward, Drift and Fox close behind her. She reached out and touched the wall with just her fingertips. No way was Rook risking her whole hand on something that trapped magic.

The stone vibrated ever so slightly beneath her fingers, as if threads of energy ran through it. It was also warm to the touch, though not unpleasantly so. Still, Rook felt a strange pulling sensation inside her, as if the red stone was trying to draw out her power. Quickly, she removed her hand.

"This stone is like your power," Rook said, glancing at Dozana. "It drains magic, doesn't it?"

"As a matter of fact—" Dozana turned to look at Fox, but before she could finish the sentence, he abruptly transformed back into a human. He wobbled on his feet, looking bewildered and frightened. "Yes, it can," Dozana finished.

"Are you all right?" Rook asked, rushing over to grab Fox by the shoulder before he fell.

"I—I think so," he said. He looked down at his hands as if he didn't know what they were. "How . . . Why did I change?" he asked.

"You didn't transform on purpose," Rook said, realizing what had happened. "It was the red wall. It took away your power."

"It's messing with mine too," Drift said. She closed her eyes and wrinkled her forehead in concentration. She managed to levitate a couple of inches off the ground, but no more than that. "I don't feel weak, but it's like someone's pulling me down by the ankles."

"That's why we couldn't open a door here," Dozana said. "The barrier is absolute. Rook's magic either wouldn't have been able to penetrate the wall, or it would have gone wild and we might have ended up anywhere. The wall is meant to contain magical calamities. The Regarans who built it didn't think anyone would ever be trying to get *into* the Wasteland."

"No kidding," Drift muttered.

Hardwick pointed to Jace and Garrett. "The two of you climb up first and see what you can see from the top of the wall. Then you'll help the rest of us over."

Rook, Drift, and Fox stood back while the two constables nodded and approached the wall. They found handholds in the cracks between the stones and carefully pulled themselves up to the top of the wall. Fox fidgeted, clenching his jaw and wrinkling his forehead, as if he was trying everything he could to turn into an animal again.

"Hey," Rook said, putting her arm around him. "Don't try to transform here, all right? Save your strength. Once we're inside and far enough away from the wall, you can change back."

"But I can't protect you," Fox said, a forlorn look in his eyes. "Not like this." He clenched the hem of his baggy, still-wet shirt and shivered. He must be so much colder in this form, Rook realized, without the thick fox fur to insulate him.

"Don't worry," she said, hugging him with one arm. "We'll all look out for each other."

Fox sighed. He closed his eyes and leaned into Rook's shoulder for warmth. Over his head, Rook caught Drift's eye, and for just a second she thought she glimpsed that same hint of loneliness in her friend that she'd first noticed back at the roost. She started to say something, but before she could speak, Drift turned away and went to stand next to her mother.

What was happening to them? Rook thought anxiously. After all this time, she and Drift were finally getting answers to their questions about their home world, finding lost pieces of themselves. How many nights had they lain awake, whispering about their mysterious pasts, what kind of lives they must have led?

Yet she and Drift hadn't shared more than a handful of words since they'd set foot in the Wasteland. Rook wanted to believe she was just being foolish, but she couldn't help feeling as if her best friend was drifting further and further away from her.

"All clear," Garrett called down from the top of the wall, but his voice sounded strange.

"That's one way to look at it," Jace said, pacing back and forth across the top of the wall, his hands moving restlessly over the knife hilt at his belt. "I don't see any monsters, though."

"What *do* you see?" Drift asked.

Jace looked down at her and shook his head. "It's impossible to describe," he said. "You just . . . You need to see for yourself."

"Let's go, Captain," Dozana said. "The longer they stay up there, the worse it's going to get for them. No one should have to see the Wasteland all at once."

"You heard her," the captain said, and it was the first time Rook had seen the two of them so firmly in agreement.

Rook followed Dozana to the base of the wall. The captain clasped his hands together to make a step. Rook raised her foot, holding on to Dozana's shoulder for balance. Together they boosted her up, and Jace and Garrett reached down to hoist her the rest of the way.

The top of the wall was about two feet deep. Rook sat down on the warm stone and looked out over the expanse.

Her breath left her body in a rush.

The buildings and streets beyond the inner wall had been very close to the explosion site, so there was little left of what was once this section of Regara. Piles of stone, wood, and broken glass were everywhere. Weeds had grown in to cover the ruins with a layer of wild green, but here and there, curved black thorns as thick as Rook's thumb grew from vines and creepers. They would have to be extra careful moving through the jungle-like landscape.

But none of those things was as frightening as what lay in the center of the expanse.

The portal between Vora and Talhaven had been conjured on Lake Caralan because the Vorans claimed that water was a strong conduit for magic, especially portal magic. Ships carrying trade goods could easily sail through the portal into the lake and down the channel to the White Sea. From there they could travel by air or water to any part of the world.

Rook glimpsed the lake in the distance, a deep blue fringe

cutting across the horizon, but above that, silhouetted against the cloud-filled sky, a forest floated in midair.

Rook shivered as she gazed at the improbable trees. It was as if a giant hand had reached down and yanked them from the earth, roots and all, as easily as she might pull a carrot from a garden. Most of the trees were dead, floating skeletons with spindly branches and twisted roots.

Woven among them was a strange, pulsing red light, tangled in the branches like threads of cloud.

Had the explosion uprooted the trees and then frozen them in the same time distortion that held the stones?

Rook scooted to the side to make room as one by one, Jace and Garrett helped the others up onto the wall. Hardwick took in the sight of the lake and the floating forest, but his stoic expression didn't change.

Because he's seen this before, Rook thought. He and Dozana both had. They knew about the danger, the power building up at the portal site.

"Do you see it, Rook?" Dozana asked, pointing to the red light clinging to the trees. "The animus rises from the lake and collects in the branches—magic in its purest, untamed form."

"Most dangerous form, you mean," Jace muttered.

When they'd climbed down the other side of the wall, the captain took the lead again, heading in the direction of the lake. He and Garrett used their knives to chop away the worst of the thorny underbrush to make a path for the others. Jace stayed back with Rook, scanning the area for threats.

"Don't let the thorns draw blood," Dozana warned them. "They're poisonous."

"Of *course* they are," Garrett said, hacking aggressively at a branch.

The rain came and went as they walked, drawing closer and closer to the lake and the suspended forest. But for all the strangeness they'd encountered so far, the most unsettling thing was that there was no sign of any of the Wasteland's famous monsters, animals transformed by the wild animus. If Rook didn't know better, she might have thought the stories everyone told were just that—stories.

But then she heard them.

At first, she thought it was just the wind bringing in another storm. But the wind didn't make noises like this. High-pitched shrieks, moans, and growls echoed from far away. A stone shifted nearby, and a faint sound like pebbles—or clicking claws—reached Rook's ears. She whirled in that direction, but there was nothing there. Her heart pounded. The others were noticing the sounds too. The constables kept their knives ready, tensing every time the weeds rustled or a shadow seemed to move among the piles of stone.

Fox bounded up beside Rook, keeping as close to her as Jace. They were far enough away from the wall that he'd transformed back into his animal form, and he seemed much more at ease.

"Can we stop for a moment?" Dozana asked after they'd been walking and hacking at brush for about ten minutes.

"What's wrong?" Hardwick asked, turning to look at her. His knife was stained dull green from cutting the plants.

Dozana tipped her head back, eyes closed, oily raindrops splashing her face. She held her hands out from her sides and breathed deeply.

"Are you all right?" Drift asked, clearly concerned. She had been hovering in the air to get a look at the path ahead of them, but now she floated back to the ground.

"Yes, Daughter, I'm fine," Dozana assured her. The woman opened her eyes and smiled at Drift, a serene expression settling over her features. "In fact, I'm feeling better than I have in a long time."

"Then why are we stopping?" Jace asked, an irritated line creasing his forehead.

"We're *not*," Hardwick said, turning away. "We'll rest once we reach the lake. Let's go."

But Dozana didn't move. "I'm afraid I have to refuse," she said, her serene expression never wavering. "This is as far as you go, Captain Hardwick."

Slowly, the captain turned around, fixing Dozana with a cold stare. "Excuse me?" he said.

Rook instinctively took a step back from the confrontation unfolding between the two of them. She pressed against Fox, and at the same time Drift edged toward her mother, a stiff breeze swirling around her.

"What are you playing at?" Jace demanded angrily. "The captain said—"

"I know what the captain said," Dozana interrupted, and this time there was a crack in her too-calm voice. "I was standing right here when he said it. I'm not invisible. I'm not an object, or a ruined thing lying in this Wasteland." Her lips twisted in a smile that chilled Rook. "Well, maybe I am a ruined thing, a broken woman. But even broken things have power."

What did that mean? Rook wondered. A feeling of dread crept over her at the look that had come into Dozana's eyes.

Suddenly, Garrett raised his knife and moved toward Dozana with a speed that made Rook gasp. The captain came in from the other side, both of them trying to flank her. Jace drew the pistol he carried.

"Stop!" Drift cried out, raising her hands. "Please, don't hurt her!"

Dozana's pupils dilated, turning her eyes to hard black jewels. Lightning split the sky at the same instant the air shimmered, and a pulse of energy rolled out from her in an arc. Rook felt it slice into her chest, stealing her breath. Then it was gone, leaving only a faint impression of heat around her heart.

Rook watched helplessly as the pulse of energy struck the captain and his men. Hardwick and Garrett stumbled. Their knives clattered to the ground. The pistol quivered in Jace's grip, but then he too dropped his weapon, and all three men collapsed. They were still conscious, working their mouths to scream for help, but none of them could speak or get up.

"What are you doing to them?" Drift demanded, her eyes filled with fear.

"They're being taught that carrying those toys doesn't give them any real power or protection," Dozana explained. Rook watched as the woman's eyes faded back to their normal color. She stood over the men, staring down at them with a look of pity and disgust. "I am exposing how small they truly are, and I am reminding you three children how much *greater* you are in body, mind, and soul. Earlier, in the park, you resisted my power and almost fought it off. These men were laid low in one strike."

A voice in the back of Rook's mind screamed at her that they should run, flee the captain and his men and run from Dozana and the Wasteland. But she found she couldn't make herself move. She just stared, horrified, at the men twitching on the ground.

"You planned this, didn't you?" Rook said, her voice trembling. "You could have escaped from them any time you wanted."

"Not *any* time," Dozana corrected her. She bent down, collected the knives and guns and tossed them into the thorny underbrush. "Only here, beyond the red heartstone wall, where the animus flows like a raging river. It feeds me, makes me stronger than I have ever been. You see, the magic of the Wasteland is a strange, unpredictable thing, but that doesn't mean it can't be harnessed by someone who knows how."

Kneeling beside Hardwick, Dozana touched a vine coiling

across the ground, careful not to prick her finger on its wicked thorns. At her touch, the vine stirred, slithering up and across the captain's chest like rope. Hardwick's jaw clenched, but he didn't dare try to move for fear of being stabbed with the poisonous thorns.

As Rook watched, Dozana awoke more of the vines, cooing at them and coaxing them like a mother to a nervous child. One by one, they wrapped themselves around the constables, stretching, tightening, until all three men were securely bound. Dozana's final touch: a ridge of black thorns encircled their exposed throats, the points just grazing—but not breaking—the tender skin of their necks.

"You know, we—the Vorans I mean—tried to preserve our forests and medicinal plant species with magic just like this," Dozana said, gazing down at Hardwick as she spoke. "They'd almost all been destroyed in the wars, and we needed to save as many of our natural resources as we could. So we poured raw animus into them, and they thrived for a time, growing and bending themselves to our will, but the side effect was that they lost every one of their healing properties. Eventually, they withered and died. The animus was too strong for them. There have only ever been two types of vessels capable of safely holding and distributing animus. One of these is the crystals grown in the gardens of Cherith, the same crystals we brought to every corner of Talhaven." She glanced up and met Rook's eyes. "And then there are the Vorans themselves."

Next to Rook, Fox's body trembled. Protective shadows sprang to life on either side of him.

"I'm not going to kill you," Dozana told the men casually, as if they were discussing the weather. "The children don't need to see that. No, I thought it was more important to make you helpless, as helpless as you made me during all those months I spent a prisoner, doing your leader's bidding. Maybe you'll be able to free yourselves once my power wears off. Maybe you'll be able to keep the thorns from digging into your flesh and poisoning your blood. You might even be able to escape before the monsters of the Wasteland come upon you. There's always hope."

Rook cringed as Dozana stood up and turned to her, Drift, and Fox. "Time to go," she said briskly, dusting her hands on her skirt as if wiping off something unpleasant. "We are very close to the heart of the Wasteland, where our *real* work can begin."

20

THE DOOR TO DISASTER

DOZANA INSTRUCTED DRIFT TO TAKE the lead and hover a few feet in the air to guide their diminished group down the twisting, broken streets toward the lake. For a long time, none of them spoke. Rook couldn't get the image of Captain Hardwick and his men out of her head, their frozen, fearful stares as the vines enveloped them.

She had no love for the Regaran constables—they'd kidnapped her and her friends and forced them into danger—but that didn't mean she wanted to see them helpless, left for the monsters of the Wasteland to devour.

It was Dozana who had tricked them all, lured them to this place so she could escape the constables. But what was she after now? Had anything she'd told them been the truth?

Rook glanced over her shoulder at the woman, who was walking at the back of their group to keep them all in sight. Her face gave away nothing. Fox trotted next to Rook with the two shadows he'd created keeping watch. It was the best protective formation they could make to keep each other safe.

The only thing Rook could contribute was to have her chalk ready in her hand in case she had the opportunity to create a door for the three of them to escape through.

But after that display with the constables, Rook's hope of being able to break free from Dozana was slowly slipping away. She had never seen magic so powerful or used so cruelly. Jace and Garrett had been many things, but they were never cruel to her. The captain was a hard man, but he had never seemed to enjoy keeping them prisoner. He'd been doing what he thought he had to do to save the city.

Rook pushed those thoughts out of her mind. She wasn't going to end up like the constables, and she wasn't about to let anything happen to Fox and Drift either. She needed to come up with a plan.

She sneaked another glance at Dozana and found the woman's attention largely on their surroundings. The farther into the Wasteland they traveled, the more Rook had the sense they were being watched, or stalked, or both. She couldn't see anything following them, but she felt something . . . a presence, as disturbing as a breath at the back of her neck.

It looked like Fox sensed it too. Every so often, he hunkered his body down and growled, his ears pressed flat against his head. He looked as if he wanted to attack everything in every direction, but like Rook, he couldn't get a fix on where the danger was coming from.

Ahead of them, Drift came back down and held up a hand for the others to stop. "What is it?" Dozana asked impatiently. "We can't afford to stay out in the open like this."

"You'd better look at this," Drift said in a flat voice. Rook recognized that tone. It was the one Drift used when she was trying not to let on how scared she was.

Dozana moved to the front of the group while Fox and his shadows formed a semicircle around them. Rook followed Dozana to Drift's side. She was bending over a dense bush that seemed entirely made of thorns and covered with a white, stringy substance that reminded her of dandelion fluff.

Then she got closer and realized that the substance wasn't part of the plant.

It was a spider's web.

Rook stared at the dense, silky strands in disbelief and tried very hard not to think about the size of the spider that must have spun them. They engulfed the bush, but that was only one small corner of the web. The rest of it unfurled across the path in front of them, covering at least two city blocks.

"What do we do?" Drift asked, keeping her voice low. "We can't go through it." To demonstrate why, she touched one of the silken strands with her fingertip and then tried to pull it away. The strands stuck to her fingers like glue, and she had to yank her hand away to free it, leaving behind a sticky white residue.

"Don't do that again," Dozana commanded in a tense voice. The vibration from Drift's touch traveled through the web, similar to the disturbance an insect would make when caught. Was the spider nearby? Rook wondered. Would it feel that tiny movement from Drift's touch?

"We'll have to go around it," Dozana said, gesturing to a path that led southeast, away from the web, but also away from the lake and the floating forest.

"That means we probably won't make it to the lake before nightfall," Rook said, pointing at the sky, which was already darkening in the aftermath of the storm, the red twilight slowly deepening to black, with hints of green edging the clouds.

"I was afraid of that," Dozana said. "We'll have to make camp in the ruins. Keep an eye out for something we can use as a shelter."

They turned onto their new course. Rook kept glancing at the web as they walked. Fox and his shadows did the same.

So they were taken entirely by surprise when the dogs leaped out at them.

Their only warning was the sound of harsh breathing and claws scraping stone. Then, from behind a cracked wall, two mastiff hounds charged into their path. They growled and snarled, foam threads dripping from their mouths.

They were enormous—bigger even than Fox—with matted fur and thick white tusks protruding from their mouths. In the center of their foreheads, a third eye stared down malevolently.

"Get back!" Drift screamed, and a blast of wind enveloped the group. The breath whooshed from Rook's lungs as the force of it slammed into her from behind, making her stumble. She looked up to see a hovering Drift in the middle of a mini tornado. Leaves and dirt swirled in a vortex around her friend, but she wasn't using the wind to fly. She was channeling it forward, pushing against the hounds so they couldn't attack the group.

And it was working. The hounds, one black and one chocolate brown, skittered backward over the stones. Teeth bared, they snarled and snapped at the air, scrambling to regain their footing, but the wind was too strong.

Rook had never seen Drift use her power like this. She couldn't possibly keep it up for long. It would sap her energy. She was going to collapse as surely as if Dozana had drained her magic. Unless . . . maybe the power of the inner Wasteland had also given Drift's magic a boost, the same way it had for Dozana.

Beside her, Fox exploded into action, sending not two, not three, but four shadows darting toward the mastiffs. Drift eased up on the tornado so the magical foxes could leap through, the wind pulling at their bodies, fraying them like smoke until they burst out the other side, re-formed, and surrounded the hounds.

Then Drift fell out of the air, hitting the ground not five feet away. Even with the magical boost, she'd used too much of her strength at once. Now she had only foxes made of shadow to protect her.

"No!" Rook cried. "Dozana, help me!" She ran to Drift, grabbing her beneath the armpits and hauling her to her feet. Drift swayed and leaned heavily on Rook.

"So dizzy," she mumbled.

Dozana put her body in front of them, temporarily blocking Rook's view of the standoff between the hounds and the shadow foxes. All she could hear were growls, barking, and high-pitched yips.

"Run!" Dozana shouted at them. "Around the web the other way! Now!"

That was all Rook needed to hear. She tugged on Drift's arm. "Let's go! Fox, come on!"

They ran, but they were so slow—a tripping, fumbling group that clambered over stone and shifting wood piles, trying to put as much distance between themselves and the mastiffs as possible. Rook had to strain to hold Drift upright, and Fox kept turning in circles to look behind them.

Suddenly the thunderous barking of the giant mastiffs turned to whimpers, and a loud thud echoed down the street. The shadow foxes reappeared beside Fox, all four of them. Rook threw a glance over her shoulder to find Dozana standing over the two mastiffs. They had crumpled to the ground and lay on their sides, unconscious just like the constables, but there was something different about them.

The hounds were smaller, Rook realized. The magic of the Wasteland had made them grow to monstrous proportions, but Dozana's power had shrunken them back to their normal size. Did that mean they would stay as normal dogs when they woke up?

Another thought occurred to her then, along with a surge of hope.

Dozana was at least thirty yards away from them, and she was distracted dealing with the hounds.

This was their chance to escape.

"Drift, is your head any clearer?" Rook asked, out of breath. "We need to run faster. If we can get a little farther away, we can hide and—"

Just then, Drift caught her shin on an exposed board and fell, crying out in pain. "You and Fox go," she commanded, clutching her shin. "I'll say we split up. Find somewhere to hide, draw the quickest door you've ever drawn, and take Fox through it!"

"Not a chance!" Rook yelled. She leaned down and grabbed Drift's arm. Fox got on her other side, boosting her up with his body, yipping and barking all the while. It was the fox equivalent of telling them to hurry.

"You're both . . . so . . . stubborn!" Drift said angrily as Rook hauled her up. They took off again, but this time Drift was limping, and they were moving even slower than before. Rook glanced down and noticed a dark stain spreading over Drift's pants leg.

"You're bleeding!" she cried in dismay. "Why didn't you say so?"

"That's why I told you to leave me!" Drift snapped.

Still bickering, they rounded a corner, and all of them stopped dead.

The thick white spiderweb stretched across the path in front of them, blocking the way. It was at least ten feet tall and twenty feet wide.

And in the center of the web was a huge brown mass as big as both of the mastiff hounds together.

Eight hairy legs, each one the length of a broom handle, spread out from its body. Rook counted the same number of shiny black eyes staring her down as she stared back, too terrified to move, to scream, or even to turn and run.

But the *spider* could move, and it did.

Directly toward them.

21

THE DOOR TO A SPIDER'S WEB

THE SPIDER INCHED ITS WAY gracefully down the web, taking its time, as if it was sizing them up as it approached. Probably trying to see how much of a threat they posed.

Or maybe it was just planning its dinner, Rook thought.

"We have to get out of here," Drift whispered. One hand was locked on Rook's arm in a bruising grip, her other hand buried in Fox's thick fur. "Go. Very. Slowly."

Rook began to inch her way back the way they'd come, Drift shuffling step by step with her. The shadow foxes spread out around them, forming a wall between the girls and the giant spider.

But the creature was still coming. The spider crawled to the very edge of its web.

And stopped.

What's it waiting for? Rook thought as they continued to back away. It should have attacked them by now. Unless . . .

maybe it wasn't like the mastiff hounds. Maybe if they just left it alone, it wouldn't come after them.

The sound of glass crunching behind them made Rook turn slightly to glance over her shoulder.

She choked back a scream.

It was two more spiders, clinging to rubble piles on either side of the pathway.

These two were half the size of the one in the web, but it hardly mattered. They were still large enough to be terrifying, and between the three of them, they had Rook and her friends surrounded.

"Drift," Rook said in a small voice.

"I see them," Drift said. She was shaking. "I'm trying to come up with a plan, but I'm having a little trouble thinking straight."

Rook squeezed Drift's hand, letting her know she wasn't the only one scared out of her mind. "Fox, how are you holding up?"

She received a growl in response.

They pressed together in a loose triangle, the four shadow foxes ringed around them. The two spiders crawled slowly down the rubble piles, cutting off any escape route that Rook might have tried. There was nowhere for them to run, although Fox might be able to jump over the spiders if it came to that.

"Drift," she said quietly. "Are you strong enough to fly yet?"

Wind fluttered Rook's hair before Drift replied. "I don't think so," she said, regret in her voice. "I can barely stir the air."

"It's all right," Rook said, trying to sound reassuring. "Maybe if we—"

But she didn't get a chance to finish. The spider in front of them launched itself off its web and scuttled toward them, a blur of legs and shining, empty eyes.

"Fox!" Rook screamed.

Two of the shadow foxes burst into action, leaping at the attacking spider. Rook expected them to pass right through it, but to her shock, the foxes landed on the spider's back, sinking their shadow teeth into the monster.

There was a flurry of twisting legs and shredding darkness as the spider fought back, biting at the foxes, who didn't seem to be hurt by the blows. More than that, the spider was distracted. If they could get past it, maybe they could tear through the web blocking their path.

A sudden shriek and a whimper cut through the air, and a weight fell onto Rook from behind, so heavy that she dropped to her knees. She twisted to see what had struck her, fearing another spider.

It was Fox. He was back in his human form and had collapsed against her.

"Fox! Fox, are you all right?" Rook guided his body to the ground and crouched beside him to check his pulse. Had one of the other spiders bitten him? She looked around wildly, but the other two shadow foxes had attacked the spiders behind them, fending them off. As far as she could tell, they hadn't gotten anywhere near Fox.

"Is he hurt?" Drift asked. She was looking the boy up and down, checking his arms, legs, and neck for any sign of a wound.

"I don't think they touched him, but I don't know what's wrong!" Frantic, Rook shook Fox's shoulder, but the boy was unconscious. His skin was so pale. Rook laid her ear against his chest. His heartbeat was strong, but she didn't know how long that would last.

"Rook! Drift! Get him out of there!"

Rook looked up at the voice. Dozana stood about twenty feet away from them. She was cut off, blocked by the shadow foxes that were still wrestling with the two smaller spiders. Rook never thought she'd be glad to see the Voran wizard, but she would take any form of rescue she could get at that moment.

"Drift can't fly yet!" Rook shouted back. "We can't get to you! Use your power on the spiders!"

Dozana shook her head. "I've used too much already. You must run around them. Hurry, while Fox's power has them trapped! He won't last much longer!"

Of course. Rook's chest squeezed as the truth dawned on her. The shadow foxes were a part of Fox. They weren't real creatures with minds of their own. Fox himself directed them. The energy they used to exist was Fox's energy. And it was being drained four times over to do battle with the spiders.

"Help me lift him," Drift said. "Put him on my back."

Rook scrambled to do as she said, hauling Fox up and draping him over Drift's shoulders. Drift grunted and stumbled under the weight, but then she steadied herself and nodded toward Dozana. "Let's go."

They ran, pressing themselves as close to the rubble piles as they could to get around the spiders and the foxes. Luck was on their side. The foes were locked together, biting and wrestling, so the spiders paid no attention as Rook and Drift edged past them. Once they were clear, Dozana ran to meet them.

"Give him to me," she said, and Rook helped her gently lift Fox off Drift's back and into her arms. Through all the jostling, the boy never stirred. They had to get him somewhere safe in a hurry.

"What about the shadow foxes?" Drift asked as they took off, moving as fast as they could with Dozana carrying Fox. "What's going to happen to them?"

Dozana glanced over her shoulder. The sounds of fighting were already receding. "We have to hope they disappear in a few minutes," she said. "The problem is the shadows are still draining Fox's power. But the farther away we run, the weaker the link Fox will have with them. Eventually it should cause them to dissipate. Unfortunately, then the spiders will be free to come after us."

"Then just use your power!" Rook snapped. "Like you did with the hounds."

Dozana grimaced. "Nobody's power is infinite, Rook," she said. "You should know that by now. I need to conserve what I have to get us to the portal site."

They moved down the street, stopping and backtracking every time they came across another web blocking the way. The sticky strands were everywhere. Rook waited, tense, expecting another spider to jump out at them at any moment.

"Why are we doing this?" Drift demanded when they had to double back a fourth time to find a different path. "The constables are gone! Why don't we just get out of here? We're no match for these creatures on our own!"

"Because Captain Hardwick was right about the portal site," Dozana said, panting as she hauled herself and Fox over the remains of a white picket fence—all that was left of someone's house and yard. "The magic is building up to dangerous levels. It's going to explode, and we have to stop it."

"Then why did you trap Hardwick and his men?" Rook asked. "They could have helped us, protected us!"

"And thrown us all in prison when this is over," Dozana said, narrowing her eyes at Rook. "Do you really think any of the Regarans would *thank* us for saving their city? All that nonsense Hardwick was spouting about trust between us—don't believe it for a moment. Now that we're free, we'll still save the city, rid it of all the wild magic, but we'll do it *my* way, and we'll save ourselves in the process."

"What do you mean?" Rook asked, grabbing Dozana's arm, forgetting about the spiders for a moment. "What are you going to do?"

Dozana smiled down at her. "Not me, Rook—*you*," she said. "You're going to reopen the portal to Vora. We're going home."

22

THE POSSIBLE DOOR

"IN HERE," DOZANA SAID, POINTING the group to a dark, gaping hole in a large pile of rubble. It looked as if an animal had tunneled into it long ago, creating a hollowed-out space that was just big enough for the four of them but hopefully too small for the spiders to follow.

Rook helped Dozana ease Fox's unconscious body into the hole, with Drift following to keep an eye out for the spiders or any other creatures that might be stalking them.

The refuge was hardly comfortable. The smell of stone dust and wet, rotting wood soured the air, and only pencil-thin shafts of moonlight filtered through the gaps in the rubble. Splintered boards with thick nests of exposed nails were everywhere. But the space was safe enough and relatively dry, so they stayed. They all needed a rest.

Rook sat cross-legged on the ground, Fox's head resting in her lap, while Dozana helped Drift improvise a bandage for her injured leg out of her shirtsleeve. Rook watched them, quietly trying to absorb what Dozana had told her.

"I don't understand," she said at last. "The portal exploded—I can't open it again, not like the Vorans did." She had tried over and over to open her own door, but she couldn't break the barrier between worlds.

"I say you can," Dozana said, tying off Drift's bandage and then turning to Rook. "It's true that it took a great deal of magic to open the original portal in Vora, but ever since we climbed over the red heartstone wall, the animus inside you all has been growing stronger. You saw how Drift was able to create that tornado, how Fox attacked with four shadows of himself working independently. By the time we reach the portal site, you will be so filled with power that you can open a doorway to any world you want and funnel away the leftover magic as if it were nothing."

"*That's* how you plan to get rid of the wild magic?" Drift asked, her voice low and angry. "You channel all that power into Rook and she spits out a portal? How do you know it won't kill her? That you won't *cause* another explosion instead of preventing one?"

"Because the remnants of the portal arch, and the lake itself, will act as a conduit," Dozana explained calmly. "And because I've seen Rook's power. I wasn't lying when I said I believe she is stronger than all of us. I think she's the only one who can get us back to Vora."

"But you don't know for sure," Drift said, "and you said yourself that the Vorans sent us here to escape a magical war. What if there's nothing left of our home to go back to?" Her voice quavered. "Now that we've found each other, isn't it better to just try to make a home here?"

Dozana cocked her head, staring at Rook and Drift thoughtfully. "Have your memories really been swept so clean? Are you telling me that you wouldn't risk everything for the chance to return to the place where you belong? A place where you are accepted and *loved*, and where you might see the rest of your families again?" She leaned back, closing her eyes briefly. When she opened them, her face was creased with lines of sorrow. "Because if I had your power, Rook, I would use it in an instant. I wouldn't waste it staying in Talhaven."

Rook tried to gather her scattered thoughts, but her heart was in turmoil. Part of her knew it was foolish to consider Dozana's plan, especially after what she'd done to Hardwick and his men—the cruel, cold way she'd left them for dead. She had been more than willing to risk Rook's life on this desperate gamble.

But, her methods aside, could Rook truly blame Dozana for wanting to get back to Vora? It was all that Rook had ever wanted. In that lonely place in her heart, the place that had filled up over the years with the hateful words of the Red Watchers, the mistrustful stares of the people of Regara, and her constant feeling of not belonging, she wanted nothing more than to escape. To find the place where she was meant to be.

Home.

Now Dozana was offering her that chance.

"I'm sorry, but I don't think it's a good idea," Drift said, interrupting Rook's thoughts. "You've seen how Rook's power doesn't always work the way she wants. If something goes wrong while she's using it, it could be dangerous for her and for all of us."

Dozana raised an eyebrow. "I'm surprised to hear you say that, Daughter." This time Drift flinched when Dozana called her "Daughter." "I thought you had more faith in your friend."

"I *do* have faith in her!" Drift snapped. "I only want what's best. You're trying to twist that around."

They were talking about Rook as if she weren't sitting right there. Anger flared inside her. "I can speak for myself," she said, glaring at them both.

"*Think*, don't speak," Dozana said. "Come to the portal site. You'll see the power for yourself and realize that with it inside you, anything is possible."

"And what if we say no?" Drift asked quietly, but the words hung in the air, thickening it with tension.

Some of the coldness crept back into Dozana's eyes. "In the end, it's Rook's decision, not yours. But all of you *will* accompany me to the portal site."

With that, it seemed the conversation was over. Rook

looked down at Fox, who had slept through the whole argument. She brushed damp red bangs out of his eyes. At least they weren't going anywhere until he'd regained his strength.

"I should go outside and make sure the spiders aren't closing in on us," Drift said. She gave Dozana a sullen glance. "Do I have your permission to do that, Mother?"

Dozana nodded. "Don't go far, and stay out of sight. We can't let the spiders trap us in here."

Drift crawled out of the tunnel, leaving Rook and Dozana alone. Rook felt the older woman's heavy gaze on her, but she focused her attention on Fox.

"I meant what I said, Rook." Dozana leaned forward and laid a hand on Rook's arm. "You *can* do this, and think what it will mean for the children who have been forced into hiding in this world. If you reopen that portal, you will provide an escape for everyone. You'll be a hero to all exiles."

Rook's mouth had gone dry. She'd been so busy thinking about going home and what it would mean to her that she'd completely forgotten about all the other exiles. Dozana was offering her a way to save them too. She could only nod as the woman sat back, a smile of satisfaction spreading across her face.

"Rook! Dozana! You'd better come see this!" Drift shouted from outside the tunnel.

"What's wrong?" Dozana's smile vanished, and she crawled quickly out of the rubble pile. Rook eased Fox's head out of her lap and left him in the safety of their shelter.

When she emerged in the moonlit darkness, the wind had picked up, blowing stone dust and dirt into the air. Rook coughed and looked up at the sky. It felt like another storm was coming, but there was no sign of thunder or lightning.

And no sign of Drift.

"Drift!" Rook called out. "Where are you?"

Dozana raised a hand to shield her eyes from the dust swirling in the air. "Go back inside the shelter," she told Rook. "Something's coming, some kind of unnatural storm."

"I'm not going without Drift," Rook said, but a wind gust snatched her voice and almost knocked her down. She stumbled backward, fighting to stay upright.

Dozana took a step toward her, but the wind slammed into her, lifting her off the ground and tossing her down the street like a toy. She landed on her feet, skidded, and dropped to her knees.

"Dozana!" Rook cried. "Are you—"

But just then, the wind surged, at the same time hands encircled her waist from behind.

It was Drift. She lifted Rook into the air.

"Wha—" Rook struggled to make sense of what was happening as the ground dropped away. Drift had used up all her power pushing back the hounds. She'd been weak, could barely walk. So how was she flying in this wind *and* managing to carry Rook?

And then she understood: Drift wasn't fighting the wind. She'd *created* it to distract Dozana.

Below them, Dozana looked up, her eyes wide with shock and anger. "Stop!" she yelled.

Queasiness seized Rook's stomach, and for a moment, the sky upended as dizziness engulfed her. It was Dozana's power, reaching out to weaken them and bring them down. But this time, Drift was faster. Wind roared in Rook's ears, and the dizziness passed as they climbed higher and higher in the sky, soaring out of reach of even Dozana's heightened magic.

Leaving Fox behind.

Rook shouted, "No! Wait! We have to go back!" She squirmed in Drift's grip.

"Hold still!" Drift screeched, careening sideways in the air, squeezing Rook so tight that the breath left her lungs. "Do you want me to drop you?"

"YOU LEFT FOX!" Rook twisted her head, trying to get a look at Drift's face, wondering if she'd gone mad sometime in the last few minutes. "DID YOU HEAR ME?"

"*Yes*, I hear you. You don't have to make me deaf," Drift growled. "Just calm down. I have a plan."

"A plan? What kind of plan means leaving Fox behind?"

"Rook," Drift pleaded, "I don't have much strength left— Dozana hit me hard with her power as we were flying away. The last thing I want is for us to fall to our deaths before we can help Fox. Just stay still for a few minutes while I find a place to land us."

Hearing the quaver in Drift's voice, Rook quieted. Inside, her heart was raging. She was terrified for Fox, furious at Drift, and wondering where they could possibly find a safe place in the middle of the Wasteland.

Below them, dark shapes scuttled over the rubble. Rook gasped. It was the huge spider and its two smaller mates. They angled away from Rook and Drift toward where Fox was hidden.

"No," Rook whispered, "no." Tears clouded her vision. What if Dozana couldn't protect Fox? What if her power wasn't enough?

"Rook, I'm sorry. I'm so sorry, but there's nothing we can do." Drift's voice broke, and with it went her power. The wind died, and suddenly they were falling, piles of jagged stones rushing to meet them.

23

THE IMPOSSIBLE DOOR

"DRIFT!" ROOK SCREAMED AS THEY spiraled toward the ground. "Pull up! Pull up!"

Drift uttered a cry of desperation, and the wind surged one last time. It was feeble and faltering, but just strong enough to create a cushion. Rook hit the ground, hard enough to hurt but not to break. She stumbled out of Drift's arms and fell, scraping her knees on the ground. Drift landed in a heap a few feet away, but unlike Rook, she didn't immediately get up.

"Drift!" Rook scrambled over to her friend's side. She touched her shoulder and turned her until she was lying on her back. Drift's eyes blinked open, but her face was as pale as Fox's had been. She stared blearily up at Rook.

"Bad landing," she said. "Need to work on that."

"Are you all right?" A quick inspection told Rook that Drift wasn't bleeding or bruised, which was a miracle. She was exhausted, though, as if the slightest touch might knock her out.

"I'm fine. I think." Knees wobbling, Drift used Rook's shoulders to pull herself to her feet. "We don't have much time. We need a door out of here."

"What? We can't leave," Rook said, staring at Drift in disbelief. Now that she knew her friend was all right, all her earlier anger and fear returned. "How can you even think that? Fox is in terrible danger right now. He could be . . . He . . ." She didn't say it, but she imagined the giant spiders closing in on Fox's hiding place.

"I know, Rook, but I had to get us out of there." Drift looked as miserable as Rook felt.

Well, *good*, Rook thought darkly. "How could you?" she demanded. "You just abandoned Fox and your mother! Who does something like that?"

"Stop!" Drift snapped. "Don't you dare say I abandoned Fox! As if I wanted to leave him behind. As if it didn't tear my heart out." She finished in a whisper and wiped her eyes. "Rook, I did it to get you away from Dozana, so you could use your power to get out of here and find help."

"*Help*," Rook said, incredulous. She wrapped her arms around herself. "Where am I going to get help? Who's going to risk coming into the Wasteland to save us? To save *exiles?*"

"Well, we have to do something!" Drift said. "You need to tell the constables what Dozana's up to."

"Do you hear yourself?" Rook demanded. "You're asking me to turn your own mother in to the constables. They'll lock her up again!"

Drift shook her head, furious tears spilling from her eyes. "That woman's *not* my mother," she said. "I may not remember my mother's name or face, but I know she's not heartless and cruel and . . ." Drift's voice caught on a sob. "Don't you see? Even if she was my mother . . . Rook, she wants to risk your life. I can't let her do that. And if her plan goes wrong, she could destroy the whole city!"

"But she said I can get us all home!" Rook burst out. She opened her mouth to say something else, but Drift's expression was so shocked that she thought better of it.

She fell silent, gazing around to see where they were. Despite only having a limited amount of power, Drift had managed to fly them some distance across the Wasteland. The floating forest was much closer now, and Rook could even make out the lakeshore. The waves lapping the sand were brown and full of sludge. There was nothing left of the portal site but two narrow pillars of blackened stones—the remains of what had once been the legs of an archway.

Drift's hand rested on her shoulder. Reluctantly, Rook turned to face her. "Tell me what you're thinking," Drift said. Her voice was calm, but her eyes were dark pools of anger. "You *want* to do it, don't you? You want to risk opening the portal and possibly destroying the city in the process."

"I never said that!" Rook shook herself free of Drift's grasp. "But what if Dozana's right? What if the portal doesn't explode and instead leads us home?"

"And if you're wrong? You don't have to imagine what

might happen"—Drift spread her hands at the ruin around them—"this is it! Only it will be so much worse. Rook, I know you want to go home, but this isn't the way."

"What other way is there?" Rook countered. "Vora is where we belong, Drift, or have you forgotten that?" Even if they wanted to make a home here, this world wouldn't let them. "Here, everyone sees what I can do and they're afraid of me."

"That's not true," Drift said, shaking her head. "Remember what Mr. Baroman said? Not everyone is out to hate us. Even Jace was being friendly. You just have to give people a chance to get to know the real you."

"Who is that, Drift?" Tears streamed down Rook's face. "All I know about myself is what other people say I am. Dangerous. Unstable. I have no idea who I was in my old world. How am I supposed to find out who I am in this one?"

"I—I don't know," Drift admitted, her voice trembling. "But I thought we'd find out together. We lost so much, I just wanted us to be our own family and be happy. I thought you wanted that too." She shook her head and cleared her throat. "This . . . this isn't getting us anywhere. We need to focus on rescuing Fox."

Her emotions still reeling, Rook nodded. Drift was right. No matter what Rook wanted for her future, at this moment the most important thing was making sure Fox was safe.

Rook took out her chalk and looked doubtfully at the rubble piles surrounding them. "I don't know if I can draw a door on anything," she said. "And I don't know if my magic will pass through the red wall. You heard what Dozana said. It may not work, or the magic might warp and send us anywhere."

Drift put a hand to her forehead as if she was dizzy again. She sat down on the ground. "All right, let's think a minute," she said. "If we rest here for a little while, maybe I can get enough power back to fly us over the red wall. Once we do that, you can draw a door." She moved her free hand over the ground as she spoke, absently drawing patterns in the mud.

Rook followed the movement of her hands. Even hurt, distracted, and afraid, Drift was making art to calm herself. She drew a star, a leaf, a miniature fox. Seeing it, Rook's heart squeezed in her chest.

We'll get you back, Fox. I promise.

But as she watched Drift draw the pictures, the smooth lines and the gentle curve of the fox's ears, Rook's skin tingled. A ghost of an idea flitted through her mind.

Lines in the mud. Lines that connected, formed shapes, made pictures. Art created from almost nothing. It didn't matter that Drift had no paintbrush or pencil to sketch with—anything could be made into a canvas.

Weren't Rook's doors created in the same way?

Rook sprang to her feet, startling Drift into smudging her lines. "What is it?" Drift asked. "Did you hear something?"

Rook shook her head. "I should have thought of it before," she said, testing the idea out in her mind. Yes, it could work. It had to. "There are all kinds of doors, right? I mean, I make a different one every time."

"Yes," Drift agreed, but she was clearly confused, her brow furrowed in consternation. "What are you thinking, Rook?"

"I've been thinking *too much*, that's the problem," Rook said, raking a hand through her hair. She stuffed her chalk back in her pocket and dropped to her knees. "A door in a wall, a normal everyday door you just open and walk through—that's all I've ever tried to do. Sure, I've created different shapes and sizes, but I never thought about changing the door itself."

It was easier to demonstrate to make Drift understand. Using her finger, Rook drew a circle in the mud roughly the size of a wagon wheel. As she worked, she thought of the danger they were all in, how much they needed help. She willed the door to take her to someone who could help them, even if it meant going to the constables.

When the two ends of her line met, the magic churned within Rook, answering her call. Dozana was right. The power, the depth of it, was greater than she'd ever felt before. She sat back on her heels, summoning a smile for Drift.

"A *trap*door," she said proudly.

And it was. The lines in the mud rippled as if something small were tunneling beneath the earth. With a loud *pop*, a beam of golden light burst from the ground. Rook covered her eyes against the light, and when she looked again, the trapdoor was complete.

It was made of simple wood planks with a rusted iron ring to open the door. Rook reached out and ran her hands over the smooth wood. It wasn't a warped, twisted thing like the door she'd created into the Wasteland. It certainly looked like it would be easier to open. Maybe the Wasteland's power had made her stronger, stabilizing her doors instead of trying to pull them apart.

"But won't we still have to pass the red wall?" Drift asked, staring at Rook's creation.

Rook nodded. "Sort of, but we'll do it underground," she said. "We let the magic tunnel beneath the red wall, far enough down that it won't be affected by the dampening magic." At least, that was where she hoped the magic would take them, down deep and up again. It sounded impossible, but magic was all about impossible things.

She grasped the iron ring and pulled up the trapdoor.

Below them, there was a tunnel of pure darkness. Rook bit her lip and leaned as close as she dared to the threshold, straining to see where it led. But the blackness was impenetrable.

"What do you think?" she asked, looking up at Drift.

"I think we have to risk it," Drift said. "If it gets you out of the Wasteland, no matter where you end up, you can open another door to go and get help."

"I can?" Dread filled Rook as she realized what Drift was actually saying. "Wait a minute. You're coming with me. I'm not leaving you here by yourself!"

"You have to," Drift said sadly, "because I have to stay here and find Fox and Dozana, help protect them from the spiders if I can."

"No!" Rook cried, not caring if her shout drew every monster in the Wasteland. "It's too dangerous." *And I can't do this alone,* a soft, scared voice whispered inside her. She and Drift had never been separated before, not like this. Whenever something went wrong, they stayed together. They were *stronger* together.

"I'll be all right," Drift whispered. She leaned forward and pulled Rook into a quick, tight hug before letting go. "So will you. But you're going to have to trust."

"Trust what?" Rook asked, misery welling up inside her. Drift was asking the impossible. "I trust you. I trust Fox. Isn't that enough?"

"No," Drift said. "You have to trust yourself and try to give this world a chance."

Lay all of her hopes on the threshold of a door, and see if the world would trample them, Rook thought. But it wasn't just *her* hopes this time. Drift and Fox were putting their lives on the line too.

She met Drift's eyes. "I'll come back," she said. "No matter what, even if no one will come with me, I'll be back to get you."

Drift grinned, the expression lighting up her face for a moment. "You better," she said. "Otherwise, I'm stuck here with Fox. When he wakes up, you know he'll probably be starving. He'll be trying to eat cheese out of my hand every chance he gets."

Rook knew Drift was trying to make her feel better, but as

she gazed down into the darkness of the unknown, a shudder went through her. She scooted closer to the trapdoor, letting her legs dangle over the edge. She said, without looking up, "Will you give me a little push? I—I don't know if I can do it otherwise."

"Sure," Drift said hoarsely. "Take care, Rook."

"You too."

Rook braced herself as a gust of wind came up behind her, blowing her hair around her cheeks. Releasing the sides of the trapdoor, she let the air nudge her forward into the hole.

24

THE DOOR TO FOG

ROOK FELL THROUGH DARKNESS, THE air growing colder. The only sound was the raspy echo of her breath. She had never traveled so far before without finding her way to . . . *somewhere.*

Then, out of the blackness, a flock of white, fluttering shapes surrounded her.

Birds. Dozens of them, soaring and wheeling through the air, their wings brushing her face as they flew past.

But something wasn't right about them. It took Rook a second to realize it was the birds' wings. They weren't made of feather and bone—they were just paper, like the folded birds Fox had created. The air filled with a dry flapping sound, like wind turning the pages of a book.

Rook stretched out a hand, trying to grab one. She almost had it, but her fingers slipped across something wet, and came away stained black. It was ink. The sticky substance dripped from tiny scrawls of writing that covered the bird's paper belly.

She reached out again, but the bird flew away, and the flock vanished back into the darkness.

Rook flailed her arms and legs, searching desperately for something to grab onto, to stop her plunge through the endless night.

Just when she thought she was going to fall forever, the world suddenly went white, and Rook hit the ground, the air whooshing out of her lungs. She pushed herself up, realizing as she did so that her fingers were no longer smeared with ink. Had she been dreaming? Where had the birds gone? She rolled onto her back, trying to catch her breath.

A thick white mist covered the world. It was as if Rook had landed inside a cloud. She couldn't see more than a few feet in front of her face. She felt the ground next to her to see what she'd fallen on.

Wood. She was lying on a wooden floor in the middle of a fog.

Was she at the docks, or just near the harbor? That might account for the heavy fog, but why was it so cold? Rook shivered, releasing a thick cloud of her own breath.

"Somebody give me a report! What was that thing?"

"A pelican, ma'am, swear it!"

"You're not seeing pelicans up here, Gavin! Don't be stupid!"

"Nate, I'm telling you, it crashed into the deck somewhere. Just get your lazy bones up and look for it!"

The voices echoed from the depths of the mist, startling

Rook. She sat up, clutching her knees against her chest. Should she try to escape? But where could she go? The mist was so thick she had no idea which direction to run.

"Pelican hunt! Pelican hunt!" another voice shouted.

"It's *not a pelican!*"

Now Rook was confused. She was sure the very first voice she'd heard had been a woman's, but the rest of them sounded like children of varying ages.

"That's enough! Everyone get ahold of themselves." The woman's voice punched through the fog, calm and command-ing. "Cassandra, give us a hand, if you please. We're on ap-proach to the manor, and I want to see what we've picked up."

"Aye, Captain!"

Then, to Rook's shock, the mist around her abruptly dis-sipated, revealing white sails, masts, and the elegant lines of a ship's main deck.

She had landed near the harbor after all. Or maybe they were out at sea. There was still too much fog surrounding the ship to tell.

Blinking, Rook slowly stood up. The woman whose voice she'd heard was standing on the quarterdeck, her form par-tially obscured by a long red leather coat and hood. Tight coils of salt-and-pepper hair escaped on either side of her face.

Arranged in a semicircle around her were six children. The youngest was an olive-skinned girl who couldn't have been more than eight, and the oldest was a pale, lanky boy with a missing tooth who looked to be about fourteen or fifteen.

This was not what Rook had expected at all.

Apparently, the strange crew hadn't been expecting her either, because as soon as the children clapped eyes on Rook, they all started talking at once.

"Where'd *she* come from?"

"Captain, it's an intruder!"

"A stowaway!"

"You're right—she's definitely not a pelican!"

The woman held up a gloved hand, and the children instantly fell silent. Her gaze swept over Rook, assessing her. She peeled back her hood, letting it drop to her shoulders. "Hello there," she said. "I'm Captain Danna Poe, and you're standing on the deck of the *Chase*. Where did you come from, girl?"

Danna Poe. The name was familiar somehow, and so was the woman's face. The image of mischievous dark eyes, light brown skin, and the thick, coiled hair streaming around her cheeks stirred Rook's memory. She stared, when suddenly it hit her where she'd seen that image before.

Her face was the same as the woman in the Wanted poster that day in Gray Town—Red Danna was her name.

And she was a sky pirate—or at least, she had been a pirate, when ships could still fly.

Rook slowly backed up, inching toward the nearest railing. She didn't know what was about to happen, but the woman had said they were on approach to some port. If she threatened her, Rook could jump overboard and swim for it.

"Hey, watch it!" one of the children—the youngest girl—shouted at Rook. "You're gonna fall!"

The others were moving toward her now. Rook grabbed the railing, turning to look down at the sea.

But there was no water beneath her, no waves lapping gently against the hull. In fact, there was no sign of *anything* except clouds, and beyond them, a faint glimpse of solid ground—thousands of feet below.

Rook gasped. They weren't in the harbor or sailing the White Sea. This *was* a skyship, and somehow, impossibly, it was still flying.

Rook spun, no longer thinking of running. What was the point? There was nowhere to go. Instead, she surveyed the deck, searching for the animus crystal that was making the ship fly. She finally spied it mounted on a pedestal behind the mainmast. To her shock, it gleamed with an inner red light, the light of a vessel fully charged with animus.

But how was that possible? There was no one left in Talhaven who could charge the animus crystals. Only the powerful adult wizards of Vora could do that, and they were all gone.

At least, that was what she'd thought, until she met Dozana.

The children spilled across the deck, surrounding Rook, while the captain trailed behind. Rook met the woman's eyes. They were not particularly friendly, but somehow Rook sensed the captain wouldn't hurt her. Maybe it was because the children didn't seem afraid of her—or afraid of Rook, for that matter. They chattered nonstop, peppering her with questions.

"Where did you come from?"

"Are you a stowaway?"

"Were you really going to jump off the ship?"

On and on it went, until the woman shooed them away.

When it was quiet, Rook took the opportunity to speak. "Are you a wizard?" she blurted out. Her gaze flicked to the animus crystal.

The captain didn't seem surprised by the question. "Well, since you're standing on the deck of a skyship hovering thousands of feet in the air, it's safe to assume there's a wizard involved," she said, her voice rich with amusement. "The question is, what are *you*? And what am I going to do with you now that you've seen what no outsiders have?"

Rook licked dry lips. The captain hadn't actually admitted she was a wizard. Did that mean one of the children was responsible for charging the crystal?

"Are they exiles?" Rook asked, staring around at the small faces. Silence met her question. The children stared back at her with wide, wary eyes. Taking a chance, Rook lifted her hands slowly and gathered up her wild black hair. Then she pivoted so the captain and the others could see the back of her neck and the white roots.

Gasps echoed all over the deck.

"Because I'm an exile too," Rook said.

25

THE DOOR TO THE MANOR

AT ROOK'S REVELATION, THE CHILDREN exploded again, talking so loud and fast it sounded like there were two dozen of them on deck instead of six. She got just enough from their chatter to realize that they were *all* exiles. And they were obviously very happy to see another person like them. They pressed closer to Rook, crowding her, plucking at her clothes, until Rook started to panic. The urge to flee surged inside her, but she had nowhere to go.

The captain clapped her hands. "That's enough! Have you all forgotten that we still need to land this ship? Get to your stations! Prepare for descent! Cassandra, widen the fog cloud. Keep us hidden all the way down. Nate, you go on ahead to the house and let them know we have a guest. The rest of you know what to do, so get to it!"

The children scattered. One of the boys ran to the railing and in the blink of an eye transformed into a sleek, shiny black crow. The bird launched into the air, soaring off with a loud *Caw! Caw!*

The girl the captain had called Cassandra raised her hands above her head, and tiny puffs of mist leaked from her fingers, thickening and swirling out from the deck to form a barrier on either side of the ship. The fog was so dense no one watching from the ground would ever be able to tell there was a sky-ship hiding in it. They'd just think an unexpected mist had drifted in to cover the world.

With the children gone, Rook edged toward the railing again, risking a glance below. Through wispy breaks in the clouds and fog, she could just make out a snow-covered forest. They were in another part of the world entirely, far from Regara.

The captain came up beside her at the rail. "Quite a view, isn't it?" She seemed much friendlier now. It must have been because Rook had revealed she was an exile, just like the other children. It was the first time in her life a person had actually been *glad* to find out her identity.

Rook kept her eyes on the trees. "I'm sorry I . . . er . . . dropped in suddenly," she said.

"I must admit, I'm curious how you managed that," the captain said. She smiled. "Then again, I imagine there are a few things you're curious about as well."

Was she ever. A thousand questions tumbled through Rook's mind, but none of them mattered as much as saving Drift and Fox. Still, she hesitated. Could she trust this woman, a sky pirate? What if the children here were prisoners forced to work on the ship?

Although they seemed awfully cheerful for prisoners, Rook

thought. She glanced over her shoulder at the children running up and down the deck, laughing and teasing each other. Hadn't Drift said she was going to have to trust someone in order to bring back help? In the end, did she really have a choice?

"My friends are in trouble," she said, looking back at the captain at last. "They're exiles like me, and they're trapped in the Wasteland, which is where I just came from. I used my magic to open a door and asked it to take me to someone who could help."

She didn't know how she expected the captain to react, but if she was a wizard, or at least familiar with exiles, Rook's story shouldn't sound as strange as it otherwise might.

The woman was quiet for a long moment, staring at Rook thoughtfully. Finally, she nodded. "A *door*, you say? And your magic brought you here?"

"That's right."

"Then the question I'm about to ask you is very important." The captain swept her hand out, indicating the sprawling forest. "Have you ever opened a door to this area before?"

"I don't know," Rook said. "I don't think—" But then she stopped. She stared down at the trees, remembering the day Fox had leaped through her door into the alley in Gray Town. He'd come from a snow-covered forest—Braidenwood, Mr. Kelmin had called it. The haunted place her doors kept returning to.

What were the odds this was the same forest?

Rook stared at the children running around the ship—all of them exiles like her and Drift.

Like Fox, who claimed to come from a sanctuary.

Sank. Chewy.

Rook clutched the railing. "You're taking us to a sanctuary, aren't you?" she asked. "My friend—Fox—came from a place like that. That's what he called it."

When she heard the name, the captain's eyes lit with relief, and her smile widened. "Yes, this is where your Fox came from. My husband and I made our home here in the forest, and we've been using it as a safe place for people like yourself. At least, we thought it was secure, but then a few months ago, something strange started happening in the forest. The children noticed it first while they were outside playing. I thought they were telling stories when they said that doors started appearing on the trees."

Rook was taken aback. "My doors?"

"Most of them disappeared before we could get close," the captain went on, "but Fox was fascinated by them. He'd spend hours trekking through the forest, searching, waiting for one to appear. He never told us why." Her face clouded. "And then one day, a door did appear, close enough for him to get to it. It opened, and he didn't hesitate. He just jumped through before anyone was able to stop him."

So that was how it happened. It was what Rook had been afraid of, ripping Fox away from his home. But why hadn't he wanted to go back to the sanctuary, where he was safe, cared for, surrounded by other children like him?

"After that, my husband and I started searching the forest

for the doors," the captain said, "and we did approach a small one once, but there was no knob on our side to turn. I knocked on the door, but it disappeared without ever opening."

Rook's heart stuttered. That night, in the closet, when she'd heard the loud knocking . . .

"That was you," she whispered. "I heard you, but I was . . ." She'd been afraid. And all along, it had been Danna trying to make contact with her. She'd been looking for Fox.

"In a way, we've been expecting you," Danna said. "Or rather, we've been hoping that whoever was behind the doors might someday show herself."

"Coming up on the manor!" shouted one of the boys from the crow's nest, waving a brown cap. "Prepare for landing!"

"You'd better find something to hold on to," the captain told Rook. "The descent can be rough if you're not used to it. Once we're on the ground, we'll talk more."

With that, she strode back to the quarterdeck and stood next to Cassandra. She moved with surety and grace, as if she'd been on the deck of a ship her whole life. Rook, on the other hand, tripped and stumbled as the *Chase* suddenly tilted, the prow angling toward the treetops. Then, all at once, they began to drop.

Fast.

Rook's belly clenched. She leaned over the rail, afraid she was going to be sick. Everything was happening so quickly. A sanctuary for exiles. A vessel that somehow still had enough animus to fly. And behind it all was a sky pirate.

Below her, the trees grew larger and larger as the ship descended, and the cold, crisp air was thick with the scent of pine needles. But where were they going to land? The forest went on for miles in every direction. Threads of fog drifted around the ship, reducing visibility to just a few feet. Rook's fingers dug into the wooden rail.

"Land ho!" shouted the boy in the crow's nest, and suddenly, there it was—a break in the tree line, a thin sliver of a clearing within the dense forest. Nestled in the center was a large two-story brick house with four lighted windows in the front. Smoke curled from two chimneys, one at the front and one at the back of the house.

The *Chase* was headed for a landing right on its front lawn.

Rook braced herself as wind gusts buffeted the ship, but the captain guided them smoothly between the trees and settled the ship on a landing platform. With a creak and groan, the ship slid into place, and the dense fog slowly dissipated.

Once they were docked and secure, two of the children ran to the rail to lower the gangplank. Rook followed the crew as they disembarked, but she hung back while the other children pelted toward the front door of the house, which was already opening, spilling yet more children onto the snow-dusted lawn. There must have been a dozen in all.

One of them was a tiny girl with tight braids clutching a stuffed elephant in one hand and a stuffed mouse in the other. She ran right up to Rook. She wore a long coat over a rich brown dress that matched her eyes, and a smile that reminded Rook very much of the captain's grin.

"H-hello," Rook said to the girl.

The girl didn't answer. She continued to smile as she held up the stuffed elephant and mouse, as if for Rook's inspection.

"Those are really nice," Rook said, though, if she was being honest, the stuffed toys had seen better days. One of the elephant's button eyes was missing, and the mouse, well, it was a little bit too—

Real.

Rook yelped and jumped back as the mouse, which turned out to be very much alive, flicked its tail and twitched its whiskers at her. The little girl giggled, and before Rook could react, she *tossed* the mouse into the air.

"Hey, what are you doing?" Without thinking, Rook reached out to try to catch the creature, but it curled into a little gray fur ball, evading her as its form stretched, grew . . . and transformed right before her eyes.

An instant later, a man stood on the lawn in front of Rook. He wore a small pair of spectacles, and had wavy brown hair that hung down in his eyes.

More pieces of the puzzle fell into place in Rook's mind. It wasn't the children who had provided the animus for Danna's skyship. It was this man. He was a shapeshifter.

Another wizard of Vora.

26

THE DOOR TO ROOK'S HEART

"WHAT HAVE WE HERE?" THE man's voice boomed. He swept the little girl and her stuffed elephant into his arms and smiled down at Rook. "Your name's Rook, yes? A little crow told me you were coming. I'm Heath Poe, Danna's husband, and this little one is our daughter, Henrietta."

The girl waved her stuffed elephant at Rook and then put her head on her father's shoulder.

"You've already met some of the children," Heath went on when Rook didn't immediately reply. "Don't worry about keeping any of the names straight yet. Just come inside and we'll get you settled and fix you something to eat."

"She's not here for food, love," Danna said from behind Rook. Rook turned to see Danna striding up to the house with the rest of her crew in tow. "She came for our help. I think you'd better hear her out."

Heath's friendly smile faded, and his face sobered at once.

"Come into the kitchen then, and let's talk. Children, give us some privacy, if you please."

Something in his tone must have told the children not to argue, because none of them said another word as they filed quickly into the house. Heath set Henrietta down when they reached the foyer and nudged her to go play with the younger children.

Before she left, the little girl skipped up to Rook again and, before Rook realized what she was doing, threw her arms around her waist for a tight hug. For a second Rook stiffened, unsure what to do, then she gave in and put her arms around the girl's shoulders. For a moment, Rook, the girl, and her stuffed elephant were all squashed together in the narrow foyer.

"Got you," Henrietta whispered, giggling, and then she was gone, running off to find the other children.

Rook glanced up at Heath, but he didn't seem at all surprised by his daughter's actions. "As you can see, Henrietta isn't shy," he said, chuckling. "She likes you, though. She doesn't waste any words—or hugs—on people she doesn't like."

Heath led her to the kitchen, where a small fire burned in the fireplace, casting flickering shadows across a floor of multicolored flagstones. Danna was already there, cleaning some mud off her boots. Heath went to the big old cast-iron stove in the corner and poured mugs of tea for himself and Danna, and then got a glass of milk for Rook. Together, they all sat at a long, scarred oak table. Heath folded his hands on the tabletop and leaned forward, shoulders hunched, eyes kind.

"So tell us, Rook, how can we help you?" he asked.

Again, Rook hesitated. Fox came from this place, she reminded herself. He'd been cared for here and called it a sanctuary. But something had also made him leave. What if it turned out these people weren't who they said they were?

Rook shook her head. She didn't have time for doubt. Fox and Drift needed her help. She had to take a chance.

Maybe it was the man's kind eyes, or the little girl with the stuffed elephant, or the exhilarating journey on the ship with all the other exiles, but something tipped the scales, and Rook told them everything, starting with how Fox had come bursting through one of her doors.

She explained how they'd all been tricked and kidnapped by Captain Hardwick and Dozana. She told them about their journey into the Wasteland, and Heath confirmed that the time distortion had caused almost a week to pass in the outside world while their journey through the Wasteland had taken less than a day.

That meant the constables outside the Wasteland would no doubt be sending a search party to look for them. Maybe they could even rescue Captain Hardwick and his men before the Wasteland's monsters got to them.

Heath's and Danna's expressions darkened with worry when Rook described what Dozana had done to the captain, Jace, and Garrett and what she wanted to do at the portal site. Heath stared down at the table, lost in thought.

When she'd finished her story, Rook sat back in her chair

and gulped down her milk, not realizing until that moment just how thirsty and exhausted she was.

Danna went to get more milk and refilled Rook's glass. "I'm glad Fox found a home with you," she said. "He was always a stubborn one."

"They all are, in their own ways," Heath commented, though he seemed distracted.

Rook took the opportunity to slide in a couple of questions of her own. "How did you come to have so many exiles here?" she asked. "Are they really part of your crew?"

"Nowadays, they're my *only* crew—the only ones I can trust with our secrets, anyway," Danna said. She leaned back in her chair, crossing one leg over the other. "In my younger days, I was a merchant, but then I turned pirate—well, privateer—for the kingdom of Izfel, back when they were feuding with their sister kingdom, Moravel. I raided ships, stole cargo, and had more than a few cannons fired at me. But the feud ended eventually, so I went back to hauling cargo—magical this time—and it was about then I met Heath."

"Dozana told you the truth," Heath said, picking up the story. "I came to Talhaven in secret to escape the wars in Vora. I stowed away as a mouse on one of the Voran merchant ships, hiding among the cargo they intended to trade with the people of Talhaven. Turns out that cargo ended up on Danna's ship, the *Chase*."

Danna laughed. "I nearly fell overboard when Heath transformed in front of me," she said.

Heath grinned at his wife. "I apologized over and over again, but I'm not sure she's forgiven me."

"Give it a few more years," she said, winking at him. "After we got married and after the Great Catastrophe brought the exiles to Talhaven, I petitioned the queen of Izfel to let me take some of the children into my care. I couldn't tell her about Heath, of course, but I'd served the queen well, and she owed me more than a few favors. Yet she turned me down. Said the leaders of the six kingdoms would handle the situation, and that I wasn't suited to looking after the magical children." She flashed Rook a dangerous smile. "But I, never being one to take no for an answer, decided it was best to turn pirate again. So after the exiles escaped, I took the *Chase* and began searching for them. That's how we found Fox and all the rest. With Heath secretly providing the animus, and the children helping to hide the ship from prying eyes, we've managed to sail the skies undetected."

"And we'll help you too," Heath said. His expression was grave. "Especially after hearing about Dozana and her plans. I believe we can rescue your friends without involving the constables or anyone else in Regara." He glanced at his wife, who nodded her agreement. "The trickier part will be figuring out a way to stop the wild magic that threatens the city. I'll have to see it for myself before I can formulate a plan."

Hope, which had before been only a spark in Rook's chest, expanded to an actual feeling. Heath and Danna were going to help her. But they didn't know what they were getting themselves into.

"You haven't seen Dozana's power," she said. "She didn't even touch us, and she drained all our magic." How could a shapeshifter hold out against that?

Heath got up from the table and wandered over to the fireplace, standing with his back to the flames.

"I know that pose," Danna said to him. "What's on your mind?"

"I'm thinking if Dozana's that powerful, and if we can't make her see reason, then the element of surprise is all we have," Heath replied, his face pale in the light of the fire. "I hope it's enough."

A thought occurred to Rook. "If you were able to sneak into Talhaven, does that mean there are a lot of other wizards here in hiding?" she asked. "Do you know them? Would they help us?"

Heath grimaced. "I've searched over the years, but if there are other wizards here, they're very well hidden," he said. "It's entirely possible that Dozana and I are the only adult wizards left in Talhaven. You see, my power isn't just shapeshifting. When wizards use their magic, the animus gives off an aura that's visible to other wizards—those who are trained to look for it, anyway. I'm able to dampen that aura so that other wizards can't sense me. That's how I was able to stow away on board the ship without anyone noticing me. As I understand, it's a rare enough talent that I might be the only one to possess it."

Rook was disappointed but not surprised. "But do you really think you can use your power to sneak up on Dozana?" she asked.

"I hope so," Heath said, exchanging another glance with Danna. "Because one way or another, we have to stop her. The portal site is too unstable to support the kind of magic she wants to unleash. Which is why I think it's best if you stay here, Rook, and open a door for me to go and rescue your friends."

"What?" Rook couldn't believe what she was hearing. "Of course I'm not staying here. I have to go back for Fox and Drift. I *promised* them I'd be back, and you need me to escape the Wasteland."

"She has a point," Danna said. "A quick escape is always best. Of course, that's the pirate in me talking." She winked at Rook.

Heath shook his head. "I don't like the idea of delivering Rook back within Dozana's reach," he said. "If we do that, she will almost certainly try to get Rook to use her power to open the portal."

That gave Rook pause. Heath was right. She and Drift had fought about that very thing before they'd parted. Dozana had tempted Rook with her promise that she could open a door home to Vora. It was what Rook wanted most, and despite knowing the risk, a part of her still wanted it. The longing was an ache inside her that wouldn't go away.

Rook stared at the crackling fire while Heath and Danna watched her. Finally, she worked up the courage to meet Heath's steady gaze. "I *do* want to help Dozana," she confessed, bracing to see his reaction. "I know it's dangerous, especially when my magic goes wrong so often, but when she said that all I needed was more power, I thought . . ." She ducked her head. "I thought it was worth the risk."

Heath didn't seem surprised by her confession. "You thought you'd finally found a way home," he said, "after all the time you spent trying and failing."

Rook's head jerked up. "How did you know?" She hadn't told him about all her failed attempts to get to Vora over the past two years.

"It's written all over your face," Heath said, smiling sadly. "You have the power to open doors to anywhere you want. Of course you'd try to use that magic to take you to the most important place of all."

He had guessed what was in her heart without her saying a word. The idea that he saw through her so easily . . . for some reason, it woke the anger sleeping inside Rook, stoked it like a fire. "That doesn't mean you know me," she said, setting her empty glass on the table so hard a crack spidered up the side. Abashed, Rook folded her arms, pressing them against her stomach. "Sorry."

"It's all right," Heath said, taking the glass from the table in front of her and setting it aside. "What I mean to say is that I can see you're frightened and exhausted. You're fighting so many different things—your magic, the people of this world—and I'm willing to bet that every time you open one of your doors, some part of you is hoping that maybe, just maybe, you'll find your parents waiting for you on the other side."

Rook flinched and stared down at the table, refusing to meet the wizard's gaze.

"That's why your powers get twisted up and fail you," Heath went on, his voice gentle, but the words bored into Rook. "It's because your heart's wishing for one thing while you're trying to use your magic to take you somewhere else. But some doors are closed for a reason, Rook. They're not meant to be reopened, no matter how much we wish it were otherwise."

Rook blinked, and tears dripped onto the tabletop, staining the wood dark. She hated that Heath and Danna were seeing her cry. She clenched her jaw, but the tears wouldn't stop. "You don't know anything," she repeated, "and neither do I. Don't you see that's the problem? Not knowing. Not knowing if my parents are still alive, not even remembering what my world looks like. And if I don't get back there, I'll *never* know!"

Heath nodded, and the sorrow in his eyes was almost too much for Rook to bear. "I wish I could help you remember, but that's beyond my power. I can tell you that I've seen what uncontrolled magic can do," he said in a rough voice. "I'm not talking about the portal explosion either. I was there for the first few years of the wars in Vora. In a short time, it reshaped the world—destroyed entire cities and devastated the land. That's why our people began reaching out to other worlds. It's why I stowed away to this one. I had no family, nothing keeping me in Vora. It wasn't safe, and it certainly wasn't a home anymore."

Rook was struck by Heath's words. "You mean Talhaven wasn't the only place the wizards traveled to?" she asked.

"It was the first," Heath said, "but not the last. Each world we contacted had a specific resource we wanted. With Talhaven, it was basic necessities—herbs and medicines because our forests had been decimated, and red heartstone from your quarries to dampen destructive magic. But I think near the end it was about more than resources. I think our leaders *knew* Vora was becoming unlivable. I wasn't there to see it, but I believe they were planning to relocate as many people as possible to other worlds. To give them a chance at a new life and to preserve what was left of our people."

They sat in silence for a time, each of them lost in thought. Rook felt exhausted and numb. Deep inside, she knew Heath—and Drift—were right. She couldn't help Dozana with her plan. But she didn't know how to let go of her dream. She didn't know how to keep that door in her heart closed for good, not when it hurt so much.

"It wasn't just for me," she whispered. "I wanted to help everyone else. I wanted to save the exiles."

"But you did save some of them," Danna said, folding her hands on the tabletop. "Rook, look at me."

Reluctantly, Rook met the gaze of the former pirate who had married a stowaway wizard and adopted over a dozen exiles. There are stories in her eyes, Rook thought, incredible tales that had to be lived to be believed.

But the woman's eyes were soft and kind as she gazed at Rook. "What about your two friends?" Danna asked. "You made a home with both of them. To hear you talk, it sounded like you were happy together. Doesn't that mean anything?"

"Of course it does!"

Danna's question jolted Rook. Drift had said something similar to her before they'd parted in the Wasteland. Drift and Fox meant everything to her. How could Drift not know that?

But had Rook given her any reason to be certain of it? How could she, when Rook spent so much time hidden in the back of a closet, opening door after door, keeping secrets, not confiding in Drift? Then, when Fox dropped into their lives, had Drift thought the boy was pulling her even further away? Rook remembered the look she'd given them that night when Fox had made the paper birds. She finally realized what Drift had been feeling in that moment. It was the same feeling Rook had seeing Drift and Dozana together as mother and daughter.

Like she was losing her best friend.

Rook swallowed a lump that had risen in her throat. More than anything, she wished she could talk to Drift right now, to tell her that she was sorry. Sorry she hadn't noticed that she was leaving Drift out. The truth was she relied on Drift for so much. Rook imagined she could handle anything this world threw at her, as long as Drift was with her. She should have told her that more often.

Things were going to change, Rook vowed. Somehow, she'd make everything right again.

"I *have* to go with you," she told Heath. "I have to save my friends, no matter what."

Heath looked unhappy, and Rook's hope faltered. Would he refuse to let her come? Panic gripped her at the thought. He couldn't deny her this. He just couldn't. She'd find her way back, with or without his help.

Danna spoke up again. "Heath," she said, catching her husband's eye. "This is her choice. *Her* future. Remember?"

Heath let out a sigh, and his face slackened. "All right," he said. "I still don't know if it's a good idea, but all right. We'll leave in the morning, after you've had some sleep."

"No, we have to go now!" Rook insisted. "The longer my friends stay in the Wasteland, the more likely the monsters will hunt them down. You didn't see that spider." She spread her arms to show him the size of the beast. "They won't last till morning!"

Heath laid a hand on her shoulder. "Rook, think. Remember the time distortion. For every day that passes here, it'll be minutes or hours at most in the Wasteland. You're exhausted, and I need time to prepare. We'll only get one chance to rescue your friends."

"But . . . even in that time, something could happen," Rook pleaded. She imagined Fox in his weakened state, trying to survive in the Wasteland.

"All the more reason we need to plan carefully," Heath said. "But I promise you, we'll go first thing in the morning."

His tone told Rook that he wasn't going to budge. She could only nod and try to push aside her misery, but she would never be able to sleep.

"We have an extra bed upstairs with the rest of the children," Danna said, "or if you'd be more comfortable down here, you can sleep on the sofa in front of the fire."

"Downstairs, please," Rook said. As much as she was curious about the other exiles, she didn't think she could handle the avalanche of questions they'd have for her tonight.

Danna nodded and stood up. Rook followed her back into the living room while Heath tended the kitchen fire. Danna retrieved an extra pillow from a closet in the front hall and arranged some blankets on the sofa.

"You're safe here, Rook," Danna reminded her. "Try to get some sleep."

"Thank you," Rook said. She took the pillow, noticing as she did a pair of crisscrossing scars on the back of Danna's right hand. "You're really a pirate?" she asked, staring at the old wounds.

A crooked grin spread across Danna's face. "One of the best that ever sailed." She raised a finger to her lips, then turned and headed up the stairs.

27

THE WHITE DOOR

ALTHOUGH SHE'D BEEN CERTAIN SHE wouldn't be able to sleep, Rook's exhaustion had the last word, and she was out as soon as her head hit the pillow.

She dreamed of the paper birds again, the ones she'd seen on her journey from the Wasteland to the deck of the *Chase*.

As she floated in darkness, the flock encircled her, messages dripping from their white wings, but no matter how hard Rook tried to read them, the letters were too blurry to make out, the words just out of reach.

Please, come back! Rook shouted after the flock. *What are you trying to tell me?*

She woke to the sound of logs shifting on the fire. Sunlight streamed in the front windows of the house, and pleasant breakfast smells trickled in from the kitchen.

There was a stuffed elephant sitting on her chest.

Rook locked eyes with the toy, then turned her head, craning her neck in search of its owner. The little girl—

Henrietta—had to be nearby. Judging by the worn patches around its neck, the elephant was never very far from the girl's hands.

A blur of motion caught Rook's eye. Dust motes swirled in a sunbeam in one corner of the room, as if something had just been standing there and then streaked away.

Rook sat up, cradling the stuffed animal in her lap. "Thanks for keeping me company," she said to the empty room.

A nervous giggle echoed from the front hall, but when Rook turned to look for its source, Henrietta was gone.

Rook hugged the stuffed animal. The strange dream was still fresh in her mind, along with the feeling that she was missing something. It was almost as if her mind was trying to tell her a secret, using all those paper birds and their unreadable messages.

Messages. That was what Fox had called them when he was folding the birds' delicate wings and tails. A shiver of premonition brushed the back of Rook's neck. Why had she seen those things in her dream? Why did Fox make all those paper birds?

At a loss, Rook hugged the little elephant tighter, rubbing her cheek against its soft, worn fur. She could only hope that she would figure things out eventually.

Heath and Danna came downstairs soon afterward. Danna showed her to a washroom so she could clean up and change into a set of fresh clothes they had found for her. Rook thanked her and stepped into the closet-sized room.

She looked at herself in the washroom mirror, and as she stood there, she gathered her hair up in her hands to expose the white roots at her neck. The dye was starting to wear off, so there were more of the pale strands visible now.

Something flickered at the back of her mind. It wasn't a memory—nothing so clear as that. It was just a feeling that she'd done this before. She'd stared into a mirror with her hair gathered up in her hands.

White hair is good luck, you know.

Rook gasped and dropped her hair, letting the strands fall around her face. Where had that come from? She had never believed her hair was good luck—quite the opposite, in fact. And Drift had never said anything like that to her. But at the same time, she knew as surely as she knew there was magic inside her that someone had spoken that sentence to her, sometime in the past.

Rook was shaky and sweating when she came out of the washroom and headed for the kitchen. Heath and Danna sat at the table, sipping tea. They both looked up in concern when she entered.

"Are you all right, Rook?" Heath asked. "You look pale."

"I'm fine," she said. She wasn't ready to tell them what she'd just experienced, not when she didn't understand it herself. Maybe she would tell Drift, when she saw her. Yes, Rook decided, she would definitely tell her friend. No more secrets.

But what a secret it was, if she was right.

Hey, Drift, you know I can't be sure, but I think some of my memories might be coming back. Giddy warmth spread through Rook's chest at the thought.

"Are you ready to go?" Danna asked, interrupting her thoughts.

Rook snapped her attention back to the present. "I'm ready," she said.

"Once we're in the Wasteland," Heath said, "I'll transform and stay out of sight so we can sneak up on Dozana without her being able to sense my magic. But, Rook, no matter what happens, if you get the chance to open a door and escape with your friends, I want you to take it."

"And what about you, love?" Danna asked, raising an eyebrow at her husband. "You'll be left behind in the middle of the Wasteland. How will you escape and get back here?"

"The same way I did once before," Heath said, grinning at her. "I'll make my way to the docks and stow away on a ship going across the sea. It might take me some time to get back here, but I'll make it eventually."

"Or perhaps I'll come collect you myself," Danna said. "I do have a very fast ship, you know." She leaned forward to kiss her husband on the cheek. "That means good luck and hurry back, in case you didn't realize."

He pressed his forehead against hers. "I will," he said softly.

Rook shifted uncomfortably, wishing she could melt into the floor so she wouldn't interrupt their private moment.

She was saved by thundering footsteps on the stairs. Seconds later, the kitchen was full of children, laughing and greeting Rook and the others. The exiles crowded around Rook, demanding to know if she'd slept well, asking for stories of where she lived and what the Wasteland was like. Rook didn't know where to begin answering their questions.

"We'll go outside to make your door," Heath said, interrupting the excited chatter. He raised his voice above the cacophony in the room. "Danna, if you could—"

"I'll keep this bunch indoors," she promised. The children objected in a loud chorus, but she held up a hand. "That's way too much whining and groaning for this early in the morning. Time to wash up, then breakfast. When Rook gets back with her friends, you can pester them for stories to your heart's content." She glanced at Rook, and her stern features softened. "We can also talk about your future, Rook. Heath and I didn't get the chance to tell you last night, but we're both prepared to offer you and your friends a sanctuary here, if you want it."

Now the children oohed and aahed and stared at Rook wide-eyed.

"Say yes!" shouted the boy who'd turned into a crow yesterday. "Yes, yes, yes!"

The others agreed, but Rook's head was spinning, and she couldn't answer them.

A home with Heath, Danna, and the other exiles, far away from Regara? They wouldn't have to worry about the Red Watchers anymore, or the Frenzy sickness. They'd never have to be afraid of going hungry.

It was too much. It was a dream.

"It's a lot to take in, I know," Danna said. "First things first. Rescue your friends. When you're all safe, you can think about what's next."

The group broke up, the children scurrying off to clean up and change out of their pajamas, with Danna herding them here and there. Rook followed Heath out the front door and into the snow. A fresh layer of powder coated the lawn. The trees at the edge of the forest were weighted down with it.

"Would you like to use a tree to make your door?" Heath asked, his breath fogging in the cold, crisp morning air.

"No, I need to use the ground," Rook said. "That way we won't pass through the red heartstone wall. It's hard to explain, but I think we'll go underground and come out of the sky. At least, I think that's what happened the last time."

Heath nodded. "I've seen similar magic," he said. "Remember to focus, Rook. The stronger your heart is fixed on finding your friends, the more reliable your magic will be."

Rook nodded. If that was what it took to keep her magic stable, then she wasn't worried. There was *nothing* she wanted more at this moment than to see Drift and Fox again.

The freshly packed snow was as good a canvas as any. Rook was willing to bet she could make it work.

"All right. Here we go." She knelt next to an unbroken patch of snow and began drawing a line through the powder. A thought struck her, and she glanced up at Heath, shielding her eyes at the blinding sun. "If you've seen magic like mine before—"

"Not exactly like yours," Heath interrupted. "I've never seen a wizard who could create doors out of nothing, but I've seen ones use teleportation. That's another word for what you do—transporting people across great distances in a short span of time."

"Still, if you know enough . . ." Rook hesitated. She knew it was asking a lot of Heath, who had already offered her so much.

But Heath had already guessed what she was going to say. "Yes, I can help you learn how to use your power. You've already discovered variations you can take advantage of, but I think together we can stabilize your doors as well, let you keep them open longer, and so on."

"But you'll help me use it *safely*," Rook said. That was the critical point, to her mind.

Heath smiled gently. "I'd be happy to."

The idea was tantalizing. Rook clasped her hands together to keep them from shaking. The thought of having people who could help her understand and control her power—it opened up possibilities she had never dreamed of.

She bent and resumed her drawing, until she had traced another trapdoor. The magic stirred within her and rose up, stronger than ever.

The lines glowed gold, and there was a hiss as the magic melted the snow, turning it to steam. When it cleared, before her was a rectangular trapdoor just like before, but this time made of wood painted white. The hinges were delicate crystal snowflakes that sparkled in the sunlight. The doorknob was made of faceted glass, and cast dozens of tiny rainbows onto the snow. There was no sign of jutting nails or warped wood planks. The door was stable and beautiful.

Rook looked up at Heath. "Well?" she asked, hoping for his approval.

He rewarded her with a look of wide-eyed amazement. "It's beautiful, Rook," he said, bending to examine the door. "I was never able to get a close look at your doors before, but this is truly remarkable. I think we can build on this in your future magic lessons."

"You mean I can do more than this?" Rook asked.

Heath nodded. "How you express your power is unique to you, Rook. You draw doors because that's how you see your power, as a doorway to another place. But you don't have to draw a physical line to open a door. The chalk, the lines— they don't fuel your power. It comes from inside you. You can make a door wherever you want. If we had more time, I'd show you, but we'll have to save it for another day." He reached down and took hold of the glass knob, extinguishing the rainbows. "Get ready," he said.

He opened the door all the way back to lie in a snow-drift. Beyond the threshold, there was darkness, just like last time.

"I'll go through first," Heath said. "Wait a few minutes before you follow me. I want to make sure there's nothing dangerous waiting for us just on the other side of the door."

Rook didn't argue. The last thing she wanted was to step into a monster pit.

Heath scooted to the edge of the trapdoor and, with a last smile to reassure Rook, slid off the edge and let his body fall into darkness. Watching him disappear, Rook counted the seconds in her head, waiting to follow.

When it was time, she took a deep breath, and before the fear could overwhelm her, she dropped through the trapdoor. Darkness swallowed her, and Rook couldn't help remembering the vision she'd seen of Fox's paper birds soaring around her. Would she see them again?

No sooner had the thought crossed her mind than something went wrong.

28

THE DOOR TO MESSAGES

SOMEWHERE CLOSE, HEATH'S VOICE SHOUTED at Rook. It sounded like a warning, but she couldn't make out the words. There was the sound of pounding, like fists on wood, but then all noise was swept away, and Rook was alone, floating in a deep dark void.

No, she wasn't quite alone. For all around her, specks of white appeared out of the blackness. At first, Rook thought the gleaming dots were starlight.

But they were Fox's paper birds. Back again, circling her in a flock. They flew close, allowing Rook to reach out and touch a paper wing. The bird turned toward her, landing in her open palm. Rook brought it near to her face to read the messages scrawled on its back.

The bird squawked once, startling her, and then its wings unfolded and flattened in her hand, until it was just a piece of paper covered in writing. Rook held up the message. The words didn't make any sense. The language wasn't one she recognized. But then the little black lines on the paper re-arranged themselves, and the message suddenly became clear. It contained two different sets of handwriting, one messy and shaky, as if the person was in a great hurry. The other was made of tiny, elegant letters.

Let's skip lessons today! We'll go to the Livian Fields. Bring lunch. Answer back—I'm starving!

That's because you never eat breakfast. Where are you anyway?

Balcony. You coming or not?

We'll get in trouble with Mother and Father.

You're no fun.

I didn't say I wasn't coming.

Yes!

But the message wasn't just words. As Rook read on, she could *hear* the voices of the two people echoing in her head, as if she were eavesdropping on their conversation.

Or remembering it.

Because Rook recognized those voices. The voice of reason, the one that said they'd get in trouble with their parents, was hers.

The other voice, the voice of trouble and the promise of fun, was Fox's.

And just like that, it was as if a wall in Rook's mind came crashing down, smashed brick by brick. It was a strange, lightening sensation—the removing of a barrier she hadn't even known existed.

A barrier to her memories.

Not all of them. There were still stubborn, obscured patches—like her name—but other important details were becoming clear, and a sob of joy and grief rose in Rook's throat. She tried to relax and take it all in, but it was impossible.

Because even though she didn't know his name, she knew who Fox really was. What the paper birds really meant.

And maybe, just maybe, that knowledge would help save her friends.

Rook came out of the dark in a rush. She was falling, but this time she landed in something soft. When she looked down, there was an endless sea of white all around her. For a moment, she thought she'd landed in a snowbank. Had she made a circle and come out back in the forest near Heath and Danna's house? It didn't seem likely, but if Rook's power had failed her, there was no telling where she could end up.

But as she lay there in the bed of white, a creeping sensation worked its way up Rook's spine. If she was lying in snow, why wasn't it cold? Or wet? And why, Rook thought with mounting panic, couldn't she move her arms and legs?

Because she was lying in the middle of a giant spiderweb.

Rook's chest heaved. She tried to push down the panic, but it wasn't easy, not when she was the bug in the middle of a massive trap. *Don't thrash*, she told herself. If she disturbed the web, it would surely draw the giant spiders.

Looking around, Rook couldn't see the edges of the web, but so far, there were no spiders in sight. The strands were like glue sticking to her clothes and skin. To make matters worse, the deep twilight of the Wasteland had finally turned to night, and the only illumination came from the stars, the moon overhead, and a few animus globe streetlamps scattered about the area. Their magic hadn't yet failed, probably because of the time distortion.

"Heath?" Rook called out, hoping the wizard was near enough to hear her. Maybe he'd escaped the web using his shapeshifting ability. She waited, but there was no sound except the wind, the distant rumble of thunder, and the cries of animals out in the dark. Rook suppressed a shiver. "I need help," she called, daring to raise her voice a little louder.

No answer.

The sound of her breathing was harsh in Rook's ears. She was trembling now, vibrating the strands of the web, but she couldn't help it. Where was Heath? The door should have put him right in the middle of the web with her, but he was nowhere to be seen. Had he somehow ended up elsewhere in the Wasteland? Was that why he'd called to her?

"Help!" she shouted, abandoning caution. "Help me!"

Still there was no reply. Rook forced herself to take deep, calming breaths. She had to think. She couldn't fall apart right now. Her friends were waiting for her, and with or without Heath she was going to rescue them.

First she had to get out of this web.

Rook examined her surroundings as best she could from her position. She was lying on her back, staring up at the night sky. Her arms, legs, and hair were deep in the web, and the whole thing was suspended about four feet above the ground at an angle, using the surrounding rock piles as supports. The web didn't seem to have any trouble holding her weight, so Rook grabbed a handful of the sticky silk strands and pushed against them. Wincing in pain as the web pulled her hair, Rook forced herself upright. The strands attached to her back stretched and clung, but a few of them tore free. The trap wasn't inescapable. It would just take time and patience. Neither of which Rook had, but she gritted her teeth and forged ahead. She raised her right arm, trying to force it above her head, tearing more strands in the process.

That was when she saw the spider.

Rook went absolutely still, but it was too late. The monster had already spotted her, and it was the big one. Rook choked back a scream as it scurried onto the web from a rooftop about ten feet away from her. It slowed and made a careful circle around her, staying just out of reach, as if it was trying to decide how helpless she actually was.

And then it inched closer, the claws of its mandibles clicking together.

Click. Click. Click.

Rook had never in her life been as terrified as she was at that moment. Even when the Frenzy mob was closing in on her in Skeleton Yard, she hadn't felt so helpless. She couldn't tear her gaze away from the spider's glassy eyes.

Do something! Rook shouted at herself. *Don't just sit there!*

Click. Click. Click.

Rook found her voice. It was either that or die. "Help!" she screamed as loud as she could.

The spider paused, rocking back on its legs, poised to leap.

29

THE DOOR TO TRUTH

A SHOUT ECHOED IN THE night, startling the spider into skittering a few feet away.

"Rook! Rook, where are you?"

Rook knew that voice. It was Dozana's, coming from somewhere in the darkness, too far away to see. She'd either heard Rook's call or she'd been able to sense her magic, just as Heath said.

"I'm here!" Rook shouted, as the spider began inching closer again. "Over here! Hurry!"

"We're coming!"

Rook's breath caught. The answering shout had not been Dozana's voice, but Drift's.

Running footsteps sounded over the broken stones, and seconds later, Dozana came into view below her. Drift and Fox were on either side of her. They were still Dozana's prisoners, but at least they weren't hurt.

Dozana's eyes widened when she saw the spider bearing

down on Rook. She raised a hand, sending out a burst of power, and the spider shrank back, legs twitching, recoiling from the woman's magic. It turned and scuttled away across the web. Rook sagged with relief.

"Hold on." Dozana drew a knife—she must have taken it from one of the constables—and sliced at the web strands. They stuck to her blade, but she was strong and fast. She cut her way to Rook and reached up to grab her arm. "I can get you out, but this is going to pull your hair."

Rook grimaced. She shot a quick glance over her shoulder, but the spider had disappeared. "Just hurry," she said.

Dozana cut the remaining strands holding her prisoner, allowing Rook to wiggle free. As Dozana had promised, the silken cords snagged her hair painfully, and Rook was sure she'd lost a good bit of it, but at last she dropped to the ground.

All at once, Drift and Fox came running toward her. Fox was still in his human form, his magic obviously not replenished enough to change him back. Drift looked tired but much stronger than when Rook had left her. The two of them nearly knocked her off her feet, throwing their arms around her. Rook hugged them back fiercely, relieved, afraid, and happy all at once.

I didn't bring help, she wanted to say. *I tried and failed again.*

But neither Drift nor Fox seemed to care about anything other than that she was back.

"Are you all right?" Dozana asked, looking and sounding impatient.

"I'm fine," Rook said, pulling away from her friends to look back up at the shredded portion of the web. "But the spider—is it really gone?"

"Not for long," Dozana said. She took Rook's arm none too gently and hauled her away from the web. Drift and Fox followed and they set off at a quick pace.

"That big one's been hunting us ever since you disappeared," Dozana said, keeping a tight grip on Rook's arm as they ran. "I've used my power to keep it at bay, but I almost didn't get to you in time. That was foolish, Rook," she said, glaring at her. "You risked your own life and your friends' lives trying to escape. Fortunately, the lakeshore is nearby. Now hurry!"

The lake. A chill washed over Rook as she realized how much trouble they were still in. They were almost to the portal site. Heath was gone, if he'd ever made it to the Wasteland at all, and Dozana held her and her friends captive again. Rook was right back where she'd started, and Dozana was on the verge of getting everything she wanted.

Heath, Danna, and Drift had all warned her not to try to open the portal to Vora. But Rook had to save her friends, no matter what. Her thoughts raced as she tried to come up with a plan. At least this time she had her memories to help her.

Rook thought of all those paper birds. Fox had been right—they *were* messages, but not the kind you wrote down on paper. These were magic. She remembered composing a message in her thoughts, then imagined herself folding it into the shape of a bird and sending it through the air to another person, who would magically receive it in their mind as part of a psychic connection.

In this way, she'd exchanged hundreds of messages with Fox in their old lives. And maybe, just maybe, she could get the magic to work again to contact Fox and communicate with him. The only problem was she had no idea how the Wasteland would affect it. All she knew for certain was that it was an old magic, a special power that only certain people could share.

Because they had to be siblings.

30

THE DOOR TO FRIENDSHIP

TURNING A CORNER AND CLIMBING over one last pile of broken stone, the group finally reached the lakeshore. The ring of trees floated at least twenty feet in the air, hovering like specters in the moonlight. Skeletal branches and roots dangled over the water, and the red lights floating in the trees cast menacing shadows over the whole area.

Then there was the lake itself.

The sight of it brought back another memory, of the moment Rook had entered this world. She'd been standing at the railing of a ship, leaning out as it passed through an immense stone archway. The portal had been a circle of light within the stones. She'd stretched her arm out to try to touch the archway as they sailed past, but she was unable to reach it. Then she and the other children had found themselves in the middle of a calm, deep blue lake, with buildings dotting the shoreline. There were shops and restaurants full of people, while pigeons and sparrows lined the rooftops hunting for scraps of food. There was even a park not far from the water, filled with beautiful old trees.

Then the portal light brightened behind them. Rook remembered turning, the light blinding her, and then there was a deafening sound, the loudest thunder preceding the worst storm. When the explosion came, Rook and the other children were thrown to the deck, blinded, deaf, not knowing whether they would live or die.

When it was all over, everything Rook had seen in that brief moment of peace was gone.

Now, the lake had become a churning mass of whitecaps, as if a great beast thrashed at the center of it. Drawing closer, Rook realized the disturbance was a whirlpool at the heart of the lake, swirling around the ruins of the portal archway. There was hardly anything left of the stones, just two broken pillars sticking up from the water.

Dozana stared out at the ruins of the archway. "There it is," she said, her voice hushed. "Our way home—or at least, I hope it will be." She turned to Rook, giving her a sharp look. "You tried to go get help, didn't you?" she accused. "With the time distortion, I have no way of knowing how long you've been gone or what you've done. Tell me, Rook, are there constables out there somewhere, waiting in the dark to ambush us?"

Rook thought about how to respond. Obviously, she couldn't tell Dozana about Heath, but she had to give her some believable story.

So Rook clenched her jaw and fixed a look of sullen anger on her face. It wasn't hard to do. She just summoned all the rage she'd ever felt at the constables and the Red Watchers and let it show on her face. "I did escape the Wasteland, and I tried to get the constables to help me," she said, putting a bitter edge in her voice. "They thought I was lying. Then they tried to capture me. I barely escaped."

"So you managed to get across the red heartstone wall all on your own?" Dozana's brows rose in surprise and suspicion.

Rook shook her head. "I used my magic," she said. "You were right. It's stronger now, strong enough to get through the inner wall. But it didn't matter. No one would help an exile."

Rook had no idea if Dozana would believe the story, but her friends seemed to take her words at face value. Drift's face fell in disappointment and sorrow. Fox tugged at strands of his wild red hair, a look of misery pinching his freckled face. Rook hated lying to them, but an idea was beginning to take shape in her head, one that required her to be patient and sly. She had no intention of trying to open the portal to Vora, but if she could get Dozana to believe that she would, that she had come around to her way of thinking, maybe the woman would drop her guard long enough for the three of them to escape.

Dozana's lips twisted into a sneer. "I'm not surprised the constables tried to capture you," she said. "Do you understand now, Rook? I'm trying to help you and the other exiles. I'm the *only* one who wants to help you."

"Yes, I understand," Rook said, keeping her voice steady and her eyes on Dozana. "If no one cares what happens to us, then I don't care what happens to them." She took a deep breath. "I want to try to open the portal."

No sooner were the words out of her mouth than Drift exploded.

"You can't mean that!" She grabbed Rook's shoulders and actually shook her. For a moment, Rook was too shocked to do anything. Fox backed away from the shouts and anger. He crouched on the ground and, with a shudder, managed to transform back into his animal form.

Seeing that and her friend's angry face almost broke Rook's resolve. But she forced herself to put on a cold expression, to turn her heart to stone.

"This is the only way, Drift," she said. "I want to go home."

"But we *have* a home!" Drift insisted. "We were happy there!"

Rook steeled herself. She knew what she had to say. Dozana had to believe that there was nothing Rook wanted more than to go back to Vora, that it was all she cared about now. She just hoped that Drift would be able to forgive her later, if they made it out of this.

"Maybe *you* were happy," she said, forcing her voice to go flat. "But that was never my home . . . and you were never my family."

Silence fell. The only sounds were the swirling water and

the wind rattling the dead tree branches. Drift let go of Rook's shoulders and staggered back, her eyes wide and anguished.

"You . . . you don't . . ." She shook her head, but the words had already been said. There was no taking them back.

And in that moment, as Rook lied to her dearest friend, she found the truth inside herself. It didn't matter what world she lived in, as long as she had Drift. She and Fox were every bit of home she ever needed. She could let go of the dream of getting back to Vora—for them.

"That's enough," Dozana cut in. "Rook's made her choice, and we need to get going."

Drift didn't respond. She wasn't even looking at Dozana— or Rook—anymore. She retreated from all of them, sinking to her knees beside Fox, who butted his head against her hand until she wrapped an arm around him.

"Do you have a plan?" Rook asked Dozana, eyeing the lake and the deadly whirlpool at its center. Along the lakeshore there were pilings sticking up at odd angles from the water, and the broken remnants of a dock. Two lonely boats were still moored there, but Rook didn't think they would survive the deadly current at the lake's center.

"There's enough space for two people to stand on the left pillar of the portal arch," Dozana said. "Drift, you'll fly Rook over there so she can draw a door on its surface. That's all it should take to—"

A bark of laughter interrupted her speech. Dozana and

Rook turned to see Drift, still sitting next to Fox, her arms crossed, her mouth set in a stubborn line.

"Something funny, Daughter?" Dozana asked, her eyes narrowing.

"Stop calling me that," Drift snapped, meeting the woman's gaze defiantly. "You really believe I'm going to fly Rook to the center of the lake so she can draw a door on the stones and blow us all up? You may as well think up a different plan, because that's never going to happen."

"Oh no?" Dozana's voice was dangerously calm. It was clear that her patience with Drift's rebelliousness had run out. "You don't think I can convince you to help me?"

"Drift—" Rook warned, but before she could finish, Fox let out a pained whimper and fell prone on the ground. He managed to stay in his fox form, but he curled up into a tight ball. Rook hadn't even realized Dozana had used her power until she saw Fox fall.

"Stop it!" Drift shouted, leaping to her feet. "You leave him alone or I swear you'll regret it!"

"You're the one responsible for this," Dozana said. "Every second you fight me and behave like a child, your friend gets weaker and weaker under my power. Do you really want to keep seeing him suffer?" She glanced down at Fox, and there was no remorse, no pity in her eyes. Fox whined again, and Rook put her hand over her mouth to keep from sobbing.

Drift's face twisted in anger and fear. "Stop hurting him,"

she said, and her voice had changed. She was begging now. "He's one of your own people. He's a *little boy!*"

"You have the power to end this," Dozana said, gesturing to the remains of the portal arch. "Make your choice, Drift. Once and for all."

"Drift," Rook said, reaching out to her. "Please. Just do as she says."

Drift looked at Fox, at the pain in his amber eyes, and a tear slid down her cheek. Her shoulders slumped in defeat.

"You win," she whispered. She wiped her face. "Let's get this over with."

"Thank you," Dozana said, and she must have released her power, for Fox climbed shakily back to all fours. "Now, you're going to fly Rook out to the pillar. If either of you tries to escape—if you try to fly anywhere except straight out to those stones—I will drain Fox's power until there's nothing left of him but an empty shell. Do you understand?"

"I understand," Drift said, her face pale.

Rook nodded. "We won't try anything."

She and Drift walked to the edge of the lakeshore. Rook felt the weight of Dozana's presence behind them, and the idea of leaving her there on the shore standing next to Fox made Rook dizzy with fear. But she had no choice.

She stared across the lake's expanse to the ruins of the portal arch, two lonely pillars rising from the middle of the lake. Dozana was right—there was barely enough room for two people to stand on the stones. If they fell, the whirlpool would almost surely take them.

And that gave Rook an idea for how they could escape Dozana. A terrible, reckless idea that had an excellent chance of getting her killed.

Or it might save them all.

Pushing back her fear, Rook turned to Drift. "Are you ready?" she asked, but Drift didn't reply. She was staring out at the dark lake, the fierce whirlpool lit by the animus shining in the trees. "Drift," Rook prodded. "We have to go."

"Whatever you say," Drift said, her voice flat and empty. She put her arms around Rook's waist, and a gust of wind plucked them from the shore and into the air. In seconds, they were flying over the churning water.

When they were out of earshot of Dozana, Rook cleared her throat nervously. Before she did anything else, she had to earn back Drift's trust, if that was still possible.

"Drift," she said, angling her head so her friend could hear her. "I know you're furious with me, but you have to listen. I'm so sorry. I didn't mean any of what I said. You were right all along. I should never have listened to Dozana and— Oh!"

She faltered as the wind died, and they dipped sharply toward the water. Drift gasped, and her hands tightened around Rook's waist. The wind surged upward, so fierce it left Rook's eyes watering, but it did the trick. They were rising again, safely above the moving current at the edge of the whirlpool.

"Are you all right?" Rook asked, her voice squeaky with panic. "Drift, say something!"

"I'm . . . I'm okay," Drift replied.

And then Rook felt Drift lay her forehead against her shoulder. There was a pause as moisture soaked through Rook's shirt.

Tears.

"I was so . . . so scared," Drift sobbed. "I thought you might be lying, but you looked so serious, it was like . . . oh, Rook, it was like I didn't know you anymore."

"I'm so sorry," Rook said, close to crying herself. "I know I'm not easy to live with. I get scared, I don't talk to you when I should, but you never complain. You're there no matter what. You were right. I've been so busy trying to find a way back home that I didn't notice we were already making a good home in this world. I didn't realize how important it was until I went through that trapdoor and left you and Fox behind. Which I'm *never* doing again, by the way. Ever. Don't even ask."

Drift chuckled. "All right," she said. "I won't even think it."

"Good," Rook said. "I want to talk more about this later, but we're almost to the pillar, and we need to go over the rest of the plan."

"So there is a plan?" Drift asked, lifting her head. "That's *amazing* news."

"It's a work in progress," Rook said. "The first part was getting you to be my friend again."

"I will *always* be your friend," Drift said fiercely.

"So that part's a success," Rook said, sniffling and blinking back tears. Drift's words gave her strength, buoying her as much as the wind that carried them. "The second part is to get a message to Fox so that he knows what we're about to do."

"But what do we do about Dozana?" Drift asked. "Her magic is getting stronger and stronger."

Rook glanced back at the shore and saw with a sinking feeling that Drift was right. The same red light that was in the trees overhead was now surrounding Dozana like a halo, as if animus were flowing directly into her body. Was it too late to stop her? Was she asking too much of Fox and Drift? For her plan to work, they would have to put their lives in her hands and their complete trust in her magic. And for Rook, it meant believing in her power with everything she had inside her.

"Tell me," Drift prompted her, tightening her grip on Rook's waist in a reassuring hug. "Whatever it is, we'll do it. We believe in you."

Rook closed her eyes and let the hug give her courage. "Okay," she said. "Okay, I have a long story to tell you, but there's a short version. It starts with paper birds."

31

THE DOOR TO FOX'S HEART

ROOK FINISHED EXPLAINING HER PLAN just as their feet touched down on the slick stones of the left pillar of the portal arch. They took a moment to steady themselves before Drift's wind died away. Oily spray from the whirlpool splashed the stones, and soon she and Drift were drenched. Rook shivered and looked around. The view was even more frightening than she'd imagined while standing on the shore.

The pillars stood roughly sixty feet apart, with the center of the whirlpool between them. The churning water moved so fast that Rook couldn't stare at it for long without feeling dizzy. The stones they stood on were narrow and cracked, the only remnants of the portal that had once brought wizards into the world of Talhaven. Rook marveled that they'd managed to hold up this long.

In the distance, Fox and Dozana stood on the shore, watching them. From this far away, it was impossible to read Dozana's expression, but Rook didn't think she suspected anything. Yet.

"This isn't going to be easy," Rook said quietly.

Drift nodded. Her short blond hair was plastered to her head. "Nothing's been easy so far," she said with a smile. "Why start now?" But then her expression grew serious. "How will you know if Fox has gotten your message?"

"He'll give me a signal," Rook said, squaring her shoulders. The only thing left to do was try to summon the magic. "Here we go."

Closing her eyes, feeling Drift's reassuring presence next to her, Rook focused on the visions she'd seen when passing between the doors. This time, she added a few changes. Instead of picturing a paper bird, she went in reverse. She called up a blank piece of paper, and in her mind, she composed a short note in the same style she and Fox had used in their own world. She wished she remembered more about where she'd learned the magic, but there wasn't time.

Fox,

Don't be scared when you get this. It's just me, Rook. I think when you read this you'll remember—at least, I hope you will. How we used to pass mental messages back and forth when we should have been doing our lessons. How we decided to make them birds because it was easier to send the message by picturing them flying through the air. All this time, I never knew I had a brother, but I think you felt our connection somehow. That's why you came through that door to find me. You were starting to remember before I was, when you took those pages out of Drift's sketchbook and made them into birds. I think they were still in your mind somewhere, waiting. I hope so, because you getting this message is the only way we're going to be able to escape Dozana.

In a few minutes, you're going to see something that'll frighten you. Don't be afraid. Dozana will be scared, though, and angry, and I'm hoping that what she sees will make her come out on the lake with you in one of the boats. When you're close enough, I'll give the signal, and then you need to jump. Jump, and trust me, little brother. When this is all over, I can't wait to meet you again.

Your sister,
Rook

P.S. I almost forgot! If you can hear this message, jump up and down a few times so that I know.

In her mind, Rook folded the message up into the shape of a soaring eagle. Concentrating, she sent it flying across the lake to Fox.

Rook opened her eyes and found Drift holding on to her shoulder, keeping her steady on the slick stones.

"Everything all right?" Drift asked.

"We'll see," Rook said. She returned her gaze to the shoreline, watching Fox for some sign that he'd received her mental message. "Come on," she murmured. "Come on, Fox. I know you can hear me. Please."

And then, just when she thought the magic wasn't going to work, Fox leaped straight up into the air. He landed, crouched, turned in a tight circle and jumped again as if he could barely contain himself. Dozana was too absorbed watching the red light gather around her to notice his excitement.

Rook's heart was full. Well done, little brother, she thought. Well done.

"I think he got the message," Drift said, squeezing Rook's shoulder. "Now it's our turn."

"Are you sure you're up for this?" Rook asked.

Unexpectedly, Drift grinned. "Everything's going to be fine," she said. "Clear skies and smooth strides."

No sooner had she spoken than shouts sounded from across the lake. Rook looked up in alarm to see a dozen armed constables charging the lakeshore toward Dozana and Fox. Captain Hardwick led them. Somehow, he'd escaped Dozana's trap and gone to get help, or maybe he'd been rescued by the other constables when they'd sent out a search party.

"You're surrounded, Dozana!" the captain shouted. "You can't use your power on all of us at once. Surrender now and you won't be hurt!"

For a moment, no one moved. Rook held her breath. Her gaze went to Fox, standing in the middle of all the chaos. He was exposed and vulnerable, just like he'd been that day in the alley when the constables had drawn their pistols. Rook grabbed Drift's hand for comfort, but she couldn't tear her eyes away from the shore.

Dozana raised her hands. For an instant, Rook thought she was going to surrender, that it was all over.

But then she swept her arm toward the group of constables, and a line of red energy exploded from her hand. The magic slammed into Hardwick and the men and women lined up on the shore, blasting them off their feet. They landed on the ground at least ten feet back from where they'd been standing.

None of them moved.

Rook covered her mouth with a trembling hand. Drift had been right. Dozana was so much stronger now. She'd dealt with the constables as if they were nothing more threatening than ants.

Dozana calmly turned toward the lake. She raised her arms above her head and a crack of thunder split the air, making Drift jump and cover her ears.

"What's happening?" Rook shouted, but Dozana wasn't looking at her. Her attention was on the floating forest. The wild animus swirled in the trees, flowing upward to form a red river of magic that cut across the sky in front of the portal ruins.

Dozana clasped her hands together, and a smaller thread of red light flowed from her body, rising to join the stream. The two sources of magic crackled as they came together, showering the lake with red sparks that hissed when they hit the water.

Rook's skin tingled, the hairs on her arms and neck standing up. She watched the light stream from Dozana's hands, and with a growing horror, she understood.

Dozana was feeding her own magic into the stream of animus gathered around the portal site. She was making it stronger, more powerful than ever.

"Dozana, stop!" Rook cried. "That's too much!"

"That's right," Dozana said, and her voice was strangely amplified, deep and menacing as it rang out over the lake. "Take it, Rook. With this power pouring into your door, you'll tear the veil between worlds as if it were paper."

"But you're overloading it!" Drift screamed. "It's sure to explode now!"

"Yes," Dozana said, her booming voice full of satisfaction. "Once we pass safely through the portal, the power I've unleashed will destroy Regara. All those in the city who have hated and wronged us will be swept away in the chaos, and the rest of the world will know the price of angering a wizard of Vora."

Her words turned Rook's blood to ice. She understood it all then, the frightening shape of Dozana's plan.

She'd never intended to fix the magic trapped in the Wasteland. She didn't care about sending the rest of the exiles home. All she wanted was to escape and take revenge on the people who had held her prisoner. Revenge that would level the city of Regara.

"Rook," Drift said, clutching her arm. "Rook, I . . ." Her voice trailed off helplessly.

Rook forced herself to look away from the gathering animus and clear her head. No matter what happened, she had to get Fox and Drift out of here.

"Keep going with the plan," she told Drift, but her friend didn't reply. She was staring in horror at the red light gathering above their heads. "Drift!" Rook tugged her friend's arm. "Look at me. We can do this!"

Drift blinked, tearing her gaze away from the animus. She looked at Rook as if seeing her for the first time. "All right," she said, her voice shaking. "I—I'm ready."

Nodding, Rook crouched on the stones as if she were going to draw a door. Beneath her, waves of roiling lake water broke against the legs of the portal arch, cold and deadly.

Swallowing her fear, Rook closed her eyes and leaped off the stones.

She hit the surface of the lake, the water dragging her down. It was so cold that for a moment, Rook couldn't move. She was alone and trapped in a frigid, dark vortex. Forcing her numb limbs into motion, she kicked and fought her way back to the surface. She came up sucking in air and raking her hair out of her eyes.

Above her, there was a blast of wind and another splash as Drift plunged into the water after her.

Rook fought the vicious current, her muscles straining. It was so much stronger than she'd thought it would be. No matter how hard she swam, it pulled her back, dragging her toward the deadly center of the whirlpool.

Maybe this hadn't been the best plan after all.

Rook turned toward the shore, searching for Dozana. As Rook had hoped, she and Fox had climbed into one of the boats and were headed out on the lake. For a second, Dozana caught Rook's gaze. The woman's eyes burned with red animus light, visible even from this distance.

That's right, Rook thought with grim satisfaction. *You have to come out here and save me.* Dozana wasn't about to let her ticket back to Vora drown in the lake. She was afraid and distracted now. That gave Rook the advantage.

To her right, Drift's head broke the surface. She wiped her eyes and started her own battle with the current.

This was going to be close.

Rook counted down from twenty in her head as Dozana's boat drew closer. She could see Fox's red pelt and swishing tail as he crouched in the bottom of the boat, waiting for her signal.

And then it was time.

"Fox!" she shouted.

Without hesitating, Fox leaped over the side of the boat. He hit the water, caught the current, and let it whisk him away from his captor. Dozana cursed and tried to make a grab

for him as he flew by. She caught nothing but a handful of water.

They were all trapped in the whirlpool's current now. It swirled them in a wide circle that got narrower as it drew them into the center. Dozana stared at them, all spread out and for a moment, a look of helpless rage twisted her face. She'd never expected her captives to escape by plunging to their deaths in the whirlpool.

But Rook wasn't about to let that happen.

She gauged the distance between her and her friends. Fox was closest, swimming about twenty feet to her right. He bared his teeth as he strained to keep his head above water, red pelt plastered to his body.

That's it, Fox. Stay with the current, Rook thought, tracing the whirlpool's pattern so she could guess about where it would take him. In her mind, she repeated the last thing Heath had told her about her magic.

How you express your power is unique to you, Rook. You draw doors because that's how you see your power, as a doorway to another place. But you don't have to draw a physical line to open a door. The chalk, the lines—they don't fuel your power. It comes from inside you. You can make a door wherever you want.

Praying Heath was right and that her power wouldn't fail her, Rook reached out a hand and pointed to a spot in the water near Fox.

Please. Please. I need a door.

The lake's surface flashed golden. Beams of light burst from the white-capped water.

Rook shouted in triumph as the water parted, revealing a yawning black hole, a doorway to safety in the middle of the churning lake. Water poured into it, disappearing as if down a drain.

And Fox was on a course straight for it.

"No!" Dozana's shout rang out over the lake. Rook looked up just in time to see her drop one of the boat paddles and point at her. Rook braced for the weakness, the light-headedness that meant the wizard was draining her power.

But it never came.

Dozana screamed in rage. She grabbed the paddle and began rowing faster.

Hope surged in Rook. Something was wrong with Dozana's magic. Had she used up too much when she fed it to the cloud of animus? Or had so much power built up in Rook that Dozana could no longer take it all?

Either way, her door stayed open, and Fox slid right into it, disappearing into the darkness. Rook cut off her power, and the door vanished.

One down. One to go.

Drift was on the opposite side of the whirlpool from Rook, but they were moving faster now, trapped in the current. Almost out of time.

"Rook, stop!" Dozana screamed, and there was desperation in her voice. "Fight the whirlpool or you're going to drown!"

She was right. Rook's limbs felt like they were weighted down with stones. The longer she stayed in the water, the closer she got to the center of the whirlpool, the point of no return.

Rook did her best to ignore the pain and pointed to another spot in the water. Gold light speared toward the sky as a second door opened. She started to call out for Drift, but her friend had already seen the door and was swimming for it as fast as she could. With the current pushing her, it was only a matter of seconds.

Casting one last frightened glance at Rook, Drift disappeared through the door to safety.

Leaving Rook alone with Dozana in the heart of the Wasteland.

32

THE DOOR TO RUIN

ROOK CLOSED THE DOOR BEHIND Drift, and a wave of relief swept over her. No matter what happened now, Drift and Fox were safe.

But for herself, things weren't looking so good.

Rook trembled with the cold. She could barely feel her arms anymore, and she'd given up trying to fight the current. Her vision blurred, and she dipped low, sucking in a mouthful of lake water. Choking and gasping, Rook tried to pull her head up, but the lake was too strong for her.

The water pulled her down into the dark.

Frantic, she fought back, clawing her way toward the surface, but she couldn't even tell if she was moving anymore. The water was a wall pushing against her, draining her physical strength just as Dozana had tried to drain her magic.

This is it, Rook thought. She wasn't going to make it. She hoped Drift and Fox could forgive her. She'd tried as hard as she could, but it wasn't enough. The Wasteland was too powerful.

A hand grabbed the back of Rook's shirt, yanking her out of the water. Rook sucked in air, gasping and coughing, dimly aware that she was pressed against the hull of Dozana's boat. She heard a grunt and felt herself hauled up and over the side. She collapsed in the bottom of the boat, unable to do anything for a moment except breathe and shiver.

Dozana had saved her, caught her again, but it didn't matter this time. By now, Fox and Drift were safe back at Heath and Danna's house. Dozana had no power over her anymore.

When some of her dizziness had passed, Rook rolled onto her back and looked up at Dozana. But the wizard wasn't paying attention to her. She was too busy trying to steer the boat out of the current's grip. Her arms shook, and her lips were pressed into a line of determination.

Above them, the red light of the animus was getting brighter, its strands twisted into a ball that shone down on them like a second sun. The air pulsed with power. It was building to a critical point. If they didn't do something quickly, it would explode and turn the whole city to ruins.

Rook looked in the direction of the shore. The constables were coming to, sitting up and staring out at the raging magic storm in the center of the lake. But even if they could get to her and Dozana, there was nothing they could do about the magic.

The boat stopped with a jerk, throwing Rook off balance. She looked up and saw that Dozana had managed to steer them into one of the pillars of the portal arch, the current temporarily wedging the boat in place against the stones. Dozana stood, wobbling for a second, then reached down and seized Rook's arm.

"Climb or we drown," she said. She dragged Rook to her feet and pushed her onto the stones, scrambling up the pillar behind her. As soon as they were out of the boat, the current snatched the craft and spun it back into the whirlpool. It circled once, twice, capsized and was gone, sucked beneath the roiling water.

Rook and Dozana climbed to the top of the pillar, a narrow, broken ledge directly beneath the swirling red light. Rook instinctively ducked away from the magic, which was now giving off a disturbing amount of heat.

"Use your power," Dozana told her, raking wet hair out of her face. "Let the animus be drawn into your body and out through your door. It's not too late."

"I'm not doing it!" Rook shouted. "I made my choice! I won't destroy this city!"

"Regara is already doomed," Dozana said, gesturing to the ball of bright light hanging above their heads. "If you care so much about the people who hate you, open the door between worlds. It may drain some of the magic away, lessening the explosion. If you do this, some in the city might even survive."

Rook shuddered at the coldness in Dozana's voice. "Do

you really hate them that much?" she asked. She raised her arms, encompassing the lake and the Wasteland. "Look at what magic did to this place. It turned the plants and animals against us, turned them into monsters! That's enough to make anyone terrified!" She dropped her voice. "Is that what it was like in Vora? Is that what you want to go home to?"

"This place is *nothing* compared to our homeland," Dozana said. "No matter what our world has become, I would rather live in a wasteland of magic than spend one more day in this hovel."

"What about the exiles?" Rook tried to take a step forward, but her foot slipped on the slick stones, and she had to go down on her knees to keep from falling back into the lake. "You told me you were supposed to protect them. If you destroy Regara, the people here will never even try to trust magic again. They'll hunt all the exiles down. They'll hunt your daughter down! Is that what you want?"

For an instant, Dozana's cold mask cracked around the edges, and there was a flash of regret in her eyes. She looked away from Rook, staring up at the deadly sphere of animus.

"Help me stop it," Rook pleaded. "There are still exiles out in the world you can protect. They need you."

Dozana continued to stare up at the bright ball of animus. Rook didn't know if she'd heard her. Then suddenly the wizard raised her arm above her head, reaching toward the wild magic.

A faint thread of power rose from the palm of her hand,

but it was silver this time instead of red. It drifted up to join the animus, disappearing into the red ball. In response, the sphere brightened, flashing briefly to pure silver before deepening to red again. Heat blazed from its surface. Rook had to duck down and protect her eyes. The power scorched her back, heating her skin like sunburn.

After a moment, Rook raised her head, shielding her eyes to look at Dozana. "What have you done?" she shouted.

Dozana had her eyes closed against the brightness, but her expression was serene. "I fed it the last shred of my power," she explained. "Some wizards choose to do that, at the end of their lives. We give up all our magic to a greater cause." She opened her eyes, took a deep breath and let it out. "I never had a daughter, Rook."

Stunned, Rook grasped the lip of stone to steady herself. "Drift was right," she said. "You . . . you were lying to us."

Dozana shrugged. "I thought it would make you more inclined to help me," she said. "I lied then, but I'm not lying now. You may yet save lives if you do as I say and channel the magic through the portal. It's time, Rook. Open the door, or die alongside the people of this world who never wanted you."

Cowering beneath that ball of heat, Rook knew she was beaten. Dozana was right. The only thing left to do now was try to open the door between worlds, to draw out some of the magic so that the explosion wouldn't kill everyone.

She had to draw out the magic.

Using a door.

A prickle of awareness teased Rook's scalp.

Of course. That was the answer. There *was* a way to get rid of the magic safely, just not the way Dozana wanted.

A tremor shook the ground, followed by a deafening rumble. It was as if the Wasteland itself was straining under the weight of the magic. On the shore, the constables who'd managed to get back on their feet were thrown to the ground by the force of the earthquake. Beneath Rook, the pillar cracked right down the middle, chunks of stone breaking off and splashing into the lake. Rook dropped flat, clutching the remaining stones to keep from falling.

Dozana wasn't so lucky. With a shrill scream and arms flailing, she fell backward and plunged into the water. Immediately, the current seized her.

Rook crawled back up to her knees. She was almost out of time. Calling on all her strength, she stood up, raised her hands, and began making doors.

33

THE DOORS TO EVERYWHERE

ROOK IMAGINED DOORS ALL AROUND her. She didn't try to draw them. She simply looked at a spot in the air and pictured a door, and it appeared, a column of gold light tearing the red sky. Hands shaking, she stretched her arms high over her head and let the animus from the glowing sphere flow through her. It fueled the magic, just as Dozana said it would, using her body as a conduit.

Doors began appearing between the skeletal trees. Five of them. Then ten. Twenty. More doors than Rook could count. She never could have created so many on her own. The sphere of gathered animus made them possible. Rook didn't even feel a tingle of light-headedness from expending all that power.

Rook willed the doors to open, but she didn't try to tear the veil between worlds. She directed them all over the world of Talhaven, to every kingdom, every remote location she'd ever opened a door to in her practice sessions back at the roost.

And the magic flowed through each and every one of them, slowly draining out of the Wasteland.

Rook closed her hands into fists, willing the magic away, and the power coursed through her like a thousand threads of heat. It wasn't painful, but it was strange, unsettling, the light of the animus surrounding her in a cloud.

Shouts rang out from the shore as the constables saw what she was doing. Another scream echoed from the lake beneath her as Dozana fought the raging current, at the same time realizing that her magic, everything she'd sacrificed, was being torn apart.

"Rook, stop!" Dozana shouted, but she could do nothing. Her power was gone. Rook tipped her head back, closed her eyes, and channeled it away into dozens of doors, letting it flow harmlessly out into a world that had never known magic until the wizards of Vora came.

Thunderous booms shook the pillar, but Rook held herself steady and kept her power from faltering. Gradually, the magic and the light began to fade.

As the power ebbed from her body, Rook opened her eyes. The first thing she noticed was that the trees of the floating forest had fallen from their suspended poses. They now floated in the lake, half-submerged, dragged down by the whirlpool. But even the lake's current was slowing, no longer churned up by the magic raging in the area.

Dozana was still in the water, but she'd managed to swim free of the dying current and was making her way back to the shore, where the constables were waiting, lined up to watch as Rook funneled the last of the wild magic through the doors.

One by one, the doors winked out of existence as Rook let them go. The last shreds of power drained out of her, and she collapsed on the pillar. Her body trembled. She was cold, weak, and sick. She needed to get off these stones before she fell in the lake and drowned. She raised her hand, trying to summon one last door so that she could follow Drift and Fox.

Nothing happened.

Rook dropped her head into her hands. What had she been thinking? She hadn't left enough power for herself. It would take time to replenish.

On the shore, the constables hauled Dozana out of the water and put her in chains. The wizard had no strength left to resist as Captain Hardwick led her away. Then a voice rang out over the lake, one Rook recognized.

"Rook! Are you all right?"

It was Jace.

Rook looked up to see the young constable standing at the shoreline, hands cupping his mouth as he shouted to her. "You did it!" he cried, his voice quavering with excitement. "You saved us!"

The rest of the constables were pressing forward now, clapping each other on the back. A few cheers even went up along the shoreline.

And Jace sounded . . . grateful. It was the last thing Rook had expected. She'd been sure the constables would be terrified by her display of power, that they'd put her in chains like Dozana.

"Hold on!" Jace called out to her again. "We're coming to get you!"

And then what? Rook thought. She'd saved the city, but she was still an exile. Would the constables really let her go after everything that had happened? Rook let out a sigh and leaned down to press her forehead against the wet stones. She was too exhausted to think about it. All she wanted to do was sleep.

Suddenly, there were more shouts from the shoreline, this time in agitation. Rook raised her head to see what was going on.

A thick mist had gathered around the pillars, rolling across the surface of the lake. In seconds, it obscured the constables and filled the sky above her, until Rook was lost in the dense fog. All she could see was the stone ledge beneath her.

What was happening? Was it some leftover magic of the Wasteland? Rook had no strength left, no power to draw on. Whatever happened next, she was helpless.

A shadow fell over her.

Rook looked up in time to see a large shape descending from the fog. It parted the mist, revealing a long, graceful wooden hull and white sails.

Rook's heart leaped.

It was the *Chase*.

Danna stepped into view on the main deck, putting her

boot up on the rail. She grinned and called down to Rook. "Need a hand?"

One of the crew lowered a rope to her, and together the children hauled Rook up on deck, where Heath was waiting.

"Are you all right?" he asked, looking her over in concern. "You're drained almost to nothing, aren't you?"

A girl hurried over with a blanket and wrapped it around Rook. She didn't realize how cold she was until the warm softness fell on her shoulders.

"How did you get here so fast?" Rook asked, her teeth chattering. "You were . . . halfway around the world."

"The time distortion," Danna reminded her. "To you it hasn't seemed long, but it took us a day and a half to get here after Heath got pushed back out your door. We don't know what went wrong, but we set a course and came as fast as we could. Some of the children have been using their magic to help speed us along. It was a wild ride, I can tell you that."

"Let's get you belowdecks," Heath said. "We can talk later."

The *Chase* was already rising back into the fog. The pillars and the lake disappeared from view amid the confused shouts of the constables, who had never even known the ship was there.

34

THE DOOR HOME

ROOK SLEPT THROUGH MOST OF the journey back to Heath and Danna's house. When they docked and approached the door to the manor, it opened before they could reach it.

There, standing in the doorway, were Drift and Fox in his human form.

At first, no one could speak. Rook was too busy being swept up into Drift's arms. Fox hugged her from behind, and they wouldn't let go as they led her into the house.

"Are you all right?" Drift demanded. Without waiting for an answer, she guided Rook to sit by the fire. Some of the older children were there too. They must have stayed behind to look after the younger ones while Heath and Danna and a skeleton crew went to rescue Rook. Everyone pressed close, wanting to hear the story of Rook's adventures.

"Give her some air," Danna said as she kicked off her boots, but she was smiling in amusement. "She still needs to rest."

"I'm all right," Rook assured her, hugging Fox and squeezing

Drift's hand. She smiled at her friend, feeling safe, feeling at peace for the first time she could remember.

The children gave her space but still demanded she tell them everything that had happened at the portal. So Rook did, leaving nothing out. She told them about the plan of escape she'd come up with and described how her memories had started to return each time she passed through a door into and out of the Wasteland. Was it the strong magic gathered in that place that had done it? Rook would never know for sure, but no matter how it had happened, she was grateful.

She told them about the moment she realized who Fox was and what his paper birds meant, and how she used one to get a message to the boy and help foil Dozana's plan. She described all the doors she'd created to funnel the magic out of the Wasteland, and the children gasped in wonder, while Heath just watched her with a slight, proud smile curving his lips.

By the time Rook finished her story, she was exhausted again, so Danna herded the children out of the room and left Rook, Drift, and Fox alone by the living room fire with Heath. The wizard hadn't spoken much. His brow was furrowed, and he appeared to be in deep thought as he stared at the flames.

"What's going to happen to the Wasteland now?" Drift asked.

Heath scratched the beard stubble at his chin. "I'm not sure," he said. "It's possible now that there's no longer magic running wild in the Wasteland that the area and the affected plants and animals will begin to heal and return to their natural state. That's what I'm hoping, at least. Once things have settled here, I'll travel to Regara to see what I can do to aid the process." He glanced at Rook, smiling. "Maybe I'll take a shortcut, if someone will open a door for me."

Rook grinned and nodded.

"Well," Heath said, standing, "I'm sure you three have a lot to talk about. I'm going to see if Danna needs help calming the other children. We've had enough excitement around here to last for weeks." He paused on his way out of the room. "You should also think over our offer of a home here. We'd love to have you all."

He left the room, but before Rook could say anything, Drift stood up as well. "I don't know about the rest of you, but I'm starving!" she declared. "Maybe I'll go to the kitchen and dig up a snack for all of us."

Fox perked up immediately. "Cheese?" he asked.

"Well, of course, cheese," Drift said, as if that should have been obvious. She glanced at Rook. "Any requests?"

Smiling, Rook shook her head. "Just hurry back," she said. Heath was right. They did have a lot to talk about.

When Drift was gone, Rook was struck by the realization that this was the first moment she and Fox had had alone together since before they'd gone to meet Dozana that fateful day in Rill Park.

It was the first time they'd been together since finding out they were brother and sister.

Rook clasped her hands in her lap, feeling suddenly awkward and shy. What could she say to Fox? It had been so much easier to talk when she'd been sending him a message in her mind. Part of her wished she could do that now.

No, they'd spent too long apart already. She'd almost lost him so many times. Never again.

"Fox," she said, and the boy looked up at her, blinking curiously. She could start with the question that had been on her mind ever since her memories came back. "Did you know?" she asked. "Did you know all along that I was your sister?"

Fox's eyebrows scrunched as he considered the question. "No," he said, but then his mouth twisted, as if he was unsatisfied with this answer. "But I knew . . . something. Like knowing a story without the words."

Now Rook was confused. "I don't understand," she said.

"I had the story, but it didn't have any words," he said. "They were missing. 'Sister.' 'Brother.' 'Family.' But I felt it here." Fox pressed his hand against his chest, over his heart.

"Oh," Rook said, suddenly finding it difficult to speak. "You felt it, and that's why you came through my door in the forest. That's why you came to find me."

He nodded. "I didn't know where I was going, but I knew it was a door to the right place. I just had to get through."

Rook's vision blurred. She wiped the tears from her eyes. "I'm glad you did," she said. It had taken her a long time to figure out where she belonged and with whom. All those nights she'd spent trying to open a door back to Vora, her magic had been trying to take her to the next best place—to Fox, and to Heath and Danna's sanctuary. She'd thought her magic was failing her, but it had been trying to save her all along.

Now that they'd started talking, Rook realized she had so many questions she wanted to ask her brother. She wanted to know whether he remembered anything about their parents or their life together in Vora. If she closed her eyes and concentrated, Rook could almost see her mother's and father's faces. All the missing pieces of herself were slowly coming together, memories mending. She knew that with them would come sorrow and grief, but having Fox there would help ease the pain.

And as much as Rook wanted to talk about the past, the question remained of what their future held.

"Fox, what do you think about what Heath offered?" Rook asked. "Do you want to stay here with them?"

Fox shrugged and settled back against the couch cushions. "We can stay wherever you want," he said. "Here or there—doesn't matter as long as we're together." He added, "As long as Drift's there too."

Rook smiled. "Agreed," she said. "Why don't I go find her so we can all talk it over?"

Thinking about it, Rook realized Drift should have been back from the kitchen by now. She rose from the couch, leaving Fox snuggled under a blanket by the fire, and went to look for her friend.

She checked the kitchen, but there was no sign of Drift, no

sign that anyone had been in there. Concerned, Rook went to the window and looked out at the snow. There were footprints everywhere from when they had come in from the ship. As she scanned the ground, she noticed that a single set jutted off from the others and headed back in the direction of the ship.

Without hesitating, Rook grabbed one of the coats from a hook by the door. It was too big for her, but she didn't care. She threw it on, buttoned it hastily, and went out into the snow.

She followed the footprints back to the skyship. Drift was nowhere in sight, but Rook looked up at the masts and caught a flash of color in the crow's nest.

Drift was leaning against the crow's nest railing, staring off into the distance. She hadn't heard Rook approach.

"I think she's too big for you to fly her," Rook called out.

Startled, Drift looked down and saw her. "I didn't hear you," she said.

"I noticed." Rook walked up the gangplank to the main deck.

"I can come down," Drift said.

"It's fine," Rook said, approaching the crow's nest ladder. "What are you doing up there?"

"Nothing really," Drift said. "I was just . . . getting some fresh air."

Her friend's voice was strained. Rook scowled as she began climbing the ladder. "Wow, that was a terrible lie. Your worst ever."

Drift snorted. "Thanks."

Rook didn't understand. Everything should have been all right now. They were safe, and she thought that her and Drift's friendship was safe too. But maybe she'd been wrong. The thought of that, that she could still lose Drift, filled Rook with dread as she climbed.

When she reached the top, Drift was waiting to pull her up, using her wind to hold Rook steady until she could secure a grip on the railing.

"I could have just come down and flown you up," Drift said.

"You're changing the subject," Rook countered. "Why won't you tell me what's wrong?"

"It's *nothing*," Drift insisted. "I've just been thinking, that's all. Mostly, I'm relieved that everyone's all right. When I disappeared through that trapdoor, leaving you alone with Dozana—Rook, you don't know what that did to me."

Rook reached out to take her hand. "It's all right," she said. "It's over now."

"We're not separating like that again," Drift said, mimicking Rook's tone when she'd said the same thing.

"I won't even bring it up," Rook promised. She looked closer at her friend. "That isn't all you're upset about, is it?"

Drift hesitated. "You know when you had that vision about Fox? When you went through the doors? Well, I had a vision too, and some of *my* memories came back."

"Really?" Rook was delighted. "That's great! What did you remember?"

Drift's face clouded. "For one thing, I remembered enough to know for sure that Dozana wasn't my mother."

Rook nodded, recalling what Dozana had confessed to her, that she'd never had a daughter at all. Of all the things the woman had done, Rook hated that the most, that she'd used her friend in such a cruel way.

"Was there anything else?" Rook asked. "Any *good* memories?"

"Yes," Drift said. "I remembered something my parents left for me, a part of my power I didn't know about, like you with the messages. They were the ones who created the house, Rook. The place where we've been staying."

Rook's mouth fell open. "But how?"

"I'm not sure," Drift said. "It's strange. They put it sort of . . . between worlds. It exists in this little pocket, a place that's just the house and the meadow outside. Because the world is so small, it's easy to get to, or something. I don't understand it all, but I know my parents created it for me when the wars in Vora started. They left enough animus there to do little things to take care of me. I think originally they meant it to be temporary—a safe place to hide. But when the chance came to send me to this world instead, they took it."

"But a part of you must have remembered the house," Rook reasoned. "Or my power must have tapped into your memory somehow, and we found the house again, even between worlds."

"I think so," Drift said, looking thoughtful and sad.

"Drift, what's the matter?" Rook pressed. "You remembered something from your past, a part of your family. Doesn't it make you happy?"

"It does," Drift said, but there were tears in her eyes. "I just thought maybe I'd remember something different. I didn't see *you* in any of my memories," she confessed, and Rook didn't think she had ever seen her friend look so miserable. "I thought . . . I hoped that we might have been sisters. I've just always felt so connected to you. We were drawn together from almost the first night we got to this world."

And it was the best thing that could have happened to me, Rook thought. Drift's friendship had saved her that night and every night after.

"But it was you and Fox who were related all along," Drift went on. "And I'm not jealous," she said quickly, her gaze straying over her shoulder toward the house. "I'm glad you two found each other. I just thought maybe if you found out *we* were sisters, that would mean we'd stay together. You'd always have a reason to come home."

Rook looked up sharply. "I already have a reason," she said, surprised that Drift would even think it. "I don't need for us to be sisters for me to come home. All I need to know is that you and Fox are there. I couldn't always see that—I was too obsessed with finding a way back to Vora—but I see it now."

"You've faced every one of your fears," Drift said, looking at her in wonder, "while I haven't even had the courage to tell you what *I'm* afraid of."

Rook blinked. She hadn't thought Drift—bright, unquenchable, unstoppable Drift—was afraid of anything. "What is it?" she asked.

Drift hesitated. "I'm afraid of being alone," she said. "Every time I saw you and Fox together, you looked so happy. It made me think I was losing you. I know that's a terrible thing to say, because I *want* you to be happy, Rook." She stared at the ground, biting her lip. "But what if you and Fox left, and I was all alone? Dozana turned out not to be my mother, and that hurts, but it's . . . it's okay. I knew I could survive if I had you and Fox. But I couldn't lose the ones I loved a second time. I knew I wouldn't survive that."

Rook was speechless. She'd been so worried about losing Drift's friendship, that the terrible things she'd said, all the times she'd neglected Drift, would mean she wouldn't want to be around Rook anymore. But Drift had been worried about losing her too.

Unexpectedly, a giggle rose up inside Rook. She tried to stifle it, but it escaped anyway, and she found herself grinning at Drift.

"What?" her friend demanded. "What can be funny right now?"

Rook shrugged. "I can't help it," she said. "I just—" But she couldn't finish because she was laughing. She was laughing and yet there were tears running down her face. And because she didn't know what else to do to show Drift how she felt, she threw her arms around her friend and hugged her so hard Drift squeaked.

"I love you," she whispered in Drift's ear. "Sister or not, we're family. With us, it's clear skies and smooth strides."

Drift hugged her back, sniffling. "You promise?"

"Always."

When they pulled apart, Drift wiped her eyes on her sleeve and cleared her throat. "What about Heath and Danna?" she asked. "I want to live here with them, but . . ." She trailed off, wearing a faraway expression.

Rook thought she could guess what her friend was thinking. "You want to live in the house your parents gave you," she said.

Drift nodded. "But I want to be with you and Fox most of all, so if you decide you want to stay, I'll . . . I'll let the house go."

"Oh no you won't," Rook said. "It's your house—Drift's Roost now—and it's kept us safe for years. We're not abandoning it either." She tapped her chin, considering. "I think I have an idea," she said.

She wasn't sure it was possible, but with Heath there to help her understand her powers, she might just be able to pull it off.

"Come on," she said, "let's get back to the house. Flying this time, not climbing," she added. "It's time to go home."

EPILOGUE

THE PERMANENT DOOR

IT WASN'T THE MOST ORNATE or complicated door she'd ever created, Rook thought as she, Drift, and Fox crowded together at the back of the roost's tiny closet, the place where she'd spent so many late nights trying to make a doorway to get back to Vora. But in order to make a door permanent, Heath said she needed to use as little animus as possible. Simple was better.

In the weeks since she'd first met the wizard and the pirate, Rook, Drift, and Fox had learned so much about their powers. They'd gotten to know the other children, and Heath had kept his promise to go to Regara to check on the Wasteland.

He reported back with some surprising and promising news. Now that the wild magic had been cleared from the portal site, the constables and the people of Regara had stepped in to try to reclaim the Wasteland. The animals and plants within had returned to their natural states, making the prospect much less dangerous. Even the instances of the Frenzy sickness in the city were dwindling.

And Heath said that the constables and Regara's mayor continued to search for Rook, the one who had saved the city from certain destruction. Not to hunt her down, but to give her their thanks. Heath said that the actions of Rook, Drift, and Fox on the city's behalf had already done much to change the people's attitudes toward the exiles. Even the Red Watchers, who proclaimed it had all been a trick to gain sympathy for the children, were losing support in the city.

It was a start, a hope for the future of the exiles in Talhaven.

Hope, Rook thought, was something she was learning to believe in. The door in front of her was another symbol of that change.

It was small, plain wood, with simple hinges. The doorknob was brass. When Rook opened it, a cloud of snow blew into the back of the closet.

There, in front of them, was Heath and Danna's house. They could come and go as they pleased now.

Rook stared across the threshold, and as she did so, she felt Fox and Drift take her hands. They stood quietly, breathing in the fresh, cold forest air. No matter what happened next, they would stay together. They'd promised each other that.

Two worlds connected. Two homes had become one.

It was all possible because of an open door.

And an open heart.

ACKNOWLEDGMENTS

Starting something new can be terrifying, especially if you feel like you're working without a net. Thankfully, when I delved into this new fantasy world and story, I had multiple people standing by to catch me if I started to fall and support me whenever I wobbled. There's always a lot of wobbling where I'm concerned.

To Krista Marino and my dream team at Delacorte Press, you continue to go above and beyond with your encouragement, your enthusiasm, and the hard work and support that make me think I can take a leap of faith and you'll be there for me.

To my amazing agent, Sara Megibow, thank you for telling me to follow wherever the world of Talhaven took me and for reminding me to enjoy the ride.

To Elizabeth, Gary, and Kelly, thank you for taking the book off my hands when I was too frustrated to look at it anymore. I knew you would help me make it better, and of course, you came through.

To Mom, Dad, and Jeff, we're on number nine. Can you believe that? You always did believe, of course, but I'm still waiting to wake up.

And to my husband, I promise I'll finish writing these acknowledgments and come help make dinner now. Thank you for always making sure I have the time I need and for understanding when I'm going nonstop. Love you tons.

ABOUT THE AUTHOR

Jaleigh Johnson is the *New York Times* bestselling author of *The Mark of the Dragonfly*, *The Secrets of Solace*, *The Quest to the Uncharted Lands*, and *The Door to the Lost*. A lifelong reader, gamer, and moviegoer, she loves nothing better than to escape into fictional worlds and take part in fantastic adventures.

Jaleigh lives and writes in the wilds of the Midwest, but you can visit her online at jaleighjohnson.com or follow @JaleighJohnson on Twitter.

READ MORE MAGICAL ADVENTURES BY JALEIGH JOHNSON!

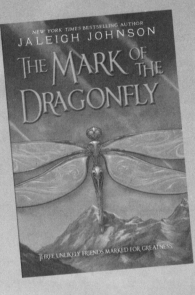

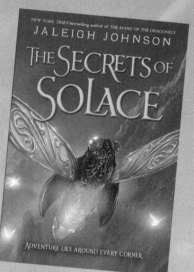